D0262063

The Chase

Also by Candida Clark

The Last Look
The Constant Eye
The Mariner's Star
Ghost Music
A House of Light

The Chase

Candida Clark

headline
review

First published in Great Britain in 2006
by Review

An imprint of Headline Book Publishing

1

Cataloguing in Publication Data is available from the British Library

ISBN 0 7553 2331 9 (Hardback)
ISBN 0 7553 3004 8 (Trade paperback)

Typeset in Perpetua by Palimpsest Book Production Limited, Polmont, Stirlingshire

Printed and bound in Great Britain by Clays Ltd, St Ives plc

Headline's policy is to use papers that are natural, renewable
and recyclable products and made from wood grown in sustainable
forests. The logging and manufacturing processes are expected to
conform to the environmental regulations of the country of origin.

HEADLINE BOOK PUBLISHING
A division of Hodder Headline
338 Euston Road
London NW1 3BH

www.reviewbooks.co.uk
www.hodderheadline.com

To G

With many thanks to the brilliant Charlotte Mendelson, Leah Woodburn, Ami Smithson, Hazel Orme and all at Headline; and, again, to Jonny Geller. Also, with much love to Frances, Guy, Nancy and Freddy Rasch; and to Christine's Toby, for taking such good care of me; finally, to S.C, for Major Cole, and S.H, for Jeremy.

'Affection! Thy intention stabs the centre:
Thou dost make possible things not so held,
Communicatest with dreams . . .'

A Winter's Tale, Act I, scene ii

part | one

1

Celia, Lady Domeyne, gave the egg a third, and harder, tap until the shell at last broke beneath the blows of the knife. She had woken just now with the dawn, which in February, in Wiltshire, came around six o'clock, the light freshening that day with the chance of snow.

She prayed it would not fall. If it must, she would like it to come the following night, at the earliest – although if it was the night that could mean ruin for the camellia in flower the previous week, because it would certainly harden then to frost. But if it came sooner . . . She did not even like to think of it. It would be the final straw.

Everything else had turned against them. If the weather also went that way she felt that a last and decisive piece of the mosaic would be set, the picture it revealed too terrible to look upon. No, it must not happen. That egg-tap had been her private test: any more than three to make a clean break and, superstitious, she would have anticipated bad weather. She smiled. They would be fortunate. The weather would hold. Tomorrow would be a perfect day for hunting.

Now she set aside the knife, took up the silver teaspoon and, with care, scooped out the yolk. The toast popped on the far side of the kitchen. She went to fetch it and heard the dogs slouch from sleep in the outer hall.

Today, Friday, was the housekeeper Marjorie's late day: she would begin at nine; otherwise she brought Celia and her husband, Leo, tea in bed. Now it was six thirty. The kitchen was still cold. She turned up the sleeves of her navy blue jersey: the arms were too long; it was her husband's; she wore his brown shooting-socks also, pulled up over tweed trousers, because in a moment she would go round to the stables in her boots. Leo would sleep until eight, but the children would begin to racket at seven, which gave Celia half an hour of breakfast and contemplation.

Never more so than before this weekend, that short stretch of private time felt like a glass wall blown into existence with every breath. When it was done, she would be safe behind it, and composed. But it was not done yet, and she felt ill prepared for the days ahead, because it was impossible to say with any certainty what they would contain: they depended on other people. What if everyone stayed away? They had promised they would not, but it was by no means certain. Or what if they came, and there was trouble? Celia glanced up as one of the peacocks cried out on the terrace. They were her husband's, too; after ten years of marriage she still had not got used to them.

With decision, she sliced butter for her toast, a large hunk of it removed from the dish to the edge of her plate, a curl applied to the warm rough bread, the crust thick with poppy seeds, which scattered across the oilskin tablecloth at the first bite, swarming there black and still as caught mosquitoes.

She thought of Egypt. Her brother, Gerald, had agreed to return to England in time, but she had not yet had word that he had arrived. His affairs often kept him away. After diplomatic service, he now worked in the private sector. Her younger sister, Henrietta – Henry – had no excuse: she lived in Holland Park; she could do as she pleased. Neither was married. Both had promised to come down by this evening.

But when Celia had called her sister to remind her of her promise, the younger woman had been at a party. There were shrieks of laughter, and what sounded like breaking glass in the background, the thump of a door being shut to seal their conversation. Henry's reassurance had had a note of irritation in it, and Celia imagined her turning to her friends to break off other engagements: 'My damn sister. Completely forgot she wants me at the weekend.'

Anxious, Celia filled the spoon with egg white and put it into her mouth. Toast followed, cooler. Everything depended upon her – the weekend, the house itself – and the responsibility felt like an obstacle around which she would have to steer them all. The kettle surged and clicked. She went to empty the hot water into the pot for coffee. Sumatra Mandheling, sweetened with Demerara.

Physically, the three siblings were similar: blond, blue-eyed, lean, energetic. But it was a mistake to imagine that their similarity ran any deeper. Gerald, Celia was afraid, drank much too heavily; Henry was perpetually, and astronomically, in debt, and her wilfulness about that, and much else, had started, Celia thought, to make her dangerous: the youngest sibling, already at the bottom in terms of age, it was as though she was intent on pulling her elders down there with her.

Celia leaned forwards. The sky was pale but not heavy enough to carry snow. Rain was a possibility, though even this looked doubtful. There was every indication that it would be a fine weekend, perhaps one of the loveliest of the season. She bit her lip. She had a number of things to do, both for that evening's dinner and for tomorrow's meet. She prayed that there would be a good turn-out, and wished that her family, at least, were more reliable. Her cousin, Will, was also expected. They should be nine that evening, if her siblings kept their word.

But there were reasons beyond this why Celia particularly wanted Henry and Gerald at Eastleigh that weekend. The second and, on the face of it, most straightforward reason was their aunt Bea's estate.

She had died last year and Celia, as executor, was keen to discuss the will. In 'discuss', Celia supposed, her siblings would have heard the chink of profit, and withdrew from letting this cloud her delight, should they arrive.

At first, the fact that she, and not Gerald, had been chosen as executor had caused some comment. But it was readily explained: he was seldom in the country, she was next in line; also, Celia had spent a good deal of time at her aunt's house in Hampshire. A hunt met there too, and Bea, like Celia, had been a keen horsewoman. These facts made the choice seem unremarkable.

What Celia intended to keep secret, however, was that Bea had left the entire estate – which was considerable – to her. She had no intention of keeping it to herself: she would divide it three ways and not mention what Bea had done. She knew the reason why. It was enough.

But with the inheritance came the certainty that, whatever happened, nothing now would be the same. Even her family's home in Devon had been lit up with potential – a decision waiting to be made. When their parents died, it had been rented on a short lease to a cousin and his wife, when by rights Gerald should have taken it on. He, however, had not wanted it 'just yet', citing lack of funds as the main reason. He would have no excuse now not to think about marrying and taking up his life there. Celia meant to press him about it when he arrived. And with Gerald in Devon, Henry more soundly established in London, her debts cleared, the family might again grow strong.

Celia thought all this with determination, much more than confidence. A door slammed shut on the upper landing. The girls' nanny had the peculiar characteristic of being both stealthy – in Celia's opinion, she crept around – and so clumsy at times that it might be thought deliberate. She was young, from Kiev, and had so far been satisfactory; Leo found no fault with her. Celia breathed out sharply, and straightened her engagement ring: Leo's grandmother's aqua-marine, a large, chilly stone, framed with diamonds.

The third reason for Celia particularly wanting her family there this weekend, and for the weekend to be a success, was more diffi-cult to explain. It was Leo. It was herself. It was the silent pact – a glided image of themselves – that had seemed to keep them bound together from the start, which now she felt had begun to slip. Thinking of the weekend, Celia had an intimation of its success in spite of everything, the hope that if they could all play their parts, carry on in spite of the ban, as though everything was unchanged, they might be reminded of themselves, the image would move back into place, and they would be returned to one another. She had the sensation of Leo having fallen back, rapt in private thought, some way distant on the path – she had let him do it, it seemed to be a form of trust – but instead of quickening his pace to meet her, he had stayed away.

She clasped her left hand in the right; the stone beneath her fin-gertips grew warm. She missed him. She did not like to confess to it, but there were times when it was unbearable.

Now the toast was cold, only half eaten. She pressed hard butter on to the remaining piece, reached for the Seville orange mar-malade, changed her mind and chose the honey. Their friend, the master of foxhounds, Charley Sutton, whose estate, Sanbourne, neighboured theirs, brought it over to them. He kept a dozen hives in a field sheltered by pines, bordering his water-meadows – the honey had the scent of sap and wild flowers locked within it. Now there wasn't much left. She eked it out. It tasted almost treacly in its richness.

When Celia had heard the extent of her aunt's legacy, her first thought had been of Leo: the land he farmed was a mirror that reflected back through his family's generations. He had only to look into it to see how he measured up. Yet since he had inherited, just after they were married, Eastleigh's estate had rapidly diminished, the loop of the perimeter tightening as it shrank, a rope run through cold water.

She ate the honeyed toast, glanced at the jar, estimating how many days were left. Over the last year the hives had been badly managed: Charley's attention had been elsewhere. It really was almost gone.

The letter had arrived last month from Bea's solicitors, Turnbull and DeMonchaux, and Leo had stood up quickly from the breakfast table. Celia had almost winced at the expectation that he would ask her, plainly, how much money she had come into. She did not think she could have borne hearing him voice that need: to know it was there was bad enough. Now, thanks to her aunt, she had sufficient means, if not to reverse the decline of the estate at Eastleigh, at least to stem the flow. But it would take some delicacy.

Her hope had been to discuss it with Gerald and Henry this evening, then be in a position to tell Leo before dinner. It would be a reason for him to hurry ahead to join her again. There might be another reason, too, but she was doing her best not to think of it: it was too much what she wanted; she feared that thinking of it might jinx it. It had been why she had had to get up so quickly this morning: she had had to dash downstairs to be sick in the loo. She had a doctor's appointment at midday. She didn't want to tell Leo until she was sure. It was another reason she wanted her siblings there: as she wouldn't ride, she needed them to swell the ranks. If she had confirmation, she hoped to tell Leo before that evening's dinner.

A car turning into the driveway made her glance up. She crossed to the window. No one was expected until nine. It looked like Charley Sutton's. He often dropped by unannounced. From the kitchen window, she could just see its roof; he had stopped by the gatehouse. The groom, James Dunbar, lived there. She supposed he might have business with him about tomorrow, but she didn't think he'd find him at home: Dunbar was usually in the stables by now. She took her breakfast plates to the sink.

Things might have been a good deal worse: the land had not, as it were, gone far. Charley had bought up much of it, not because he needed it, or wanted it, even – and a good parcel had been leased out – but simply to avoid its falling into the hands of outsiders. At least this way, the understanding went, Leo might buy it back on fair terms when his situation improved.

But it was not something she and Leo could discuss. It was too intimate to approach head-on. She had overheard him talking to Charley about it a few weeks ago. He had been laughing in an attempt to sound light-hearted, but she had heard the strain in his voice, and hesitated in the hallway to listen. 'Yes, you bastard, it's the first thing I'd do after the roof – see that you give me back my land.' He had looked embarrassed when she entered the kitchen at that moment.

Celia rode out with Charley a couple of times every week. It had been Charley who had suggested to her how Leo had acted too often on what later turned out to be poor advice. According to him, Leo refused to adapt to all the new ideas as quickly as he should; nor did he have the heart, apparently – Celia read it as 'heart' although the word Charley had used was 'guts' – to fire a number of people in his employ, who, according to him, were either 'no good' or 'simply bloody useless'. The farm manager, who fell into the second category, supported a wife whose ill-health meant that she was often, expensively, in hospital; their groom James Dunbar, who belonged in the first, had been sent their way via Gerald.

Proportionately, meanwhile, Charley had flourished. He was much occupied with the hunt, but the rest of the time he was in finance, private equities. And as Eastleigh had become shabbier, less heated, badly patched up, Charley's house, Sanbourne, was maintained so well that, although it was Victorian, it looked almost new-built. It had been Charley's great-grandfather's – that man also had been master of foxhounds. But the family line had been weak before then. Nor did Charley have any children: the line ahead seemed fragile too. The result had produced a bottleneck – all the Suttons' wealth gathered in the present generation. It seemed a shame to Celia that the money had nowhere to go, until she remembered Leo, and felt guilty to have been sorry for a friend who, in more ways than one, was her husband's rival. But they had known each other since they were boys, and for that reason Celia also felt an instinctive loyalty to her husband's friend.

Celia turned from the window, away from these thoughts, as it were, and contemplated Marjorie's list pinned to the kitchen notice-board. The butcher would deliver at ten. It was all in hand. Marjorie could be relied upon.

From the hall she could hear the dogs shuffle closer against the oak door, pressing to be let into the kitchen. Upstairs a footfall revealed the children, testing the morning, but not entering it. Their obedience saddened her, as though they had sensed that something was wrong. She waited for a screech, or laughter, but none came. She held her breath to listen and on that in-breath seemed to feel the gravity of history rushing in – so much reduced so quickly to the space of one weekend, no more than an exhalation and everything would be over. The law had been passed: after seven hundred years, it was illegal; it had been written out of existence.

She stopped there. She could not bear to think of it. She would not. She would go on as if today was one of all the many other pieces of mosaic that made the picture, and not the one to complete, to kill it.

She heard a car approaching on the gravel at the front of the house. That must be Charley now. She hesitated by the pot of coffee, wondered if he might like some, added more water, stirring the grains, watching a lone breeze run through the stumps of lavender not yet sprouted into hedge. She glanced down at her hands. They suffered in the cold. She took out a tube of cream from the drawer and rubbed her palms together. The scent of roses. Penhaligon's Elizabethan. She looked at the label and felt a sudden stab of hatred for it. That this false scent should win the day appalled her. The roses were not yet in bloom. It was not even spring.

With a fingernail, clipped short and sharp, she picked the label from the tube, tearing at the gluey edges until it came away ragged. It stuck to her fingertips. She washed it off.

Charley came through from the side of the house into the kitchen. He had a way of walking – a tall man, in his early forties, fine-boned and dark enough to pass for an Italian – that made him seem perpetually in thought, head bowed, one hand often deep inside his coat pocket. Today he carried a brown manila envelope tucked under his arm. He dropped it on to the table as he came in. 'It's for Leo. I'd asked Esther to post it, but she forgot.' He shrugged.

They stood facing one another for a moment. She handed him a cup of coffee, and thought he looked exhausted.

He sighed and shook his head. 'God, Celia.' Through the open door the cold air fell, steady and windless.

She wanted to say something to set aside that chill but it was too heavy, too full of years. 'I was just thinking about you,' she told him, truthfully.

He glanced at the manila envelope. 'Let's go outside.'

They put their cups together on the table and went out.

2

Eastleigh had become Leo Domeyne's through a series of tragedies. Built in 1725, it had belonged to his family always, but the succession had not been smooth. The sons either farmed or served in the army. Many had been lost in battles and foreign skirmishes: the siege of Gibraltar in 1779; the Crimean War in 1850; two close together, one in the first Balkan War of 1912, and another in the siege of Kut in 1915, in present-day Iraq. A third from that generation had survived the First World War only to fall victim to the flu epidemic that followed it.

Leo had given Celia a potted history the first time he met her. He went on to tell her how the place might easily not have been his, but for a reckless nanny, vague with gin, who had left his older brother to stray wild across the main road as a child – amazingly, that far in safety – and from there into the stream that ran along the ditch, following the road towards town. The stream wasn't deep, only a few feet at that time of year, late summer, but the boy drowned, and because of it, Eastleigh fell in time to Leo.

Celia was a distant cousin of Leo's, distant enough not to know the stories yet close enough for him to feel that she should have that sense of their shared dimension, the family tree breaking off into drama. She had had a look of indestructibility, an unchippable glaze, which he read as the veneer of a deeply passionate nature – that had been his impression of her when she was pointed out to him by his mother.

'That's the chilly Stevenson girl,' his mother had said, and Leo had seen Celia standing in the doorway at Eastleigh – he was outside, walking with the older woman up from the gate.

Leo had heard Celia described in such terms before, and had built up a picture of her in his mind as aloof, perhaps cynical, her chilliness a form of extreme disinterest. But that she appeared to him indestructible in no way added up to chilliness: an unbreakable exterior did not have to be icy; it could just mean that a person was private – a good thing. He had imagined, also, that when he met her he might have the impulse to slap her on the back in a brotherly way, bring her down a peg or two, loosen her up a bit. But he found, seeing her for the first time, that he gulped, his hands clammy, a stammer rising to his lips at that vision: the thought of slapping such a girl was out of the question.

There was a tennis party: Celia was in whites, her blonde hair tied back in a plait, her legs pale and on just the right side, he thought, of slender. She seemed anything but chilly. Her eyes, in their delight at the scene in front her, were almost hungry in their expressiveness – the exact reverse of the cynicism he had anticipated: a kind of secret ambition of optimism that she could not conceal. A person who feels so lucky to be alive, he thought, is, of course, most aware of not living the life they yearn for, and it was this, he suspected, that kept people distant from her: she had an aura of risk. It was her definiteness that made her seem liable to go either way, into black or white, and he wanted to take hold of her and steer her to the middle course.

A number of people had gathered in front of the house, waiting for instructions – directions to the courts, the order of play. Leo did not know the other guests: his mother had arranged things. He was twenty-six, down for the weekend from London, a little bored already by the summer, and then there was this girl.

As he approached, his friend Charley Sutton suddenly stepped out from behind Celia, coming from inside the house. A few years older than Leo, he had just returned from Malawi after six months' working on a game reserve. Leo had seen him the previous week in London and had heard all about it, and when he saw Charley now, he sincerely wished he would go back. He was very tanned; even in tennis whites he gave the impression of being armed, or as though he might suddenly use his racket as a weapon; and where before he had been merely dark and lean, now his good looks stemmed more from his having seen things that definitely were not Wiltshire.

Leo did not break his stride as he approached. He felt ill matched with his adversary but Celia was standing in the doorway of his house and there were unspoken rules about such things. He overheard Charley asking her if she could tell him where the loo was, which only strengthened Leo's sense of injustice: Charley had been to Eastleigh on countless occasions; he knew perfectly well where it was.

Leo noticed Celia draw back, startled, as Charley stepped up beside her. She blushed slightly, saying, 'I don't live here, I'm afraid,' and his impulse was to see off his rival, then get beside her and make her feel at home.

As he came close, Charley, seeing him, must have read in his look of intent a prior claim, for he backed off, even before Leo had told him, 'You're wanted on the courts right away.' Leo allowed himself the white lie: Charley had just done the same thing.

With Charley gone, Leo was able to introduce himself properly to Celia. As he did so, he became conscious, if not quite of a physical resemblance then of an echo: he was taller by a foot, far broader, but both were fair; and his negligence over his appearance – shirt untucked, sockless, grass stains on the knees of his trousers, his hair sticking up where he habitually ran a hand through it — somehow underlined her own composure. She seemed to be a tidied-up female version of him. It appeared to be reason enough for her to smile at him, and it encouraged him to tell her about those family tragedies. He didn't want her to be in the dark: he wanted her to be well equipped — an instinct to provide for her, spurred on by the suggestion that beneath that unchippable surface something lay burning; he wanted to be sure that it did not go out, to keep her stoked up.

His mother was wrong, he was quite sure. It wasn't that she was chilly. It was that she was homeless — her burning self was all she seemed to have; there was nowhere else that she belonged. It was this that gave her the gleam of strength, the glint of something inde-structible.

It intrigued him, because he had a sudden intimation that they might meet there: he had a home, although it did not feel like his. But it puzzled him, too. He wanted to discover how any relative of his could give that appearance of being so well lit and so unburn-dened: homeless, yet secure. He had perceived his family as deep rooted, with an immense steadiness, those tragedies the sole bright flashes of motion, but with the brightness of stars, for they were already historical, their light quite dead. When he told Celia about them, later that afternoon, tennis halted for tea, the lavender hedge behind their deck-chairs crisping and dusty with fine weather, she glanced at him in alarm: what was he trying to tell her? Was it some kind of warning? Her alarm had had a look of fatalism about it, as though she had expected as much, and this preparedness — her light-ness, she was ready for anything — replaced in his mind her gleaming surface, and set her apart from him, framing her perpetually in that first doorway of his memory, a little remote, but almost perfect for that reason.

Charley Sutton returned to Malawi, as Leo had hoped, but not before he had – as Leo put it to himself – 'lured' Celia out to lunch in London a few times and once, distressingly, to dinner. He had felt duped, he said, by Leo's appearance of intimacy with Celia on that first day, but that didn't mean he should persist in the misunderstanding, so he had asked her out. Celia, according to Charley's letters home, had not, however, been interested in him, and had, on each occasion, spoken almost exclusively of Leo, which Leo found immensely gratifying.

'Unwavering devotion to you so far, but I'm not convinced. I'll make her crack yet.' Charley had joked about battling it out with Leo on his return, but by then – six months later – it was too late. Leo had pipped him to the post: they were engaged.

Years later, after they were married and had had the two girls, faced with something that gave Celia every reason to be at least a little broken, yet she simply went away – staying with her aunt Bea for three months, as he knew she had often stayed with her as a girl. She returned mended, and Leo remembered his mother's first judgement, 'the chilly Stevenson girl', and wondered then whether she had not been partly right.

He did not want to ruin her composure: he loved her; of course he did not wish her harm. Yet wondering at her strength, he felt that it underlined a weakness in himself that, given the choice, he would have preferred to keep concealed. He found that he wanted her to step down from the picture to be beside him, outside the house, and yet the tragedy meant that, finally, she belonged there, a little more, even, than he. She was at home.

It would have been their third child, and by instinct both she and Leo were sure it was a son. They already had two girls. But without a son, the line broke off, weak with daughters and cousins.

Leo was not superstitious by nature, but he read in his wife's miscarriage the price of his own luck in inheriting the house – the presence of his brother, its rightful owner, somehow returned to steal the life of his son.

It had happened because of a fall out hunting. The going had been fair, the day slow, but recent rains had made it wetter than he had realised; her horse had slipped and fallen at a hedge he had taken. Celia had always been a better rider than he; but he could have forbidden her from going out.

'In a way, she's been lucky.' When the surgeon said this, Leo had been glad his wife was still safe inside the anaesthetic. To apply any idea of luck to her at that moment had seemed barbaric. He had not been able to reply, but had flinched at the man's hand, sympathetic, on his arm. He had wanted to punch him.

After that he did not hunt; he gave it up. But it had often struck him as being a ghoulish sacrifice – as though by stating so publicly that the hunt was finished for him, he hoped to have time die too, and that way find he had raised the dead. He still wanted a son. More, he wanted *that* son – an impossible wish. It was macabre of him, and he felt the guilt of it around him always. The guilt of the fall, and the guilt of his constant longing that the child would somehow come again.

Now Leo had promised Celia that he would ride out with her tomorrow. He knew how much it meant to her, that he would be by her side on such a day. But her reaction, when he told her over dinner a week earlier, had made him uneasy. 'Oh, you don't have to do that, darling.' She had seemed startled that he should suggest such a thing. He persisted: he would like to. Carving off a slice of apple, she fumbled with the knife, cutting her hand. 'Charley will be so pleased,' she added, but had looked almost afraid, as though Leo's staying away had been necessary for her remaining.

Leo remembered all this in a dream, his sleeping mind exact with grief, for when he woke on Friday morning – Celia had already left the room – he recalled that it was five years to the day that the child had been lost. He turned over but could not find her. Had she, too, remembered?

Now he listened out for her. It was just past seven. A door slamming shut — the nanny — had woken him. He crept out of bed and went on to the landing. He thought he heard voices downstairs. There were two doors into the kitchen. One gave on to the side of the house, the other into the hallway. Both were open. He could tell that the first was open by the draught; and the second by the sound of Charley's voice, saying his wife's name, and by her reply: 'I was just thinking about you.' Then he heard them go out, the soft click of the door being shut behind them.

Leo stood for a moment, holding the banister rail. He rubbed his forehead. Now that she was gone, the house seemed particularly quiet. It was as though it had slipped from him, not with any violence but like a silk robe crumpled to the floor, revealing him as he was. It should never have been his, but without it he was naked, out of place.

He went back to their bedroom and stood by the curtain, concealed. He could just see Celia and Charley walking together across the drive and round the side of the house towards the stables. He watched as Charley took a jar of something out of his coat pocket and handed it to Celia, who touched his arm, her hand resting there as she said something to him that Leo naturally could not hear. He supposed the gift was Sanbourne honey. He turned from the sight and climbed back beneath the sheets.

He could hear the woodpigeons in the chimneystacks, and the slow, strong flap of the doves that mingled with them and, as was always the case, at the back of his mind he was reminded of how, as a boy, shooting once in the poor light of evening, he had mistaken them. Killing a dove he had felt cursed. Frightened, he had concealed it, told no one, buried it beneath beech leaves and soft earth in the copse.

Now he was a better shot, and the woodpigeons had to be kept in check or they wrecked the mortar that held the bricks together around the chimneys. He turned over in bed. He would go out with his gun later, see what he could do about them. Certainly he would do it if the day stayed clear.

3

'Some of the lads are off down there at the weekend.'

Lance Ash raised his pint as though in encouragement at this remark, and made a noncommittal sound of interest.

'To see that they behave,' another of the men added.

But it only depressed Lance to hear them talking like this, and he didn't think it very dignified, either. He had no desire to gloat and, anyway, the thought of doing so embarrassed him: he had never watched a hunt before. He wasn't going to start now that it was over.

'Wiltshire, is it?' He tried to appear interested, as though he was considering the merits of the suggestion: a good day out. But he had no intention of joining them. Even had he wished to, he had spent so little time recently with his wife, Alison; he didn't suppose she would allow it.

It was Wednesday, 16 February, and the Court of Appeal had that day confirmed the decision of 28 January: on Friday, the ban on hunting foxes with hounds would come into effect. Although he had played his part unwaveringly in the legislation's progress, Lance Ash felt no appetite for celebrating its success. The battle had been fought where it counted, in the chambers, in the courts. The evidence had been set out and considered. He did not want to witness the defeat.

The hunt they were thinking of going to 'keep an eye on' was Charley Sutton's, the Royal Fusiliers, which rode on Salisbury Plain.

'It'd be a constitutional crisis if they do go.' He had hoped to dampen the other man's enthusiasm, imply that it would be a non-event. They wouldn't ride, surely. But it only stirred him up.

'Exactly! Queen's soldiers against her own law!' The man who spoke was from Birmingham, and too much white flour in boyhood had made his skin doughy, but with the pinched quality of dough under-yeasted, for he was also thin. Lance did not think he had ever heard his fellow-backbencher sound so much like a royalist, and had half a mind to point this out, but he checked himself.

He drank another inch of his pint, frowning at the taste. The bitter was gassy, the end of the barrel. He blamed this for his headache, but he knew it wasn't that. He wished he could get rid of the image of something he had seen last night.

He tried not to read it as a sign, but stopped short of laughing about it now. When he opened his mouth to mention it, his throat had tightened, preventing speech, and he took this to be the physical manifestation of superstition, from which he had not suffered for years. Surreptitiously, while they were not looking, he touched the wood of the bar for reassurance.

As a child, even as late as grammar school, Lance Ash had dodged lines and cracks, tugged his short pale hair at the sound of ambulance sirens and searched anxiously for the second magpie. But he had done his best to grow out of all that; at the age of forty-nine he had passed from pale to grey with only the smallest shift in physical tone, a look of milky weakening that he described to himself as purification, a whittling away of moral indecision; and in the place of his superstition there was now a kind of solid dread – a territory towards which he did not stray. To be wrong was a place to which he refused to travel.

Yet the image remained with him as they raised their pints. Even though it would have been cheaper to do so, they seldom drank in the Commons bar. They went outside, and on this occasion more

than most he had felt the tremendous weight of the place behind
them as they left; not heavy but golden, with gold's particular gleam
of authority that looked like light. An illusion, he told himself with
contempt. But still, he did not glance back, particularly not tonight.
He feared the gold might touch him at any moment and find him
sullen, too dull ever to return.

Besides, with his back to the place, he was better able to relish
the comfort of being inside. It felt like spurning home. It gave him
that sensation of power: I can do without you now. Returning, he
would often feel himself on tiptoe, and he sank into the green back-
benches with relief. He had been let back in. It always seemed miracu-
lous – a reprieve he was not certain he deserved.

The thing – he did not like to name it: he knew it was not a
vision yet he hesitated before seeing any of its consequences veiled
in fact – had happened around four a.m. He was at home in Hounslow.
They lived on the periphery of an estate, one of the new collections
of mid-priced dwellings known as 'dormitory communities'. Aimed
at service-sector workers, he had been in support of such developments in the House. He considered them democratic. He had had
reservations about the name at first, but had grown to like it for its
accuracy: people drove out there after work to sleep; it was a community of sleepers. In private, he found the idea almost titillating,
and it was made more so, for him, in that he never caught sight of
his neighbours. He knew them only by their night-moves. He knew
all those details – when they slept and rose, after-dark glimpses that
might have blanched to nothing had he seen any of them by day –
but not their faces or their names. There was a perfection in their
anonymity that he found restful.

It had been the word 'dormitory' that had bothered him fleet-
ingly when, years ago now, he had first heard it used in that new
context. Until that moment, for him, it had been cut with the taste
of exclusion: rows of snoozing boys, lucky soporifics, members of

a club even then, privileged with sound sleep that for him had not come easily. Hitched to 'community' he felt the word became no longer theirs but his, and after the initial disquiet it was this that pleased him and made him feel a subtle victory had been won. These little symbols mattered, he thought, and often more than most people imagined they might. Win the victory on each small point and in the end you would win the day. It was why he had entered politics after accountancy: ambitious, he was convinced he had the skill to make the whole picture add up. Control the numbers and you held the power.

The sacrifice, in this instance, was that he had felt obliged to live in one of those new developments. His wife, Alison, was open in her dislike of the place. She had grown up in the suburbs, in High Barnet, which, according to her, was quite a different thing.

That night she had been away, at her mother's in Cockfosters, he wasn't sure why. She had gone the day before. It was mid-February, so was it perhaps time for Mother's Day? He had noticed flowers in the shops. His own mother had passed away five years earlier. But he had been working hard to see the Bill through and hadn't been paying attention when his wife told him where she was going.

Usually he liked to be in the house alone but this time he did not. The place seemed dank and different from how he thought of it, as though at one remove from itself, when usually it was so overloud and full of smells: the radio blaring, pots always steaming on the stove, unnamed fragrances of home – an excessive motion that Lance felt sure his wife sustained to distract them from their lack of chil-dren. Neither professed to want them, but it was not something that, once decided, stayed away. They often fought about it: what if? Such arguments made both of them feel lonely, and also underlined the fact that Lance was hardly ever there. With her cooking she tried to compensate for all that. Those smells had the power to give him pleasure because they made him feel tender towards her: at least they were in it together.

He had gone to bed a little after midnight, clutching the pillow on which his wife's head should have been resting. He hugged it to himself as though it were she, and thought about her absence with surprise.

But he must have slept soon after because when he was woken by the noise at four he was groggy with shock; a deep sleep that meant he moved from his dreams with the swiftness of dreaming's ease, leaping out of bed, alert, to the window. When Alison was away, he slept with the curtains open, liking to be woken by daylight as soon as it came. But it was still black outside. He peered into the darkness. He saw that the metal dustbin had been tipped over – the clatter had woken him – and the fox was half hidden inside, its fat brush tipped with white and lit with moonlight, making him think of it at first as two separate animals. It had precisely the appearance, with its head buried in the bin, of a mythic animal spliced together: two familiar beasts making one unknown. He reached for the word, but could not find it. He knew that it was classical. He did not have that kind of education. He drew back, watching.

With its head hidden, the fox seemed industrious in its hunger, and the metal, too, gave the process a faintly mechanised appearance. What had he been dreaming of? He had dozed in front of the news – tanks still in Baghdad – perhaps it had been that. He blamed the forgotten dream for the alarm he felt at the sight of the busy fox. He did not fear it. He was safe inside the house. But he was bothered by its boldness. He watched it scragging something inside the nest of rubbish. Its head was still concealed. He thought with irritation of the mess he would have to clear up tomorrow.

He remembered his wife's report of a neighbour's Pekinese found dead beneath a bush in the garden. The neighbour had blamed a fox, and talked of toothmarks; Lance had ridiculed the notion until his wife fell into agreement with him, or at least made a show of doing so. He remembered he had cracked a joke about the Hound of the Baskervilles. It was Hounslow, for goodness' sake! But when he had said this, Alison had looked away: both of them had heard the joke flattened by the echoed 'hound'.

Now he only hoped that the animal would leave their neighbour's rubbish bin alone – ruin theirs if it must, then just get lost. He hated to be proven wrong. He would clear up the mess before it was light. Seeing himself doing this, he faltered, and thought of going outside into the wet darkness to the bin to find that the fox had not left, but was only waiting, hidden in it as though it were a kennel, or a cave, and he saw himself reaching inside, a test of his own conviction that would end in horror, the expectant teeth sharp for bloodshed   and then he remembered being in Rome on his honeymoon, and, in imitation of *Roman Holiday*, reaching inside the mouth of the fountain to prove to his new wife that he was hers, and the chill of his fingertips as they entered that emptiness.

Lance had always been a pale man, with a smoothness that suggested the blunt weight of a hammer's iron, because with time he had also made himself grow strong, so that when he was quick, which was seldom, it caught people off-guard. And as Alison reached towards the fountain's mouth, he had shocked her by snatching away her hand, swivelling her round to manoeuvre her out into the sunlight. 'I believe you. You don't need to prove it.' It had seemed to him a man's test, and not for her.

'Lance, you're hurting me!' She had craned round, her body twisting as though in exaggerated pain. But she had smiled with sly pleasure – do it again! – and he had been glad he had stopped her.

It was a long time ago. He had had conviction enough for both of them then. Now he relied on mathematics more than morals to give him clarity. It made much better sense. Foxes could be shot or gassed. That was the proper way to control their number. They didn't need to be made vivid with heroism by being chased.

Whenever he thought this, he rubbed his lips together lest the notion emerge. It was secret. He supposed it was ridiculous, but plenty was that was also felt, he reassured himself. Yet it was how he thought of those foxes: a red streak of freedom slanting across green. He was offended by them and everything they meant, just as much as he was offended by their pursuers. He would have liked to see them both wiped out. But he was conscious of the apparent contradiction: wasn't he supposed to be on the fox's side? And yet he hated all wild things equally for being free. He saw freedom as a form of privacy and cunning, a version of self-interest. He was not free. He was a public servant. Those foxes should no longer have the power of that glory, their brushes pinned up on pub walls, the kill remembered, the moment atrophied.

He rubbed his eyes. The fox rattled the bin. When he looked back, it had gone. He turned to the room with indignation on his lips. He had meant to call out to Alison, but the thought died with the in-breath: she, too, was no longer there.

That evening, raising his pint, he had felt all of this settle on his tongue like a dead weight, silencing him. Someone slapped his back in congratulations for his small part in the legislation's progress, and he tipped forwards, spilling a drop of the rusty-coloured John Smith's on his white shirt front. No, that animal's visit was not a sign of any kind, for the country would not be overrun by foxes, freely marauding pet-killers rooting through rubbish. Measures would be taken. Like vermin or cockroaches, they would be exterminated with quiet efficiency and no fanfare whatsoever. The people would forget. They had short memories. You could always rely on them not to remember. It might foul up the next election but it would not swing the vote. It was only some silliness over animals – foxes, dogs and horses. It should never have been news.

They raised their glasses in a toast. 'The weekend!'

Later, crossing the street on his way back to the Commons alone, he turned sharp left instead and went to the river. He stood on Westminster Bridge, leaning on the iron parapet, facing downriver towards the waterway opening into greater night, strung about with the stars of Lambeth Bridge.

Bolder now with drink, he thought that the palace looked particularly lovely and, yes, he had been right before, the cold February air did give the stone a certain brightness, as though the buildings themselves were cooked up out of light. He stole a glance at them, smiling, and felt pride in himself for having a place there, and the pride reminded him of everything he had felt for his wife when they were first married – fifteen years ago? Was it really so long as that? – when he used to miss her so much that he would come out here to call her from the phone-box just before the bridge. He liked to be outside the House when he spoke to her, because he felt as though the formality of the place, should he have phoned her from inside, might cloak his words in a pomp that would have meant insincerity. He had never wanted that.

Remembering this, and the previous night's empty bed, he took out his mobile phone, thinking he might ask her when she would be back – and would she remember how he used to telephone her from here? He would ask her if she did – when, with a lurch almost of sickness, he realised the reason for all those flowers: today was Wednesday the sixteenth, the date enshrined in Hansard, which meant that Monday had been the fourteenth, and therefore St Valentine's Day.

He had forgotten. He stared down at his phone. Her number was there but he was too ashamed – now that he had remembered – to call her.

4

On the same Monday morning that Alison Ash reached down to collect the post, finding only demands for money and no offers of love, even from her husband Lance, Isabella Frey, expecting nothing – she didn't have a boyfriend, hadn't been on a date in over a year – saw the red envelope, half hidden beneath bills on the hall table, and her heart almost turned over. She felt as though, finally, she had been found out. Someone had tracked her down. She couldn't stay in hiding for ever. This thought made her feel oddly guilty, and at the same time very pleased.

She had just washed her hair and, still dripping, had dashed down to fetch the post. She did not open the envelope at once, but took it upstairs to her flat on the top floor, dropped it on to the sofa with the rest of the mail and went through to the kitchen to make a pot of tea.

It was a bright day in London, and unseasonably mild. She raised the sash window; the sun was warm even at eleven o'clock. The news was on the kitchen radio and she listened to the headlines: more fighting in Faluja; WMDs elusive; fox-hunting's final days. She turned the dial for music and found Stravinsky on Radio 3. Rubbing her short hair with the white towel, she crossed to the kitchen window, raised the sash and smiled, looking out. She tipped her head up and let the breeze run through her hair. Chestnut-coloured, fine, it would soon be dry.

Although the trees were still bare, the air carried the scents of growth – bulbs and new grass on Primrose Hill, things gradually in bud. Someone had been thinking of her on St Valentine's Day after all.

Her impulse, however, was not to tear open the red envelope and see at once who had sent her a card. She had half a mind to prop it on the mantelpiece, unopened, and enjoy it that way. She checked herself as she thought this, it was idiotic, and she frowned, shutting her eyes as she leaned out of the window.

She had been working almost non-stop since the previous summer. A painter, she had had a small show in December, and another was planned for April. Rather than take a break between, she had decided to rush on straight through. Now spring had set its back to winter and she had not even noticed: her industriousness had been a kind of blindness. People were falling in love and sending Valentines' cards and she certainly wasn't ready for all that, but – she glanced at the card and smiled – how wonderful it was that such things went on. But being prolific now felt like a silly boast – look how fast I can go! – as though running on empty was an achievement in itself.

Thinking this, she thought also of her parents. It was their speciality to appear self-sustaining. They had moved ten years ago from Chelsea to live in a large white house in the Balearics, on Formentera. It was impossible to pin down how they managed to go on for so long, and with an impression of luxury that made Isabella's friends suppose they were rich. Perhaps they were? They had bought property in the sixties and sold it off bit by bit – 'One more bites the dust!' There would be a flurry of gifts and entertainments, the house full of guests, parties rapidly extemporised, and then, as though astonished at such ostentation, the pleasures would stop, and the children would name those times 'the months of beans', faces mournful as they saw the sacks of dried mungs and adukis arriving. It wasn't surprising that her brothers had shored up their lives with a skill for making money: one ran a hedge fund on Wall Street; the other was a corporate lawyer in Hong Kong. The alternative was a punishment on the nerves. Even Isabella, in secret, had investments.

Now she reached for the phone. Her mother's perennial cry was 'Just drop everything, darling, and come on over!' Isabella decided she would take her up on it: she would fly out to visit them that weekend. She sipped tea, dialled, the phone rang but, frustratingly, they appeared not to be in, and that they refused the practical device of an answerphone underlined their unwillingness to be dependable. 'We've been lousy parents,' they would often say, laughingly, 'but look how you've all turned out!' They would shake their heads in astonishment, and peer at their children, as though unsure that they were theirs. It amused them that they were so different.

Now Isabella felt dissatisfied. She supposed she could always go somewhere else. She had standing invitations to various people's houses. But to visit any of them seemed oddly purposeless, and she wondered at her desire to see her parents.

She leaned back in the armchair and heard a swarm of school-children go by in the street at the front of the house, a sudden raucous buzzing; a whistle blew; there was the sound of a woman's laughter from the flat next door – their window must be open also – and she felt a pang of loneliness. Her flat, where she also worked – her studio was on the floor above – seemed as isolating as a tower.

Her hair was dry now and she touched it critically, considered having a haircut, and, doing this, remembered one her mother had given her at the age of eight. 'Tip up!' Isabella had turned her head upside-down and her mother had swiped off her long, straight hair with a pair of dress-making shears. It had been hilarious at the time. She felt a little sad now to remember it. It wasn't how she lived – with that kind of cheerful recklessness. When she was happy, she hoarded it; she kept herself in reserve, and saved her passion for her work.

Yet her family was entirely made up of such decisive cuts and unfathomable-seeming motives: the line took off at violent tangents; in places it appeared to break off altogether; there were numerous emigrations and boat-burnings; talk of a castle in Schleswig-Holstein; an inventor great-uncle; a hermit botanist, disappeared to a Pacific island; a rash of poets and painters; a great-grandfather who buried the family library in the grounds of his house, food for wormy generations.

For a living – she thought of it as 'on the side', since her heart was not in it but in landscapes – she painted family portraits. But she did it curiously, with a sense almost of novelty, for there was no coherence in the picture of her own. She turned away from the window. She had planted herbs in the window-boxes, and the scent of lemon thyme was carried into the room on the spring air, which tugged at the buttons of her shirt: a reprimand. She touched her throat, took a deep breath and told herself that perhaps she was tired, after all. But her nerve-ends felt urgent with life, anything but weary. She was ready for something, but did not know what, and it was the readiness that bothered her: she had supposed she was running happily along a track of life that satisfied her utterly, yet now this overwhelming restlessness. She supposed she could take a run on the Heath, but she rolled her eyes at this idea and sighed. That kind of thing never worked for her: she couldn't take her disquiet that seriously.

She thought of the red envelope and stood up. She would open the wretched thing, then get down to work. She went through to the kitchen to look for biscuits and, telling herself to brace up, tore the envelope to discover, with a jolt of disappointment, that, after all, it was not even a Valentine's card. It was a note from someone called Will – the letter-head extended this to William Bowden – and it took her a few moments to remember who he was.

When she had been studying art at the Ruskin School, in Oxford, he had been at Christ Church. That red envelope had been no more than a coincidence, just something given out at a newsagent's with a card. Their paths had barely crossed. Two separate circles, the point of overlap had been theatrical: she had painted stage sets; he had acted, badly, as she remembered, though with panache. She smiled. He didn't mention what he did now. She doubted it was that. She tried to remember if she had found him handsome, and could not: the bad acting had drawn attention away from him, and clouded his personality for her too. Yet, thinking of him, she found that she could see him very clearly, and she wondered how that could be. She had not thought of him for years; it was ten since she had left college.

Snow had been falling, and he had arrived at the theatre stamping it off his boots. They were long riding boots, she remembered, and he had muttered something about being in character, which she had not believed, although his part, she recalled, had been figured in a military idiom. He was playing James Tyrone in *Long Day's Journey Into Night*. The director had put Will in uniform, asked him to play it like a returned soldier, disenchanted. She had opened the door for him – it had been locked: she was the only other person in the theatre; she held a paintbrush, and as he stood there, she had said something about how the snow had fallen on his dark hair – he was hatless – and not yet melted. It had given him a cap of white. He glanced into the mirror by the door, and groaned, ruffling his hair until the snow vanished. It had seemed to shock him; he had blushed and, as though reading the question in her eyes, said to her, 'Makes me look just like my father.'

Recovering, he had disappeared inside the theatre, but reappeared a moment later and asked her if she would like him to help her. He had arrived early by mistake, he explained, and wasn't due for another hour or so. She handed him a brush. They painted in silence. She had thought his kindness in offering to help was charming – she thought of that word again now, remembering him, and decided that

it was the light in which he was most accurately cast. His good manners – he had helped her down off a ladder as though she were
descending from a carriage in a gown – seemed to her a form of
respect that made him appear aloof, a little apart from the others,
and she added to his charm a possible reason: he could afford to be
charming, because he wanted nothing from her. It was simply a
mirror that reflected him as he wished himself to be perceived. She
recalled his discomfort at the vision of his father gazing back at him
– conjured up because of snow.

Isabella smiled as she read the letter, going to her bedroom to
put on her work clothes – paint-encrusted jeans and T-shirt, a scarf
round her now-dry hair. As she undressed, she felt a nudge of disappointment at the thought that he had wanted nothing from her,
then, if that had been the reason for his charm, and this added to
her pleasure now: he had written to her; he must want something.

She sat down on the edge of her bed as she read to the end. He
had obtained her address from a mutual acquaintance: he mentioned
the name, and she recalled that she had taken a commission from
the family a couple of years ago. The girl had been at Isabella's show
last December. Will had heard that she painted portraits, that her
speciality was children.

Once, a father – he was in insurance – commissioning her had
remarked, 'Good idea, catch them while they're young.'

Yes, it made good business sense, she joked: you had a customer
for life; and there was always the next generation to consider, too.
'Not a bad little racket.'

The man had narrowed his eyes as though she might be trying to
trick him. But his daughter had been sweet-natured, modest, rather
shy and a quiet sitter. Isabella had transformed her nervous pallor
to beauty. The parents were happy: they had got their money's worth.

But it was not on account of his own children that Will had written
to her. He did not mention whether he had any, although Isabella

assumed — something to do with the solidity of possessing headed writing-paper — that he had. It was on behalf of a cousin. She lived in Wiltshire, and had two girls — eight and six. A portrait was wanted of Celia and her daughters for her next birthday, and Will had heard that Isabella was 'just the ticket'. Isabella wondered if he knew how much such things cost: she didn't come cheap.

His letter gave a few details about the family: Celia kept horses, and rode on Salisbury Plain. Isabella felt that she could see them already. She imagined the girls fresh-faced and hilarious, full of life, only to be caught on the run in glimpses, quickly sketched before they fled, urging on portly ponies with kicks and Polo mints; Celia, she supposed, would be heavy-boned and swarthy, clumping about in wellington boots. Will mentioned that Celia's birthday was in the summer but, as a PS, he wondered if Isabella might like to 'go for a look-see' the following weekend. 'Short notice, I know, but call me up if you happen to be free. I'm going anyway and could take you along. It's a beautiful part of the world down there, too.'

Yes, he was charming, she thought. He wanted something, sure enough, but he was also offering something in return: the country-side, which for her meant landscapes. Not art, but the thing itself.

Isabella folded up the letter, and put it back inside its red envelope. She took it to the living room and placed it, as she had meant to do, on the mantelpiece. Even opened, she might still enjoy it.

She hummed to herself as she went upstairs to work. The solitude she had just felt seemed to tremble and break, a fog dispelled by heat. A weekend in the country would be lovely. She had said no to things for far too long; now she would say yes.

5

'It can go off now.' Leo didn't want Celia to see what was on the news.

The housekeeper, Marjorie, switched off the television and went back to polishing the mirror. 'It's all misty,' she said in disgust, using the opportunity of silence to gain momentum with 'and sticky!' She peered into the mirror, frowning in disapproval at her reflection, as though she had caught sight of a stranger.

It was shortly before lunch on Friday, and the last time Leo had seen his wife she had been going round to the stables with Charley Sutton. That had been at seven a.m. He had kept himself away from her, in his study, wanting to be found, but she had not come and by midday he had given up and gone through to the drawing room to see what was on the news, turning up the volume so that she might at least be lured into telling him to turn it down.

Now, with the television off, he could hear her crossing the hallway outside, the sharp click of her high heels on marble, the skidding cluttery sound of the four spaniels following. She must be going out; she had not mentioned any plan to do so. He straightened the *Telegraph* on the low table in front of him, bent forwards over it, wishing to be discovered by her intent in reading.

Marjorie, meanwhile, continued with what she termed 'having a blitz' in advance of the guests' arrival that evening for dinner and the weekend. The air, as a consequence, glittered with fine dust that rose up like fresh smoke when she began, as she was doing now, to beat at the sofa cushions with her fist. The Persian rugs were rolled up; Leo wished that she would take them outside and get on with them instead. He coughed discreetly. He knew better than to tell her what to do.

He listened out for his wife. He heard her footsteps stop, hesitant, and the sound of papers being shuffled together on the hall table gave him an accurate picture of her at that moment. When he had gone down to breakfast, he had found the brown manila envelope addressed to him left out in the kitchen. It seemed to have been dropped there in a hurry. Stamped, it had not been posted but hand-delivered and opening it, finding it was from Charley, he had seen his old friend in an unquiet light, tossing aside that envelope with a kind of hurried ostentation – as though he had been perfectly conscious of its importance to Leo, equally conscious of how little it mattered to him. The casualness of its being left lying around like that felt to Leo like provocation. Inside the envelope: paperwork for Leo to sign, an agreement they had been drawing up over a piece of land. If Leo signed, Charley would own a still larger part of the Eastleigh estate. It verged on putting him in the position of tenant farmer.

Now he could imagine Celia straightening the papers, and casting her eye over the documents he had – deliberately – left on top. He wasn't certain what he had meant by doing this. He dared not confess to himself that it was a cry for help. That was too subtle, and he was suspicious of subtlety, associating it with the French or, which was almost as bad, with lessons as a boy spent studying the rules of rhetoric, which he had hated. It exasperated him to remember this. But he had wanted to point out to Celia an equation that he felt had been arrived at not by him but by Charley Sutton: buying up bits of Eastleigh, walking around in the early morning with his wife. He went no further. But when he put those papers on the hall table, he had hesitated, anxious, staring out at the cold day, the weak sun pallid behind a veil of white that now had strengthened to a pasty blue, a little sickly-looking, he thought, and then he had turned away. The front door was shut. The house felt over-quiet, glum, the air distinctly musty.

It was why he hadn't objected to Marjorie going over the cleaner's work, which, she had said, proud with implication, wasn't 'enough for this weekend'. Now the place was discordant because of her industry, and secretly he cursed her. But the scent of disinfectant was preferable to the other scent – the wood leaching the life out from the spring air's possible freshness, holding the seasons in too tight check so that the place felt nothing like a farmer's house. He had rubbed his hair, his eyes. It felt more like a dowager's house, or like his mother's – as it had been before he was allowed, eventually, to move in. He shot a disgruntled glance at her portrait. It caught the light with too much significance for his liking, haloed in a pool of silver at the foot of the stairs. She had been a beautiful woman, but that didn't stop her also being his mother, and yet it was supposed to be his house now.

He waited for Celia to come to him, but instead he heard her footsteps retreating on the marble, going back upstairs, but more slowly, as though she had seen something she wished to digest in private, he thought, not made happy by feeling triumphant in that conclusion; or as though she had seen something she wished to discuss with someone else. He checked himself. His suspiciousness humiliated him. Having his eye on all that felt suddenly like an entrapment. He should keep his mind free for more important things.

He cleared his throat again, and this time the cough came out with some authority. Marjorie glanced at him, nervous, and apologised for the dust. She turned her attention to the tables, rushing at them with a fanatical display of diligence, raising photographs in their silver frames, lifting up boxes and china ornaments, clattering at top speed with a chamois leather and what smelt strongly like white spirit. He wondered, with vague alarm, if that was wise. It was as though her desire was to wipe away the surface of the house, erase its impression to reveal what lay beneath.

But he knew that this was not what had alarmed him: it was a red-herring, or lightning conductor. He paused inwardly, for he did not like to mix his notions, but there it was: he felt muddled. He couldn't see how the muddle would clear. The whole thing was simply a terrible confusion, a fog. He rubbed his eyes. Without a television to stare at he felt short-sighted.

Celia was suddenly at the door. He hadn't heard her approach. 'There you are!' She made it sound as though she had been searching for him in vain all morning. Then she disappeared and he felt bereft: he wanted more. He followed her, joining the tail end of the procession, behind the dogs. She had already gone into the kitchen, and he could hear her discussing something with the butler, Ellis – Marjorie's husband – who, Leo supposed, was on his break.

He went to the front door, this time opening it on to the cool midday, deciding to wait for her. The brown manila envelope was still on the table where he had left it, and perhaps, he decided, she had not seen it after all. He glanced back at it, the documents on top had not been disturbed, and felt oddly ashamed: he had hoped to catch her out. It was childish of him, he was well aware, to attempt to do so. The land was his business, not hers. He knew how much it troubled her – and not for selfish reasons but on his account – to feel that he was losing bits of Eastleigh. He should not have tried to get a rise out of her, and certainly not today. Hunting mattered so much more to her than it did to him; she had enough to think about without his suspicions.

He told himself all of this, his hand on the door, but he did not feel the confidence of that resolve and, looking outside, the avenue stretching away to a dark point in the line of yew trees at the perimeter, he felt the vertigo-sufferer's nerve – a blank desire to jump, or at least to walk away, not face up to his impression of a vast conversation waiting to be had. But what were the words? It was too much for him to begin to speak of the things he had in mind, which were without proper form, as though he'd need a poem to do it – he scoffed as he thought this, turned back impatiently to the hallway where she still was not – not something elaborate, just some *thing* to stand in place of the feeling. It wasn't words: words would not do at all.

He thought suddenly of that morning, when she had been out of bed before he'd even had chance to take hold of her. He had needed her then, remembering their son, but he had seen her instead outside with Charley Sutton. Perhaps it was that. He just wanted her in his arms.

Uneasy on the threshold, he sighed heavily as he waited for her. He was glad that she had missed what he'd seen earlier on the television – the Act of Parliament banning hunting with dogs finally coming into force, shots of pleased backbenchers and gloating saboteurs. It had been one of the last items on the news this time, like an afterthought, or an entertainment spot, he considered bitterly. Over the last year it had descended, the story somehow shrinking as it fell. Now it was about to evaporate to nothing, and soon it would appear never to have existed.

'Charley doesn't think it'll change anything in the long run.' Celia often reported bits of information from Charley in this manner. After the accident, Leo had asked his old friend to go with her on her rides, not so much as chaperone but until she got her confidence back, and the habit had stuck. When she had said this, only the previous week, Leo had kept quiet. If Charley had said this then evidently he was more worried than Leo had imagined. It was obvious that things would change. They all knew it, and Charley more than most. Leo himself had heard one of the whippers-in report that Charley had said he'd half a mind to turn terrorist and pop off those backbenchers one by one. There was little point in a huntsman who could not hunt. Obsolescence was just another kind of death.

Leo hoped the whipper-in had misheard. Charley was a good man, but inclined to rashness, and Leo thought he might almost do it. He was capable of a great deal of haste, and passion. If he was thwarted at one thing it was his nature to turn hard to something else, apply his full weight there until, inevitably, he succeeded at that. It was what made him so good at business: he just drove forwards, blinkered.

Celia's voice carried through from the kitchen. 'Yes, of course he will be riding.' Leo wondered if they were discussing him, in which case he thought that the enquiry was most impertinent. He had the uncomfortable sensation that it was apparent to everyone, even the servants, that Celia's choice of Leo, rather than Charley, had not been to her advantage. Was everyone so conscious that Charley had proved himself the better bet?

The dogs came out of the kitchen towards him and he ran his hands over them, working them up, Celia would say. They had begun to jump. They would stop when she returned. They knew what was expected of them. He stepped aside to let them out. They streamed across the gravel up to the park, feathers flying, birdlike almost in their grace. He watched them go, standing by the glass panes of the inner door, seeing them cresting the hill and gone beneath the oaks.

Leo was glad that he had been able to protect Celia from the announcement on the news. There was no pomp left at the moment of its being final; it had instead the common sadness of administration about it, and it had been partly because of this that it had bothered Leo so particularly: he had had a sudden intimation that this was how great wrongs were often perpetrated: on paper, without ceremony; and then he saw the man, and his loathing fell on him.

Who was he? No one, really. A backbencher. Man by the name of Lance Ash.

Leo seldom felt hatred but when he did it seemed to strike him at the back of the head, a swift and unexpected thump, of which he could see neither the point nor the cause. Because of this, it weakened him to hate, so he did not do it. It was partly why he had asked for the television to be switched off. He could almost not bear to touch it himself. He did not wish even to encounter his own emotion in this instance.

Seeing the man, just one of many such men, no doubt, who had in their small way set their names against him – for that was what it seemed now to amount to: the unevenness of democracy, its ability to unbalance all certainty, and just chuck it out – he felt the hatred dissolve and in its place there was a kind of despair that shocked him. He hadn't realised he minded so much. He had thought that as it was really Celia's bag his concern was second-hand.

But there had been something in that backbencher's manner that saddened Leo utterly: as though attentive to a telephone ringing in another room, the man's mind already appeared to be elsewhere; the decision, for him, possessed of little consequence. He had only been doing his job. And there was fatalism, too, Leo felt, in his assurance. It suggested that he had been driven to it, that the result was inevitable, merely predetermined, the consequence of his background, nothing more remarkable than that – a series of events that, for all anyone's outrage, actually did add up.

That was the worst part of it, Leo felt: the man's apparent conviction. What could one do, faced with that? Nothing. It was stalemate. The reason it had made him so uneasy was because, far from being a conviction he himself knew nothing about, it was not remote. It was a mirror. It was how he knew he looked, discussing the same subject, speaking from the opposing side – the reflection a little dusty perhaps, but a mirror nonetheless.

That had been when he'd asked Marjorie to switch the damn thing off. He did not like what he saw. He was sorry for them both. Something beyond both love and rational argument was in play. It troubled him to consider what might run deeper even than that. He didn't think it could be anything very good – something that reddened a person's mind until they killed. He flinched from the idea because it seemed to stand very near to him, almost a presence beside him in the shadowed hallway.

He glanced outside: the dogs were still gone from view. He wondered if Celia was going out to ride with Charley. But if that was the case, why the high heels? His own boots, unworn for five years, the leather cracked now at the ankles, were beneath the coat-rack in the corner of the hallway. He had better see to them pretty quickly if he was to wear them tomorrow. He would ask Marjorie for some wax.

He thought of his first hunt, the clear-cut fear that had come at him like a decision. He took it, and rode, and was blooded at the kill. He thought again of that backbencher: it was as though he, too, had been blooded – not in fact, but in intention. Although their causes were opposed, they were daubed with the same preoccupied conviction. It wasn't something a man needed to dwell on. Blood came up with its own answers; it was much too dark for anyone to see beneath it for a reason.

He shut the inner door. It was cold outside, although he doubted that there would be a frost. He peered upwards. The sky seemed to have sunk lower, the clouds weighted with an iron burden that looked to him like rain.

Having kept silent about that backbencher, the thought of him welled up, stronger, and now Leo wanted to perform some act of devotion for Celia, as though to lift the hex of the man's appearance, and to lessen his own instinctive guilt at having secrets from her. He missed her. Where was she going? He felt anguished to think that something deeper than love might take over; that perhaps had taken over already, between even them. He had not thought such a thing might happen.

A sudden sound from outside startled him, made him glance round. It was just the dogs, back at the front door, jostling to be let in; he went to do it; and it was like this – preoccupied with the four animals, his back turned – that she found him.

Before he had had either the chance to say any of the things he had wished to, or offer up his affection, votive – he had not been quick enough, he did not know what he should do – she had gone, a kiss lightly on his cheek as though he were one of the children. She smelt of cinnamon and star anise, and a wine-ish smell that he recalled was her favourite perfume, and as he stood alone without her in the doorway where he had first met her, his breath shortened with the question of for whom, if not for him, she was wearing that scent. She had not said where she was going. Afraid, he went to find the children.

Lance Ash. Even the name had the ring of death about it.

6

The original site on which the Domeynes' Palladian house was built had first been parcelled off in the fifteenth century, following the break-up of the centralised feudal authority. This earlier building was torn down over a century later by the Elizabethans, and the plot had stood empty until the seventeen hundreds. But evidence of that earlier habitation was visible in the land, even in the present day, as a low ridge covered with gorse and screened by beechwoods.

The size of the estate had waxed and waned over the years and now, as though at the end of its long cycle, it was again almost the exact proportion as at the very start. Its appearance had altered, sure enough, but in the manner of passing vogues, for beneath it all the nature of the place was ancient and unchanged. At certain times this nature was revealed, and the land was reminded of itself. Mist rising up from the water-meadows; a moonless dawn when no bird sang; the snow falling fast, ensuring silence.

The building then looked temporary and theatrical – a play put on in the middle of a crisis. But because it had endured for so long, the nobility of the attempt had taken on an air of faint despair. Could the play reveal the crisis in a quieter light, or was there something far stronger in the land that would win? The seasons would close. Everything tended towards the ending.

It was a house to fall in love with because it seemed, in spite of its longevity, to be so fleeting, and as such it offered the dream of catching hold of the impossible. Because such things cannot be done, its dominant characteristic was of readiness, with time grown a little exhausted – the stage-set painted, the actors and audience assembling, everything held in waiting.

Now, aside from the paddock, some woodland and a few fields, in February ploughed but still stubbly, wheat and barley coming later, the estate was almost entirely contained within the circuit of the red-brick walls: parkland with oaks; the beech coppice; the bluebell walk between a broad avenue of limes; on the eastern side of the house, a row of Italian pencil cypresses, black lead against the sky; and the Oriental water-garden, where the small lake was stocked with golden carp and lilies, the perimeter sedgy in places but elsewhere, in early summer, sprouting ferns and wild rhubarb. A massive elm brought down in the 1987 hurricane had been left. Upturned, it showed the chalky earth beneath; the roots were home to a badger's sett.

Closest to the house were the formal gardens: a rose arbour, a white gravel and dwarf box maze, a herb garden, a lavender border remarkable for being composed of each of the different varieties, and terraces in shallow banks leading the eye towards what was once an open vista, and now had been screened off by pines: the noise of the road had become intrusive.

The garden, a little ragged but still fine, had been designed in 1735 by the young Capability Brown – the main lure for its spectators in the summer. However, it was not the result of a formal commission, but a weekend's suggestion. The plans still existed, such as they were – really no more than rapid sketches, executed on the encouragement of a friend. The Domeynes had not had the funds at the time to see through the commission. Their own gardener had followed Brown's design. Brown had not minded. The garden, therefore, was perceived by the Domeynes as serendipitous – an unexpected gift, something not absolutely theirs.

The beauty of Capability Brown's garden at Eastleigh was that it was a different place, depending from where it was viewed. From one vantage-point, it was Arcadian; from another, rustic; elsewhere a vista opened up a clear line on towards the house, and the view then might almost have been urban, a direct sight-line across one of the royal parks in London.

The windows of the house reflected the view back out across the land. But instead of a mirror, the suggestion was of a clear way through – the windows opening straight out on to the other side. This strengthened the impression of the place being almost one-dimensional, a stage-set, or a painting that had been suspended; and the effect was a puzzle, because the building was made of red bricks, which were anything but airy.

The pleasure of the garden was also in precisely this puzzlement: the mind balked at what the senses perceived as true – concealments creating what logically seemed impossible views; baffling angles suddenly revealing a clear run towards the horizon; a glimpse through woodland that set the vanishing-point in darkness.

The plan had been executed with casual geometry in the space of one afternoon. It was an early attempt, but it sketched out Brown's ambition. He saw no obstacle in that meeting of mind and emotion: the play between them was the point, to reveal it his intention. In the present day, the garden seemed a charmed place, everything it represented dropped in from another world, and its loveliness was insistent for that reason.

The tennis courts, set in the 1920s, also still remained at Eastleigh – the reason for Celia having been there when she first met Leo – but the nets sagged, weighted with green mildew, the string rotten in places; and the courts themselves also needed reliming: the traces were too faint to play with any degree of accuracy.

In summer, and on certain days in spring – for the aconites, snow-drops and, later, the bluebells – all of this could be seen by the public: tickets were sold from a small wooden hut erected at the north gate.

The garden, and the small income derived from it, was Celia's affair. Most of the revenue went to the cottage hospital in the village. Leo understood that it all went there. But, using her own funds, Celia embellished the remainder to match the original amount and donated it to the women's refuge in the town. Leo did not know she did this; nor had she ever discussed her motive in doing so. It was the one thing she meant to keep secret from her husband always.

Opposite the hut, also just within the limits of the Domeynes' estate, was the gatehouse, built in a flush of industrial wealth in the late eighteen hundreds. There was no use for it now: the gates were seldom locked – people just drove through, parking their cars where at one time carriages would have pulled up, or garaging them in the part of the stable-block not occupied, as it mainly was, by Celia's horses. She had three; four others were also kept there, at livery, looked after by the resident of the obsolete gatehouse, James Dunbar.

An ex-cavalry officer, James Dunbar lived in the gatehouse gratis, employed by the Domeynes in the capacity of managerial-style groom. 'Managerial-style' was never stated, of course, but it was the idea: his status as an ex-officer made them reluctant to employ him simply as groom. Notionally, he was of more worth to them than had he risen from a lowlier rank, even though he performed a lesser task, and when they spoke of him, they would often say that they were 'lucky to have him', and the company in which they said it understood perfectly what was meant. He had descended, rather than risen, to his present status, which gave his position an aspect of vagueness, of a role inadequately performed but still beyond reproach: fallen on hard times, to criticise him would have smacked of gloating.

Nevertheless, he was not very good at his job, and with some reason. He characterised himself, much more than the gatehouse, as obsolete: even he could no longer fathom out his purpose; he did not do what he was built for.

James Dunbar had left the army with an honourable discharge two years after what had become known as the first Iraq war. He had been injured, fighting in the Gulf. Departure had already been on his mind. The bullet entered his right shoulder and, ahead of the pain, he had felt the injury's justice: it was what happened to you when you lost belief in the rightness of the enterprise. He had not lost it utterly but, like a poor dye, it had seeped from him. He had felt the ebb, and been disgusted with himself. His family's male line had all been military.

But it was how decisions came upon him: they crept up, until eventually he would find that he had been hijacked by them; in retrospect, they seemed inevitable. Yet he had thought it all through, turning things over each night until the idea of leaving began to shine, and he perceived it to be as well made as the gun he had just oiled, set aside. It was well made, but like love, which he also regarded with suspicion, as a kind of hijacking, impossible to catch hold of. Had he not been shot, he doubted that he would have had the courage to leave.

That equation, running so tightly together, was what made him see how far his faith had slipped. He had lost the firmness of his control. His finger slipped on the idea of his belief. It might have been enough to get him killed. The bullet might have lodged lower, in his heart.

He had been stumbling at the time. Wind had made the sand rise and he had been blinded by it – a kind of gritty fog – just before he heard the whiz and pop. The enemy had found him by his heat, he later discovered; it was entirely unexpected, an ambush. His men had not known the others might be there.

Even now the wound still caused him trouble, especially in damp weather. It was enough to make him unfit for service, but not so unfit that he was unable to operate as a civilian. Certain things he could not do, but they were not now required of him: fire a pistol accurately at full gallop; hold a rifle steady enough to be the crack shot he once was, although, with his shoulder bound up, he could still shoot. It made him bitter – a cousin had a grouse moor in Yorkshire – and since he could not be reliable, he was temperamental instead, with a temperamental person's self-righteous logic: 'You just don't understand!'

When pressed, he would not say that he had lost all appetite for war, that he was set against it now in the way that, before, he had been set against the enemy. He would simply say that he had seen enough, which was perceived by some as dignified, others as a kind of disgrace. But the injury marked him out as an underdog, and those who found him disgraceful also understood the shame in mistreating underdogs: the fight should be honourable, otherwise it was cruelty.

Waking early on Friday morning, the dawn light silver and without warmth, James Dunbar turned over awkwardly in bed, his shoulder aching with the damp. He drew the green velvet curtains in the bedroom, glancing outside. The yew cast a heavy shadow inwards. It was a quarter of an hour earlier than he usually woke, six a.m. He turned off the alarm clock, and went through to the kitchen to cook bacon for his breakfast.

He didn't like to wake sooner than was necessary: it brought the day up closer than he wished, the extra time a kind of parenthesis that set aside what it contained, making him take notice.

He had been at Eastleigh for almost twelve years, and he knew that it was overdue for him to move on. It was not simply that the hunt was doomed – he certainly thought it was. It was that he no longer cared that it was so. More than that, he corrected himself, boiling the kettle for tea, sitting down at the kitchen table with yesterday's

Times in front of him, unread, it was that, secretly, he was glad. It forced his hand. He would have to leave now, find other work. Without hunting, Celia would keep fewer horses; the livery would most likely go – those horses were Irish hunters; perhaps they would go out to stud in Waterford.

He rolled his head, stretched out his arm, flexed his hand, frowned at the twinge of pain, cursing the damp cottage. It was the life of a hermit. But over the years his reflections had got him nowhere. The trees had grown closer, the small house, with his familiar movements contained within it, had grown more snug around him until it seemed svelte, in its containment, as a trap. He sipped at the tea, scalding his lips. He got up to make toast for a bacon sandwich, reaching for the HP sauce.

The day was very still, when he looked into it through the window, and he could not imagine that tomorrow would bring anything other than the end, and that it would look the same as this: pale and quiet, a slight rustling across the fields and then it would be over. There would be no next season. Thinking this, he felt the nerves of anxiety start their dance along his spine, which straightened, a military memory stirring in his vertebrae. He felt his trigger finger twitch. It was a kind of anguish and he could not rid himself of it: the memory of how everything had begun; his love of riding out with hounds; being blooded into a world where it was as acceptable as drinking tea that one day he might give the order for a kill. He had given it; he had also obeyed it. The blood had proved stronger by far than habit; it had decisively recoloured him.

He sipped the strong Lapsang Souchong, cooler now. A bit of twig stuck in his teeth and he spat it out into his hand, a small black aromatic stick; he opened the window, threw it out. The air outside felt warmer than it was in the house. He propped the window open. A thrush was singing in the elder, and its call was answered from a little way off. If he had known that he would lose his faith, would he have pushed through life up to this point? He checked himself, hating the question for its ring of sentiment, inviting it closer because he knew that beneath the posture it was sincere, and he did not yet know the answer.

The alarm clock clicked past the quarter-hour in the other room. It was appropriate, he told himself, getting up with a sigh, reaching for his tweed coat, his hat, looking about for the peacock blue silk neckerchief he always wore beneath his shirt, that he lived now as a hermit, because it was impossible for him to place himself outside in the world and find a home there.

He thought of his family: they had not, quite, disowned him when he left the army, but it was as though he had fallen from the list of things in which they took an interest. When, rarely now, he visited his parents, even when invited, they always appeared shocked that he arrived, and flustered, too, fumbling and blushing, his old room not quite prepared, towels missing, the bed not turned down or aired. They made a point of not mentioning the fact that he never brought anyone to stay with him. He had five sisters. He was the youngest. They were all married. The pressure that had been on him as the only son seemed, with time, to have evaporated. But it was an illusion: the hissing steam from a pressure-cooker suddenly gone off, and the silence was dangerous – everything was going on inside there. Because of those sisters, he would come into little money, if anything. This had preyed on his mind when he started seriously to think about leaving Eastleigh. He wasn't cut out for a life of impecunity.

James considered how it had been Celia's brother, Gerald, who had set him up with the position here at Eastleigh. He wondered if Gerald would be back in time from Egypt. On the last few occasions they had met, Gerald had been distinctly off, but if he wished, he might be very useful. And if he did not wish it, James thought now, there was something of which he might remind the older man that might encourage him.

His boots were by the back door; he put them on, fingers slipping on the leather because they were still buttery from his half-
eaten sandwich. He set his cap at an angle, looking at himself in the
mirror. His green eyes were tired, but his cheeks had colour. It was
impossible not to feel a faint tug of excitement at the days ahead.
Something would happen. He would make sure of that.

He left the cottage for the stables up at the house. He did not
hurry; he munched his sandwich as he went. The early sky was turning
quickly blue between the branches of the trees. He could smell the
pines, and he lingered, eating, bending down at one point – were
the aconites coming through? It was just a snowdrop. He leaned for
a moment against a beech trunk.

Last week he had overheard a conversation that for some reason
had stuck in his mind. He asked himself whether it might have been
this that set in motion the train of thoughts he now found himself
caught up with. It had been the housekeeper, of all people, Marjorie,
and she had been agreeing with something her husband, Ellis, must
have said about him. 'Yes,' the woman's voice had been disapproving,
'you're right about Dunbar.' James had heard her speaking in the
kitchen: he had been outside, passing through the back courtyard
from the stables. 'He does moon about rather, doesn't he?'

At the time, he had minded and felt insulted. But now, setting
off again along the driveway, he reconsidered. At the age of thirty-
six he was, just, young enough to carry it off without incurring
anger although, of course, the husbands did not like it because he
was also handsome. If he must do it, he knew that they wished he'd
do it elsewhere, in other dining rooms, after enjoying other people's
brandy. The wives maintained on the other hand that he was a 'sweet
boy', but this was taken to be a blind for their affection, and even
if no more than fondness, as with affection shown to puppies, it was
still possible that the animal might some day turn and bite.

Approaching the house, he thought of that evening's dinner. He had kept himself secret for so long. A person could not stay loaded that way without eventually going off. It was right that he should leave. Now was the perfect time to make his announcement. They would all be there. He saw himself at that moment as a saboteur. If he wished, he might be dangerous. What did they expect? He could not help it: his old self would return.

To think of their anxiety gave him confidence. He broke off a switch of birch and swished it ahead of him, swiping the heads off daffodils as he walked. It didn't matter, he told himself, watching them fall – they were already over.

7

One husband in particular was anxious about James Dunbar: Charley
Sutton, the master of foxhounds. He was perfectly aware – he was
sure that he had seen it with his own eyes – that Dunbar was in love
with his wife, Esther.

Charley thought of this on Friday morning as he rose to go outside to the stables to check on the horses. It had occurred to him
because he had been thinking of that night's dinner up at Eastleigh.
He supposed that Dunbar would be there. He wished he would not.

He hesitated before he went out to the yard. In the narrow hallway
by the back door, the coat-rack was dense with coats; boots were
ranged beneath. Most of the stuff was his, although some belonged
to his wife. He touched the red sleeve of a jacket, noticing with irritation that a moth had burrowed into the wool. He let the thing
drop. It was unlike him to feel jealousy. He saw a small moth emerge
from the sleeve and, between thumb and forefinger, swiftly crushed
it.

He cleared his throat. It was not jealousy, he corrected himself,
it was the annoyance of being presented with an uneven fight. Dunbar
was swattable: he could bat him to the boundary in an instant. It
was insulting that he should have had to consider that boy at all. No,
the reason he wished Dunbar would not be at dinner was because,
while he did not want there to be a scene, he could feel a part of
himself heat up – just as it did on the day of hunting, his blood

rising, his attention becoming fine tuned – and yet it was too early for all that: it was only dinner.

He pushed his feet into wellington boots, took down a tweed coat and hat, put them on and went outside.

It was a fresh day, cold and clear, and the air felt good in his lungs, dispelling the sensation he had woken to – as though a blanket had been stretched too tight in the night. By morning he had not kicked it off: he had been too weak. It was unlike him to be thus. He was seldom out of sorts. But as he crossed the yard he felt an apprehension that was physical: a tension in his spine, his left knee aching as though he had spent the night not in his goosedown bed but bound up in a ditch. It was fanciful to think like that; he stopped himself, straightening up, but he grimaced as he did so, and brooded on what had brought together Dunbar and his own disquiet in his mind. At forty-five, he had woken for the first time with a premonition of himself as an old man, estranged by vitality from a younger wife.

Esther was only nine years younger but – and perhaps it was because they did not have children? – she had the bright looks of a girl. He often thought so and, indeed, was often told so, too; on one occasion he had even been told so by Dunbar. He had remembered this as he woke, sliding out of bed before Esther, glancing back at her red hair snaking towards him on the pillow. She did not move as he left: they had not been entwined.

He entered the stall to check on the gelding he planned to use tomorrow. He wasn't certain that he would: the animal had not been quite fit all season; he had fallen lame the previous year, and although he had mended, he still wasn't a hundred per cent. His unfitness was a hair-crack, that was all, but Charley had avoided taking him out unless the going really was fair. A frost, and he rode another horse. He ran his hands along the animal's belly now and down the leg, wondering. The day he had suspected Dunbar had been the day the horse fell lame.

It had snowed in the night, and the sound of their voices had carried clearly towards him through the trees. The hunt was over, they had made a kill, and the field had almost dispersed. There was to be a few hours' hiatus before that evening's dinner, hosted by the Domeynes. Charley had started out on a mare, and switched to a fresh horse mid-way through the afternoon – the gelding. It was not his habit to do so, but as a favour to a friend he had agreed to give the other man's animal some exercise first, before the season's close – 'the final season' as, with displeasure, he had heard someone call it. Now that tag had stuck and he could not make it shift. It entered his head against his wishes. Once it was there, it lingered like a defeat already suffered so that he could not turn from it.

Perhaps he had ridden the gelding too hard, but it had been a fast day. They had been crossing flinty ground, a ploughed field where hoar frost had made the furrows iron, and somewhere in traversing that ice-bound sea his horse had picked up a stone, which, by the time they'd gone a way down the road, had made him lame. It was almost the end of the day. One of the whippers-in took over; Charley left the field early rather than switch a third time.

He had been leading the gelding back down through the woods to Eastleigh, meaning to put him in their stable since it was nearer than his own. He'd have the vet look at him there: it meant he'd not be held back from dinner if the man was late. As he went down through the pines, the needly ground the softest way, he had been able to hear a number of voices ahead of him, gathering outside Eastleigh, the sound of a horse-box driving off, the metal of hoofs on gravel. There were other voices, too, hidden somewhere in the wood, but he had drawn almost level with James Dunbar's cottage before he could see anything, the avenue opening up between the trees. He had glanced across towards the gatehouse from the distance of around a hundred yards, startled at first partly for the view: he hadn't known that a clear way was cut through at that point; the

garden often caught him unawares, and usually he enjoyed the sensation – a man's garden, he had always thought, a garden of ideas.

But this time, looking across, he noticed three horses, loosely
tethered outside as though their riders had just that moment dismounted, and he frowned, and had half a mind to call out to whoever it was, tell them to see to the animals quickly: it wasn't wise
to leave them standing without blankets in this cold, not after a day's
hunting, they should know that; and then he noticed that one of the
horses, the bay mare, was his wife's.

He did not stop, or even break his pace but slowed enough to
hear her voice raised in laughter, along with two or three other
men's voices, clamouring slightly as though they were inside playing
some kind of game. Carrying on down the hill, he caught sight of
Esther through the window, framed there perfectly static, her russet
hair exposed – she had taken off her hat, the net must have gone
with it as her hair was loosened from its bun – and then she was
obscured by the black jackets of a couple of the men.

She was his wife. Charley had never suspected her of anything
less than devotion: he had no evidence for it. But he had often
thought that she was easily led astray: she was too sympathetic.

He had passed a little further down the hill when he heard her
call to him, her voice very natural, he judged, as though she had
anticipated his being there, but how could she? And its naturalness
at that moment appalled him: was it studied, an indication of her
guilt, or genuine? He realised that he could not tell, which hurt him.
He stopped. She was leading her horse towards him.

Charley had looked back then to see three men emerging from
the cottage. James Dunbar was in the middle, and the two men
either side of him stood for a moment with their arms round him
as though he had performed some act of heroism and they were
celebrating his victory. Charley turned away. What was the man's
victory? He did not answer Esther when she asked how lame his

horse was. It offended him that the gelding should be lame: what could she want with a boy like James Dunbar?

She caught up with him, and started to tell him how James, whom she now referred to as 'Jamie', had wanted them to have 'a straightener' – Charley assumed his wife was quoting Dunbar when she said this – before they went down to the house. His sloe gin. 'Killer stuff, darling, I think he's overdone it this time.' His gin was considered potent enough as it was, Charley was well aware. He did not respond. 'He said you'd be coming by, so I thought I'd hang on for you.'

Charley glanced at Esther. He believed her. She concealed nothing. It was all Dunbar. What was he playing at? James and the two other men, whom he did not recognise as local, were still jostling about in front of the cottage. The horses were restless in the cold, steam rising. 'He should get those animals inside and blanketed. He's a fool to have them standing about like that.' He had hoped to demote Dunbar in his wife's eyes, swiftly to the rank of an employee, but she only appeared puzzled.

'We were expecting you to pass by. We only just got down. I asked them to wait.' He heard a faint note of hurt in her voice; when he looked at her she touched her lips with her tongue, as though licking away the taste of sloe gin. They led their horses on down the incline towards the house.

The entire episode – her arrival at the cottage, his seeing her there, her leaving to catch up with him – had perhaps taken no more than three minutes. But it had exhausted him. It felt like the point of sundown, blackness coming like a revelation. He had never felt jealousy before, if that was what it was, and it darkened him; he felt suddenly very tired. He refused to be that man's rival. She either loved him or she didn't. It was how he had lost Celia to Leo. He just backed off where he might fail. He seldom failed.

Now Charley leaned against the gelding, an arm round his neck, gazing out at the empty yard. A few weeks ago an old friend had telephoned him, asking if he'd like to make up a party of men hunting big game in Malawi. It was hardly compensation for what had been lost. He had said he'd need time to think about it. But the same day he had sent his guns to be serviced. He had not mentioned it to Esther. He needed to be away from her to love her; he had started to wonder if it also worked the other way round. His spirit had risen momentarily at the thought of being able to show himself to her as he wished to be seen – at a distance that allowed him to be a man.

He unlatched the stable door, remembering the overheard phrase 'the final season', which now he could not dislodge. He cursed it for it seemed – like that impression of Esther, framed, Dunbar looking on behind her – magnetic in its influence. Words and pictures like that could make the unthinkable happen, he decided, which was why they should not be uttered, should not be seen.

He went out into the yard. The horse pressed against him, pushing him forwards. If Esther wanted Dunbar, she could have him. If it was all the other way round, Dunbar would find himself in trouble. Tonight would show decisively which way things fell, and by then he would be ready.

But, first, he wanted to see if Esther was awake; he wanted to hear her voice. Dunbar was easy prey, not so insignificant as to be ignored but sufficient to be sport.

He walked, more confident now, back into the house. Crossing into the drawing room he noticed, among a stack of magazines, a brown manila envelope he had asked Esther to post to Leo the previous week. He wondered briefly at her forgetfulness and, glancing upwards, supposed that, rather than go up to her now, he had better drop the papers round himself to Eastleigh. He needed Leo's signature.

He was half out of his coat; he slipped his arm back inside and went out to the car. It shouldn't take long. He would be back most likely before Esther woke. He might say something to Dunbar if he ran into him, and he smiled to think of this. Just as he left, he noticed an unopened jar of their honey. He picked it up: he'd take it round for Celia.

8

Rather later on Friday morning, for he was seldom an early riser, Will Bowden, Celia's cousin, was rummaging in the wardrobe in his flat in London, in Maida Vale, cursing: his black hunting jacket had fallen from its hanger and was now hopelessly crumpled. He couldn't find his stock, and his white breeches, when he unearthed them, were muddy at the knees from last time. He would try a bit of damage limitation now – have a crack at ironing and washing out those marks, but otherwise it would all have to do.

He threw the bundle on to the bed, sat on the edge in his pyjamas and, for the first time, felt nervous about seeing Isabella. He had kept his eye fixed on the hunt, the weekend in general, and had tried to outwit himself by firing off a letter to her, which, for him, more prone to using the telephone, made him think of the episode as being of the order of a business transaction – a favour to his cousin's husband, Leo, he wrote, who wanted a portrait painter for Celia and the girls. It was just the excuse he needed to get in touch with her.

He smirked to himself now – ruffling his hair, which was in need of a wash so that doing this made it stand on end, darkly spiky – as he recalled his mischievous choice of red envelope. He had known perfectly well what he was doing: it would arrive on her mat on Valentine's Day, and he knew what girls were like. He wasn't exactly a Lothario, although he supposed he might become one when he was older, but he had often heard himself described as 'fast', and that moniker he did not mind. In fact, it pleased him a good deal, because it was his intention.

The trouble with Isabella was that she had resurfaced in his thoughts in December, and somehow she had stuck. That, for Will, was most unusual. Girls did not usually stick in his mind for such a length of time. They flashed there, suddenly, and were extinguished just as quick. He didn't mean to be fickle, but he supposed it was in his nature. Part of his intention in seeing Isabella was to find out if that would dispel her. He supposed it would. He wasn't sure that he would mind if it did. He imagined, in fact, that it would be a relief because for the last two and a half months he had thought of little else. At Christmas, he had found himself wishing she was with him, which was absurd, as he barely knew her, but by New Year's Eve he had made a resolution. He wouldn't mess about. He would see her, and then he'd know what was what.

He scowled at his crumpled jacket. There wasn't time to have it dry-cleaned. He'd take a long hot bath, and hang it up in the steam. He'd dip the breeches in there too. He didn't have washing powder. He'd have to use soap. His mother was right. He was a heathen when it came to domestic arrangements. Thinking this, he felt a good deal better. He was dirty because he was a boy. It was women who wanted him clean. Still, he scrubbed at the muddy breeches, and almost whooped when he discovered his stock and hunting shirt, happily unblemished, in a bottom drawer. He saw himself in full kit and knew he would be handsome. How could Isabella not adore him more than he would her when, after so long, he saw her again? That would do the trick. They would simply be unbalanced. Her liking for him would quickly bore him.

He went to the bathroom, turned on the taps and sat on the rim of the bath. Whatever he tried to tell himself, he knew perfectly well that he would be anything but bored if Isabella liked him.

He poured bath salts into the water and considered. Certainly she hadn't sounded all that keen when she telephoned him to say that, yes, she could come down at the weekend. What had been her phrase? 'Sure, I can make this weekend, no problem.' She had sounded businesslike, terribly efficient. A radio had been tinkling in the background, something classical, the doorbell had rung mid-conversation – 'Courier,' she had said, before hanging up. If he was honest with himself, there had been faint amusement in her voice, too, as though she had seen right through him. She had seemed preoccupied with a world of which he knew nothing. Even her accent sounded a little strange – faintly transatlantic – and he felt affronted, a glimpse almost of loneliness, to think that she might have been living in a foreign country and he had not known.

The water had reached the brim. He looked down at it in surprise. It wasn't like him to daydream, and he told himself to brace up. He undressed, let some of the water run away, and got in. It was scaldingly hot, as he liked it, and in particular today because he required a degree of mild punishment to maintain his composure, and if he was to pull the thing off, he certainly needed that. It wouldn't do to let her get even the faintest whiff of his ulterior motive. Having put it like that, he felt better again, and roguish, and he shut his eyes, sinking beneath the hot water.

Although Will figured it as pure accident, fate almost, that had returned Isabella to his thoughts, in fact there were numerous points at which their lives might have overlapped sooner. In the end it had been because of her show at the Marlborough Gallery in London the previous December. The invitation came to him via a girl he had picked up in Cork Street. He had glanced with some scepticism at the image on the card, dismissing it as commercial: an inoffensive family portrait, somewhat in the manner of Augustus John, he decided, though the lighting was pure Whistler. It was a mishmash, pleasant enough but derivative. He thought nothing of it, but wedged it alongside the other Christmas-party invitations on his mantelpiece. He went out to such things a good deal; they blended one into another; and most were simply an excuse to be sociable, nothing to do with art.

He collected a little, but it wasn't really his line. He was in property, a developer, so far on a small scale but enough to 'keep him out of mischief', as his mother had argued; years ago she had been successful in persuading his father to cough up the initial sum for his son's investment. 'After this, you're on your own, understood?' His dad was rich but tight with it. Will was grateful: that handout was more than he deserved. Until then, he had been dissolute. Secretly, at least from his parents, it was a habit that had stuck, but at least he tried, economised where he could – he was a member of only one London club, and a cheap one at that: Whites had been prohibitive; he served Berry Brothers' own-brand, not Dom Pérignon – and his business now was flourishing.

The show was in the week before Christmas: as the other invitations were removed one by one, Isabella's came to the front, and by then Will had started to find the picture interesting. He had a dinner at Mirabelle later the same evening. It would be a pleasant precursor to that. He remembered the pretty girl who had sent him the invitation. He decided to go. By then he had adjusted his opinion of the portrait – not sentimental, but actually quite charming – and thought he might even find himself buying some of the art. Unaccountably, the picture had lodged in his mind with a kind of radiance that felt to him like expectation – a proposal of something to which he had not thought he might ever be responsive: family.

He could only take his own family in small doses, but there were a great many of them; they were hard to avoid – the country seemed chock-full of his cousins – and, dangling from the branches of the family tree, its roots deep in English history, a number of titles gleamed with a look of importance that depressed Will to contemplate. It was simply too bad that he was expected to merit any kind of privilege. He just wanted to muddle along. He enjoyed being irresponsible, looking out only for himself. The idea of obligation irritated him, and the thought that he should strive to be worthy of a past not of his making left him nervous, and faint of heart. He hadn't asked to be born into what others thought good fortune. To think of it threw him into panic. He tried not to think of it.

At the age of thirty-two, however, the idea of his playing a role in his family's story had gathered steam. He could feel it coming to a head in all of his mother's conversations. It was their chief subtext. A friend had remarked only the other week — they had been shooting at his parents' home in Oxfordshire – 'I expect you'll settle down to it all pretty happily.' Will's mother had been arranging a meeting between Will and a selection of well-chosen, distant female cousins. He was supposed to be ready for all that, but he certainly didn't feel it.

'I've asked the Bridgnorth girls. You remember Lucinda – she's terribly sharp.' His mother had addressed him the moment they came in from the shoot; his friend sniggered.

Will's father, stepping in from the gun-room, announced, 'Yes, he'll like the Bridgnorth girls. Hugh's a good man.' Will listened to this kind of thing with despair. They often referred to him in the third person, and as though there was no doubt that he should comply and, inevitably, become just like them. But it was not his ideal, and it was not of his choosing. He wanted nothing more than to make his own life; he feared nothing more than that it would not be possible. History would win the day. His family vision would prevail — and not that light and lovely vision in the portrait.

Leaving the house to go to the show at the Marlborough Gallery, plucking the invitation from the others on the mantelpiece, he had paused momentarily before tucking it away in his coat pocket. There was something else about it: the name of the artist was familiar but he could not place it. He hailed a cab and took off across town, pondering.

With Christmas imminent, the city was carnival with motion. It made him feel safe to be caught up in that haphazard vitality because it was perpetual: he associated cities with a quality of immortality that he felt the countryside lacked for being so brazenly seasonal.

For him, the seasons – nature's clock – spelt death much more than life. There was too much order in them. They determined each inch of the countryside in a way that he, having grown up there, felt he knew minutely. They were a finger's grip against the jugular of his spirit. Since they barely touched the town, he preferred to live there because it made him feel free.

He was expected, on his parents' death, or before, should they be infirm, to take over the house in Oxfordshire and he shuddered to think that all that would one day be his. He didn't want it. He thought of the countryside with dread. Always, leaving to return to the town, he felt oddly damaged by it – almost battle-scarred, as after a conflict not resolved but once more undertaken, and always in the certain knowledge that one day the victory would fall decisive, and not to him.

Stopped in a traffic jam in Marylebone, Will had shut his eyes and opened them moments later to see that it had begun to snow. His thoughts softened and shifted to the evening ahead, alighting on a memory of where he had heard the name on the invitation before. He sat up in the cab as he remembered.

It had been snowing then, also, and he had been so keen on the girl that he had come away early from hunting – it was a Saturday in November – expressly to be at the theatre for an hour before the rehearsal, alone with her, and to make his arrival there seem an accident. More than ten years later, he had almost forgotten her name, although he could see her clearly, her short chestnut hair, very green eyes, long limbs, and the grace of her movements, the attentiveness of her expression as though, without judgement, she was noting everything down. He remembered her as quick to smile, and how she had done this when he held out his arm to her to help her down from the ladder. She had been painting the sets.

He marvelled that he had not made the connection sooner. She had been good then, studying at the Ruskin School; it was only natural that she should have made a career from that much talent. He drew out the invitation from his breast pocket and stared down at it: Isabella Frey.

Looking out at the snow, it saddened him that he had forgotten how much he had liked her. He recalled that he had tried, once, to ask her out on a date but she had looked at him as though the suggestion that she might go anywhere alone with him was so out of the question that she could not even consider it. He had broadened the request to include the entire cast and remembered how he had spent the evening in the Turf Tavern waiting in vain for her to arrive.

Halted at a red light, he had tried to pin down what it was about her that had enthralled him. Where he felt full of so much that was not him, she, by contrast, seemed to have everything because she had so little; it gave her an aura of perfection, because her emptiness meant that she was uncatchable: you cannot corral something that is not there. Without responsibilities, she could go to hell if she wanted to. He could not. Someone would step in to prevent it. Too much depended on what he felt to be his purgatory.

The taxi had moved off and was heading fast along Bond Street. He glanced at his watch. Six thirty. The place would not yet have filled up. He wasn't due to meet the other girl until a quarter to the hour. That gave him almost fifteen minutes. He felt his heart run fast in his chest. He put the invitation back into his pocket. He wanted to see Isabella, and say something to her – thank her for that lighter vision of family, although how he'd say that he had no idea — before the show became too crowded with all the people who, usually, he might have liked to see, but whom now were for him like that cast of fellow-students in the university pub, all awful for not being her.

He felt the pressure of the minutes. Ten years shrank into a quarter of an hour. The cab jolted, braking suddenly, skidding on the sleety road. The driver apologised. The engine stalled. The man threw an insult out of the window to the straying shopper. Will felt returned to himself. What had he been thinking? That family was most likely hers. He had barely known her. He touched his forehead, took a deep breath, settled back into the seat, told the man not to worry, that he was not in any rush.

'Good job, mate, traffic's shocking up ahead.'

It was his reprieve. It settled in him like the sum of life: the map was already set out for him; Isabella was a wild card; he was being crazy. Besides, she would probably not even remember him.

He decided not to go to the show. He took out his phone. He would tell the girl he had been delayed. He did not trust himself to see Isabella now, after everything he had been thinking.

He reached across to pull down the window. He was tired. He breathed in the chill December, and thought he scented all the perils of the countryside. But he drew back, correcting himself. It was only Green Park.

Now, remembering all this as he stepped, pinker, out of the bath, Will felt amazed at his restraint in having waited for so long before he found a way to see her. It had done him good, he told himself, to show some self-control. He had bided his time; now he would reel her in. But as he peered at his face in the mirror, combed back his hair, he wondered if he had aged much in the last ten years, and whether she would like him as he was.

He paused, considering, then grinned at his reflection, speaking aloud. 'Good Lord, man, pull yourself together.' He really was losing his touch. Of course she'd like him.

He threw his breeches into the bathwater. 'Heathen,' he called himself, with pleasure.

9

When Celia left the house late on Friday morning Leo, lacking Will Bowden's confidence, went straight upstairs to see the children, Hettie and Belinda. But they were not to be found. He stood in the empty nursery. Marjorie was still clattering about downstairs, and he could hear the nanny, Anna, beating rugs outside the kitchen door. She was fanatical about dust mites and the children's asthma. He had wondered briefly at the bare floorboards as he entered the room. He kicked aside a wooden dog in annoyance. It was a house full of women. Even the spaniels were bitches. He turned quickly from his resentment as though it were an insult and for that reason beneath him.

But he lingered in the nursery, in no way comforted by the suggestion of dependence it inspired in him. Suspicious of Celia's whereabouts, he felt reduced, a gravy boiled down to something black and much too sharp to be palatable. He could still hear her telling Charley Sutton, 'I was just thinking about you.' He could still see her hand on Charley's arm as his friend gave her that jar of honey, and the paperwork for that piece of land left out to taunt him on the kitchen table.

It disconcerted him to feel like this, and threw his world off-balance: the house full of women was his; the women, too, were his, in a manner of speaking. He kicked the wooden dog a second time. But if they were his, where were they? It didn't add up.

Frustrated, he picked up a book of Russian fairytales. Anna's influence. He riffled through it, unseeing. No one had read to him when he was a boy. Were boys read to? He believed they should be. But his mother had delegated such things to the servants, and it was impossible to imagine his father might consider it — a man who regularly beat Leo for being poor at sports. He pictured those moments between being sent up to bed and having the lights turned out by the nanny and could not think of them as anything other than solitary. No one came. He put himself to bed. The nanny put her head round the door. 'No torch, mind, young Leo!'

It might have been affectionate were it not so clear that she didn't care either way whether he read beneath the covers or went straight to sleep in the dark. His behaviour was immaterial to her. She had a lover in town and meant to quit her job soon to be with him — he had overheard her discussing it on the telephone and his heart had sunk: there had been too many nannies. It was unclear whether this one even liked children. Their smallness appeared to make her think of them as being of no importance — too little to fuss over. It gave her an air of efficiency that Leo experienced as an absolute chill, for it was so unobservant as to be entirely loveless.

He was sent away to school at eight. The chance of being read to never again arose. He corrected himself, remembering. He crossed to the window. There they were. The girls were in their tree-house. They were good climbers. Their blonde heads were bobbing about just inside the window. He was comforted that they were as blonde as he had been as a boy. He raised the sash and, hearing this, they turned to see him and began to wave; he couldn't catch their voices, high and lost on the air. He felt better to have found them, and for a moment he was glad, too, that he had found them at a distance, because he wanted the privacy of his memory uninterrupted. It wasn't strictly true that he had not been read to, for Celia had read to him once.

It was a few months after they had first met. They were both living in London at the time. He had wanted to impress her – dinner at the Ivy, cocktails in the American bar at the Savoy beforehand – but by late afternoon, having fought all week to suppress the flu, he had found himself phoning her from his bed, feverish, barely able to speak, his throat sore, the shaded bedside lamp impossibly bright, punishing his eyes.

'I'll be right round.' She had hung up, given him no chance to refuse. She had not been to his house before, although she had sent him a birthday card the previous week, which had been when he had, as he put it to himself, decided to 'go for it'. Until then, he had doubted that she thought much of him. This night, a Friday, he had been going to make his big move, the pace stepped up until she could be in no doubt of his intentions: he had surprised himself, the first time he saw her at the tennis party at Eastleigh, by wishing, very clearly, one day to marry her. It had been a stroke of luck that Charley was out of the way in Africa. It gave him the chance to take his time.

That night he had twisted in his sheets in an agony of nerves. He leaped from the bed, had tried to take a shower but staggered, slipping, on the tiles, and when he turned off the water he felt damp immediately with fever. He returned to bed. There was champagne in the fridge, he remembered, and a small pot of Sevruga, in case; strawberries, too, although now he thought of throwing them into the bin in case she spotted them. Breakfast. He had even thought they might drive down to the country on Saturday if it was fine. They had spoken of it. What had he been thinking? He had over-reached. She would find him disgusting, spluttering and sweating. He even had spots. He turned off another light. The brightness was unbearable. It was growing dark outside, just after six, the last week of September. He heard her taxi pull up. He put on his dressing-gown and went to let her in.

She wore a white dress and discounted its prettiness by saying, 'Nurse service,' as she stepped briskly over the threshold. She had brought him oranges, medicine, vivid blue cornflowers and a book: Hilaire Belloc's *Hills and the Sea*.

'Darling.' She paused to kiss his forehead, then took his hand and led him straight back to bed. She found a thermometer, frowned at his temperature: 102. She sent out for Chinese chicken soup and insisted that he eat it. She lay on the covers beside him and, understanding perfectly his horror of brightness, although his headache had abated with the medicine, she read to him by the illumination of her pocket Maglite.

'Since we won't make it to the country this time' – he could feel her smiling in the dark: she must have realised, he blushed, and yet not minded that he had hoped tonight she might stay with him – 'I've brought the country to you.' And then she read to him, a chapter about how to mow a field, 'one of my favourites, listen . . .' Her voice in the darkness had almost broken his heart; waking to find that she was still there, fully clothed on the counterpane, it was remade, and the love he felt for her at that moment ran back over all that childhood solitude, renaming it precursor to the life ahead.

Three months later she agreed to marry him. The question, he was well aware, had hung above every moment between that nocturnal read and then. He had always been a bad dissembler.

Now the sound of a door closing downstairs drew him from his reverie and he felt a faint lurch of guilt, as he always did, at the thought of being found alone in the girls' nursery. Not Celia's but Anna's steps coming quickly along the landing. She drew in her breath fast to see him standing alone by the window; she stared at him, colour rising to her high cheekbones, her black hair tied back in a long plait, its thickness somehow making her seem more slender when already she was doll-like in her smallness. He noticed that her blue shirt – the sleeves rolled up, the buttons so low that he caught

73

sight of an edge of lace, a curve of breast – matched her eyes, the colour of Celia's cornflowers. Celia often commented, as though it were a test, on the girl's prettiness, and with his wife so much in his thoughts, as though she were beside him at this moment, pointing it out again, Leo became aware of it. He felt no desire for her but suddenly he could see what such a longing might entail, and how easy it would be.

She trembled, glancing down at the book of Russian fairy-tales in his hand. Celia had joked, too, that Anna had a soft spot for him, and he sensed it acutely in the way she looked from the book back to his face, reading into his interest in it something quite different from what was the case: that vision of Celia, his memory of falling hard in love with her. He set the book back on the table. Anna went to the window, brushing lightly by him, to call the girls to come down for lunch. Her voice carried. He turned to watch them scrambling from the tree. He had a vision of Celia, and of Charley, like Anna, openly desirous, brushing past her. Why had Celia kept where she was going a secret?

He watched Anna's slim back as she bent out of the window. She turned to see him watching her and her smile then was coquettish. There were too many women in the house. Leo left the nursery.

Going downstairs to his study – he would ask Marjorie to make him sandwiches and bring them to him in there: he didn't want to be near Anna or the girls when Celia was gone, not today – he ran his hand damply along the banister, remembering that weekend of fever, and the depth of love that that sickness had uncovered in him. Illness and love ran together in his mind, and not just because of that time, but because of the powerlessness that he felt underwrote both states, from which it was impossible to break free. There were times when he hated to love Celia as he did. This was one of those. His suspicions felt like a storm he'd have to weather before he could enjoy loving her again.

He headed for his study. He would sit it out. It was absurd to be so overwrought without good reason. He would calm down. As he was crossing the hall, he noticed the papers Charley had dropped off for him earlier that day and faltered. He swallowed hard as he scooped them up: he would sign them right now, not have any of this nonsense muddying his judgement.

As he stopped to pick them up, his eye was caught by one of Celia's handbags left out by the coats. He barely hesitated, but went to it and, listening out for anyone approaching, peered inside. It was almost empty, but her chequebook was there and he took it out, riffling through the stubs. She kept a neat chequebook, entering everything in that she had spent. They were meagre amounts, all domestic, none, by the looks of it, extravagances for herself. But beyond the fact that she was so thorough, which made him feel ashamed, there was nothing to arouse suspicion. He flicked through it again. There must be something. And then he saw it, the last stub in the book: 'Frenshaw House', the sum, five hundred and twenty pounds.

He dropped the chequebook back into her handbag and went through to his study, shut the door and touched his forehead. That was it. That was his proof. He wasn't losing his mind. His instincts were perfect, and his suspicions sane, for what was Frenshaw House if not an hotel?

He stood in the middle of the room, his heart racing. He stared about him at all the things that spelt out his family and his family's line, a long intention seen through, against poor odds sometimes, but seen through powerfully for all that. Now it would be cut off and Celia had not even given him a son. This was the end of every-thing. He threw the papers Charley wanted him to sign on to his desk. He would sooner let the house fall down around him than sign away any more land. He had been tricked. His old rival had finally shown his hand. He thought of his father, the refusals and the punishments, and it was as though this blow had been dealt because he had not been more like that man. He had been too kind, too tender; he had felt too much love. He clenched his fists, and in that gesture his father came so close it felt like a kind of habitation, his blood jumping to another man's heartbeat.

He sat down heavily in his chair. He gripped the arms to stop himself trembling. He felt over-hot and dizzy, as though he might be coming down with something. He would kill them both rather than lose her to another man. As soon as that thought came to him he swatted it away in terror. But he had already glanced on instinct at the gun-rack. He shut his eyes tight. He could see himself doing it too clearly. He gripped the chair-arms as though to keep himself seated, stop himself leaping up and setting out on the course of destruction at that very moment. He must wait for further proof. He would ask her directly what that cheque was for the moment she returned.

But he shied away from hearing her say the words, as though even her lies might be poison, and to hear them would sicken him too. Besides, he told himself, he would not need to. He would see them together at that night's dinner. He would have his eye on them both. And tomorrow they would all ride out. By then he would know for sure.

He opened his eyes and stared out at the gardens, grey in a cold light, a white sky showing nothing. His breath was no longer ragged, and the feeling he had had earlier of being abandoned was gone. What was left was worse, the cold focus of the chase picking him up and deciding his actions, a deeper history taking over.

The phone rang. He answered it. It was Esther, asking if Charley was with him. There was some trouble, nothing important, at the kennels, and he was needed there but no one could find him. He felt the vision take shape and clarify, become a pure point of absolute conviction: Charley and Celia together at that moment.

His heart skipped at the sound of footfalls in the corridor, and then Marjorie was at the door: 'Sandwiches, sir?'

Even now, even knowing that it would not be Celia, that she was with Charley Sutton, even now, Leo thought with anguish, his heart had shuddered with a renewal of love, hoping that it had been her. Yes, it was a kind of sickness, and he wanted rid of it.

He nodded but could not speak. He would take sandwiches alone in the study. He would wait for his wife there.

It was just after one o'clock. His hand unsteady, he took down a book. He would read to himself.

10

The backbencher, Lance Ash, returned home on Thursday night to find that his wife, inexplicably, was also absent.

Since she had gone to her mother's on Tuesday, the only contact they had had was a few answerphone messages. He refused to call her at her mother's. He had tried her mobile a couple of times but it had always been switched off.

Now he frowned as he stood by the microwave, heating up something she had cooked and frozen in a Tupperware container. The food – a curried lamb stew that he remembered her making the previous week – brought her closer to him and made him miss her. He supposed she was all right. She always had been.

He opened a can of lager and took the plastic dish and can through to the sitting room. He didn't want to eat alone at the kitchen table. He turned on the television. The ten o'clock news led with the movement of troops in Iraq. Hunting was not mentioned until the final item, which had been out-sourced, he noticed, from the tone of it, which was entertaining, not entirely sober, the blonde girl presenting the piece in a slim blue coat and high heels as though there was not enough left in the news itself to hold anyone's interest.

He frowned. The story had been flogged half to death, needing only a final shot to kill it off for good. He wished that it would come. He had had enough. It had run them all ragged. When the girl mentioned that two hundred and fifty hunts up and down the country were expected to turn out on Saturday in defiance of the ban, coming into effect tomorrow – drag-hunting, rather than a proper chase – he gulped his lager in disgust. It was over. Why couldn't they all give up now and stay quiet? He remembered his friend the day before in the pub saying that a bunch of them were going down to Wiltshire. Maybe he would join them after all. He had the connection; he had only to call.

A noise on the road outside the house made him glance up: Alison? He spilt a drop of yellow curry alongside the blot of John Smith's already on his white shirt and cursed. She knew how to get rid of such stains. He did not. No one came. The car passed on.

The item cut to footage of earlier hunts, the girl's voice talking over the pictures. He went through to the kitchen to find a cloth to clean his shirt. He thought the girl sounded posh, her voice less RP than actually regal, and he suspected her of being a sympathiser. The images they had dug up, too, he considered highly sentimental: soft-eyed dogs tumbling together in picturesque heaps, then coming to heel in a moment – unimaginable, he thought, in a land of canine fanatics, not to admire the way they did that; children bouncing eagerly after their mothers on hairy ponies; rough-looking farmers on skilled old nags that made him think of Constable and Lawrence, and nifty labourers tilling the soil.

He snorted in derision. Such images were tantamount to propaganda. It wasn't right to show such things. He had half a mind to write a letter and complain but the thought only made him tired. When they showed a group of teenagers in trainers and anoraks, he was reassured, anticipating quips about cruelty, but apparently, they were horseless followers of the hunt, and he hated that implication of belief, which shaded their conviction with a quality of invulnerability. As though to oppose them would be to criticise their religion! It had all become too confusing: the distinctions were too blurred. He ate, narrow-lipped. They had a few pictures of toffs, as he thought of them, aloof and neat-thighed in breeches and black jackets, others in hunting pink. Pink, he thought, and scoffed again. The colour was red. What gave the rich the licence to rename even colours? Such things were public property, not theirs by rights.

The news item annoyed him. He suspected the BBC of bias often, and particularly in this. They were all Oxbridge. It was hardly surprising. A Mafia. What hope was there when such people wrote the news? He remembered that they had made a good deal of the march in 2002, showing all the wellies, as he called them, when they should have been ignored as law-breakers, and ostracised for that reason, not shown mud-covered and rosy-cheeked, not revealed as so healthy and therefore so much in contrast to the gawping city folk. They should have been dealt with as a mob, not as individuals.

He remembered the day. It had been impossible to drive through central London. He had been late for the football because of them, and missed the opening goal. Their healthiness offended him. It had seemed to him like a form of superiority. But not everyone could live out of town. Some people had jobs. He paused in that thought, concentrating on the stain, which was only getting worse with his rubbing it. What did Alison do to get rid of such things? Some kind of trick and they were gone in moments. He did not have the knack. He was only making it worse.

He glanced back at the television. Protesters milling about outside the Commons. The House going in for the vote; earlier stock footage showing the chamber and a question put way back in 1997. It had taken almost a decade, and had been a long time coming even before that.

He went to get another can of lager. The news ended. He flicked through the channels and the telephone rang. When he picked it up it was his wife. She told him that she had just seen him on television – as though she had needed that excuse, proof of his public existence, to call him. He swore. He must have missed it when he slipped out to the kitchen. He would have liked to see himself.

Alison's voice sounded cheerful in a way it seldom did. It was a cheeriness that made his palms damp with apprehension, and he had the strong impression that someone was in the room with her, goading her to tell him something she was reluctant to impart. Her mother, Lance supposed, who had always schemed against him.

'Yes, Lance,' he noticed that she did not call him 'sweetie' as usual – she did not often use his name, 'we saw you on the TV, think it was done back in the summer as you didn't have a jacket. It was just quick, outside your work.' She referred to the Commons that way, as though uncertain what she should call it, and a little nervous about naming what he did aloud: it was too remote, and vaguely dangerous.

'You were on about the hunting, Lance, and then they showed this nob straight after, so you did sound good.' It was the bit of the broadcast he missed. He had given a number of soundbites over the life of the Bill. He had been on message. They liked him to do pieces to camera, because he was – how had they put it? He couldn't recall the word. Innocuous? Inoffensive? He knew that they meant he was colourless, bland, even. He didn't mind all that much. He knew what he had inside. It was the grey hair that did it. He had always believed he had a forgettable face. Such things mattered in politics. You had to have foot-soldiers as well as generals. It was his privilege to serve. He thought it a more dignified rank than one of authority.

Alison's voice ran high. She was telling him now about something her mother had done. Her sciatica was murder. She had had treatment. Homeopathic. It had worked. 'No one's more amazed than Mum, Lance, you can't imagine!' He could. He really didn't want to. He flicked through the channels, the sound on mute in case he chanced on porn. They had Sky. He didn't want to send heavy breathing down the phone at her, or her mother. There wasn't much to look at.

Hearing her voice, he missed her less, and missing her less he found that he was reassured. Everything was as it was. She hadn't even mentioned Valentine's Day. He would make it up to her or perhaps – he thought about it as she elaborated on the theme of back pain – he should keep quiet and they'd have an unspoken pact not to mention it until next year, and then he'd do it with a flourish. The works.

It was as he was imagining himself, armful of red roses, Alison munching happily on Belgian chocolates, that it came. At a pause in the flow of her conversation he asked her when she'd be coming home. 'Lance, that's what I've been saying. I knew you weren't listening.' She sighed. 'I'm not coming back for a bit.' Was it the sciatica? He waited for her to explain. Perhaps she had to stay to look after her mother. He set the can of lager on the coffee-table in front of him.

'I think it'll be for the best. Just for a bit. I know you've been hard at it, Lance, but I was so upset over Valentine's Day and you didn't care at all, did you.' It wasn't a question. 'I mean, you never do anything, do you? How do I know, these days, if you even like me? You never *do* anything, do you, Lance?' She was speaking fast and he could almost imagine her mother clapping in her excitement that, finally, her daughter was telling him where to get off. The women would expect him to be desolate, no doubt. He turned up the sound on the television to show how little he cared what they thought. But his heart was racing. This was how such things happened, marriages ending over lager and curry, telephone and TV, long-distance, things packaged up and frozen.

She told him she would be gone for a month, 'as a trial', by which she meant, he thought, 'for starters'. She wanted to pick some things up at the weekend, but didn't think it was a good idea if he was there when she came. Could he be out? He said that yes, he could. He would see that the house was empty when she got there.

He set the receiver down. His face felt cold and damp. But it was a few moments before he understood that through the entire conversation with her he had been crying. In some part of himself he had been conscious, from the second he heard her voice, that it would be what she would say. She was going to leave him. He loved her. Of course he had known. He knew her intimately, all her shapes and patterns. How could he not? She was his wife. It was what the word entailed. His wife, his life. He bent forwards on the sofa, head in hands, and sobbed.

The next day, after work, he got into his car and drove west; the bright sunlight, he told himself, was what made his eyes stream tears. The thought of her coming to the house where she no longer lived was intolerable. It would be like trying to kiss a dead body back to life.

He remembered the connection, the lads going off to the countryside to see the illegal hunting, and he fled. He could still hear her. 'You never *do* anything, do you, Lance?' Well, he would think of something now. He rubbed the tears from his eyes. He wouldn't just keel over and let her ruin him. He would show her.

It was dark by the time he found himself driving the primrose-scented lanes in Wiltshire. He had not been into proper countryside for years and its shadowed beauty made him breathless with grief. Shapes came at him, transfigured by the headlights' beams. Everything that was lost seemed to rise up before him as he drove. So much life going on, and even his small part of it had been cut down. He had nothing left.

He noticed a low-lying white building up ahead on the road. There was a sign outside and he wondered if it was a bed-and-breakfast. He might stay there if it was. But as he drew near, he saw that it read, 'Kennels', and he caught a glimpse of a man, tall, dark-haired and straight-backed, but staggering slightly as though drunk, crossing the yard, a gun cocked under his elbow.

It didn't look like a place to stay. He drove on. There would be somewhere in the town.

11

Celia had been worried that she might be late for her appointment at the surgery – she had barely had a chance even to kiss Leo as she left Eastleigh – but she had been just in time.

Now she stepped out into the market square and tried desperately to stop herself rushing straight back to him with her news. It was as she had prayed. They would have another child. She smiled up at the sky as though into bright sunshine. Everything else would start to go their way.

It was, however, very cold, the temperature rapidly descending, and she shivered as she buttoned up her green tweed jacket, fished her gloves out from her brown suede bag. Very fine rain was falling, and the sky was steadily closing in, the light weakening as though later on there might be snow.

She checked her happiness, and remembered how Leo had been forlorn, fussing over the dogs as she left. She would go now to the tobacconists' and buy him a box of Romeo y Julieta cigars as a gift. She knew he had run out, and they were his favourites. She would give them to him to cheer him up and then, when he was happy, she would tell him.

As Celia started to cross the empty market square she noticed Charley Sutton's wife, Esther, leaving the pharmacist's. But before recognising the woman as her friend, she had noticed her extreme thinness, not slender but gaunt, with anorexia's look of distress accentuated by a big coat; it billowed weirdly in a gust of wind. Celia had half turned away in displeasure, then looked back: Esther? She had always been on the rangy side of svelte but something now had tipped her towards this panicked narrowness, her arms held tight to her body, head down.

Celia hesitated. Esther had not seen her, but Celia couldn't ignore her. She was heading for her car, and Celia reached her as she was bending to unlock the door. Esther's red hair was dull, her skin too pale, eyes hollow; she gave every appearance of sickness. Celia pretended not to notice, and was cheerful in suggesting they go to have a cup of coffee in the shop just across the square.

Esther shrank from the suggestion. 'I'm terribly late . . .' But she did not say for what. Her hurriedness had about it the false intensity of the liar, and she let Celia lead her away from her car and into the coffee shop; they sat at a table in the back room, where the windows gave on to a small garden with cherry trees just in flower.

'You were at the surgery?' Esther slumped, disgruntled, as she said this. 'But you look very well.'

Celia blushed. She felt very well. She felt wonderful, in fact, but Esther's remark sounded more like an accusation, and her appearance seemed to sit between them like a question too difficult to broach.

'Charley's bearing up.' Celia smiled, wanting to divert the subject away from her good health, but Esther flinched at this remark, and Celia supposed it likely that things were difficult at home. Reports had reached her via Marjorie – Ellis was thick with the gamekeeper at the Suttons' house, Sanbourne: Charley had sent a batch of guns for servicing; he was planning a trip to Africa. Esther had not mentioned that Charley was going away; nor, indeed, had he.

When Celia had spoken of it to Leo, he had been brisk. 'If you must pay so much attention to gossip, darling—'

'Well, do you think he might leave Esther for a long trip?' She had been considering whom they might invite to Eastleigh to keep Esther company in his absence. She had always thought Sanbourne must be a gloomy house to live in alone. The Suttons only occupied one wing; the rest was shut up for most of the time, and Celia thought this made the place feel desolate, the empty rooms dead from expectation of something that would not come.

Leo had looked at her strangely before he answered. 'You should probably ask him when you see him.'

But Celia did not like to pry. She had let the matter drop, though now, with Esther, she was curious.

Esther did not answer her immediately. 'Bearing up?' She touched the collar of her shirt. 'Yes, I'd say he's doing pretty well, wouldn't you?'

'Oh, absolutely.' Celia would have hated Esther to think she was implying that she had noticed any strain in either of them.

She changed the subject again, mentioning who would be at that evening's dinner. Esther laughed, but without humour. 'Henrietta's so unreliable, though. My jury's out that she'll be there.' Her eyes challenged Celia to disagree. Her gold bangles, loose on her wrist, rattled against the table.

'She's promised to come down.' Celia didn't like other people to comment openly on her sister's unreliability, especially as it was so well known; and it struck her as ill mannered. 'Gerald, too, though we're waiting to hear if he's back in time. He's been delayed, I think, in Cairo.'

Esther raised her eyebrows. 'Who will Henrietta bring this time, do you suppose?'

Celia's sister was notorious for arriving each visit with a different man. Few were her lovers, but enough affected that status to cause comment. 'And you're surely not expecting her to ride?'

Celia had not, until then, suspected for a moment that if her sister came, she would not ride. She had promised on both counts. Celia had taken her at her word. It was unthinkable that she should let her down on that of all days. She did not like to show her nerves to Esther. She smiled, and turned to call to the waitress for another cappuccino.

It was as though, sensing Celia's good spirits, something had shifted and reversed in Esther, a vital stone dislodged, allowing a rush of bitterness to flow through all her comments. Celia, seeing her thinness, had figured it in her mind as reason for sympathy, or at least encouragement, should she need support. But now it seemed that Esther had run angrily ahead to a spot she considered to give a better view, and all her remarks had that tone of righteous far-sightedness, as though, seeing the game, she had determined to spoil it.

This was unlike Esther. Before, she had been almost girlish, shy beside Charley's decisiveness, and Celia wondered what had happened to her to upset the security that had made that possible. It couldn't be her fault. But she had the impulse to tell the other woman her news, as though it would stand as proof somehow of a wider goodness: she would throw it into their conversation and it would dispel the poison.

Celia glanced at her watch. It was almost two. She was impatient to get away. She prayed the child would be a boy. She longed to have a son for Leo.

Esther was watching her closely, suspicious. 'I shan't be able to make it until eight. I'm sure Charley will be there sooner.'

Celia's coffee arrived. She burnt her lips as she drank. She wanted to be in her house, arranging things for that night's dinner, and she wanted the dinner to be perfect – the new life a charm that would smooth over all the terribleness of their defeat: she wanted the ceremony of that last supper to be unbroken.

Esther was tapping the teaspoon against her saucer, as though planning her next line of attack, and Celia wished she wouldn't. She thought of the puddings she had asked Marjorie to see to. She was better at them than Cook, and with diplomacy, on special occasions – as though it were a favour to the housekeeper – Celia was sure to delegate. A gentle battle went on because of it, but the chocolate mousses and strawberry coulis were worth it. She wondered if Marjorie had meant it when she said there was no chance of them running out of Jersey cream.

'I phoned Eastleigh earlier, and spoke to Leo.' Esther had fixed Celia with a hard stare. 'I was looking for Charley.' Celia was puzzled. 'But of course he wasn't there. I just thought you should know.' Esther started to stand up. 'Will you take care of this?' She pushed her untouched coffee towards Celia and turned to leave.

Celia drew back in alarm. Esther appeared almost to quiver as though she might pick up the cup and throw it at her. She bared her teeth in a smile that had an air of triumph about it and Celia wondered if she was unwell, had perhaps gone mad: Esther's gums were white, as though through extreme tension; her red hair appeared muddy in its dullness, a dirty fox discovered dead in a ditch.

Celia was momentarily speechless. What could she say? 'We'll see you tonight, Esther?' Celia tried to keep her voice level but she could hear it falter. Esther, by contrast, half shouted, letting out a short laugh that was more like an exclamation of disgust. 'Absolutely. Yes, you'll see us both tonight.' She left. Celia settled the bill.

The afternoon, when she stepped back outside, was darkening, with clouds rushing from the south. But the rain had stopped; the clouds were too dark for snow; and the temperature had risen fractionally, making the air almost clammy. She stood for a moment, disconcerted. She had a few errands to run before she returned to Eastleigh: more Jersey cream, just to be certain, from the grocer; then to the tobacconist for Leo's cigars.

As she recrossed the square, she tried to make sense of Esther's behaviour. She believed there would be a perfectly rational explanation for it, but her bitterness had been so shocking, just then, that she felt personally attacked. And what had she meant by all that talk of phoning Eastleigh? It was hardly news: it was perfectly sensible for her to phone there if she was after Charley. She and Esther had never been close, never intimate, but the distance at which they had been friends had seemed secure.

Now in the tobacconist's, looking down at the boxed cigars, her confidence shaken, she suddenly wondered if she was right about Leo's favourite: was it Romeo y Julietas or Cohibas? Both brands were familiar. She hesitated, chose the Romeo y Julietas. She reached into her handbag for her chequebook – she liked to keep a record – but couldn't find it, and used her card. Not being able to find the chequebook reminded her: she had meant to post that cheque to the women's refuge. The spring visits to the garden had been a great success so far this year. The weather had proved perfect for aconites and snowdrops. She'd added a share of her own money to the amount, as was her habit, and had meant to pop it in the post last week, but now here it was folded up in her handbag: she had been distracted. The place was almost on her way; she would run it round now.

The refuge was a large, modern red-brick building on the edge of town, where the countryside began, grey light leaden on the chalky fields of stubble. She pulled up at the front door, jumped out – she was a familiar face there – and left the cheque with the girl in the office.

Just as she was getting back into her car to drive off, another pulled up: an unmarked police car. There were two women in the back: one in uniform, the other half hidden in a red hospital blanket, only her face revealed. Celia didn't recognise her, but she could see her bruises, one eye almost closed. She had encountered such cases a number of times before. She took a deep breath, and drove away. The name of the refuge was Frenshaw House.

Her husband, of course, did not know about her donations. It wasn't a significant secret, Celia felt, and, anyway, it was her money. In the past Leo had voiced his disapproval of her method of charity, describing it as 'random' and 'haphazard'. 'Hardly very effective, darling.' But privately she held firm to the belief that if everyone was haphazard in that way – committing random acts of kindness rather than of wickedness or violence – then the world might immeasurably be improved. It was just a question of reversing the image, and it was easy enough to do. It wasn't much, but it was something.

She supposed there were more effective ways of being useful, but this was hers. She kept quiet about it. She didn't think Leo would mind if he discovered that this was what she did. Besides, she had a personal reason for sticking to her guns on this point, and over that particular charity. Bea had understood.

Now, heading home, Esther, and then that broken woman's appearance, filled her with apprehension, and she felt the gathering of another picture also in the darkening day. She drove faster as though to outrun it, but turning into the driveway at Eastleigh, she slowed down, and had the terrible sensation that she had fled in precisely the wrong direction.

The pines at the gate darkened and swayed, shivering, as she drove past. A horse-box was turning out of the gate that led up to the stables; she noticed James Dunbar, who waved at her from that distance. He had been to fetch two hirelings for Henry and Gerald. The dogs were out and, seeing the car, they crossed the park, following false scents, tacking back and forth across the grass for home, their eyes on her as they descended.

As Celia made the final turn towards the house, rounding the high yew hedge that sheltered it from the open park, she saw that Will's car was already there. She cursed lightly to herself, although she was glad he had arrived. But she had wanted to see Leo alone briefly before people came so that she could make up for that missed kiss earlier. She had wanted to give him the box of cigars and tell him their good news in private. Now it would have to wait.

She cut the engine, and sat for a moment, nervous. She had been turning over in her mind the episode with Esther, and suddenly understood what she must've meant: she thought Celia was entangled in some way with Charley. Celia was almost relieved. It was too silly, quite preposterous. She determined to confront Esther, gently, that evening. Her nerves must have been playing tricks with her; Celia should have been a better friend.

The rain had started again, and although it was only some time after three o'clock, the day had grown darker still, and a quick wind was rustling the cedars that grew close around the stable-block. Celia took up her bags and darted for the house. The dogs ran barking into the hall behind her. She shut the front door. The hall was gloomy, but when she flicked the light switch there was a faint crack as the fuse blew: the house was badly in need of rewiring. She could hear Will and Leo talking in the drawing room. A number of pieces of luggage were scattered about, and there was the sound of china clattering in the kitchen, tea things about to be brought through.

As she took off her coat, Leo came out from the drawing room, and she went to kiss him. 'Have you seen Charley, darling? Esther has misplaced him.' She had hoped to crack a joke. She could not wait to tell him her news. Just as soon as her cousin and his friend had gone up, she would take him aside.

Leo took a pace away from her, and it was only then, as he stepped back into the light, that Celia noticed his expression of mistrust. 'She phoned here to find him, yes, I know. You're later than you said you might be. Your guests are already arriving.' He turned from her and went unspeaking to his study. She could hear him locking up his gun-rack.

She stood for a moment in the unlit hallway, stunned. Then, through force of habit, she went to wind the clock that stood in the centre of the mantelpiece. It had not been done that day, and the time it showed was wrong, although the weekday and date, and the window showing the phases of the moon, all were accurate, and because of this, she remembered suddenly, and at the sound of foot-steps behind her in the hallway, she turned. The accident was five years to the day. Her own thoughts had been of the future not the past, but Leo must have been thinking of that. No wonder he was upset. That would be the reason.

But the study door remained shut, and it was Will who came through from the drawing room. She took a deep breath. He strode towards her, taking her up in a hug. 'Cousin C, don't you look well!'

Celia wished people would stop remarking on how well she looked. At this moment she felt anything but that. Leo came back out into the hall, his expression so cold that she could not believe he had remembered. There must be something else. She put her hand out to the table edge to steady herself. In her other hand she held the cigars she had bought him and looked down at the small square box, wrapped in brown paper; she thought of the news she had hoped to whisper to him, a secret of love that might change everything. She could give neither gift to him now.

Marjorie came through from the kitchen carrying a tray. 'The drawing room?'

Celia collected herself. 'Yes, thank you, Marjorie. We'll take tea in there.'

Leo strode past them all, heading for the kitchen. He was mut-tering about the fuse-box, and could be heard to call out, 'Ellis, the bloody lights again!'

Marjorie's tea-cups rattled on the tray.

12

Isabella had spent Friday morning in her studio, a large, north-facing room on the upper floor of her building. The sky grew pale around one o'clock, and she glanced out to see a fast gust of snow, eddying upwards; she crossed to the window to watch it, but it did not settle. There was no sign of it now. It might never have existed. A car pulled up and Will Bowden got out – she recognised him instantly – then crossed the street to ring her doorbell.

She was still in her work clothes and bits of paint were stuck to her face and hair. When the bell rang again, she spoke into the intercom, telling him to let himself in and she'd be down in a moment. She applied an inconclusive daub of titanium white to the background of what was supposed to be a winter landscape but which in fact was not yet very much at all, and wondered how on earth she had not noticed the time. She had been lost in a reverie, part work, part thinking of the weekend, and of him.

Now, hearing him come into her flat on the lower floor made her realise just how sunk in contemplation she had been: the sight of him outside, and the sound of his footsteps, had filled her with alarm, and when she called down to him, 'Won't be a moment. Make yourself some tea, or Coke, or something', her voice came out as an idiotic squeak. Make yourself some Coke? She felt foolish and dashed through to the bathroom with a bottle of white spirit to clean her hands.

She slipped quickly into a fresh pair of jeans, swapped her paint-splattered shirt for a T-shirt, brushed her hair, hesitated, put on makeup, rethought the T-shirt, changed it for a white silk blouse, took a deep breath and went downstairs.

'You're all packed?' He was stretched out, half lying down – almost indecently, she thought – on the sofa. This meant that when she crossed the room to say hello to him, she found herself standing above him while he stood up, and as he did this with no haste whatsoever, she had the sudden impression that he was going to pull her down to lie beside him. She stood her ground but could feel herself blushing as he smiled at her, overlong dark hair falling into his eyes.

Her bag was by the front door, and he went past her to scoop it up, jangling his car keys in the other hand. He had barely greeted her, as though they had broken off conversation just moments before, and yet she had had phrases stacked up to deliver – ten years! You haven't changed a bit! – imagining the flush of nerves at taking off for the weekend with a man who was, after all, almost a stranger.

But the oddest part of it was its naturalness, and this she found more thrilling, and more of a shock, than any sense of danger. They went outside together, and getting into the car beside him she found that she felt very much at home. She had a strong urge to touch the fabric of his shirt where it met his wrist, the dark hairs curling near the white. She wanted to tell him that it was very lovely to see him because, perplexingly, she had found that it was. She noticed fine lines around his eyes that had not been there before, and she had to look away, because for some reason they made her feel tender, as though she had missed him. A sense of profound reassurance had settled on her, as though she had just glimpsed the way home after being lost in a fog. It made her indignant: she had not been lost; and the indignation stirred her, made her feel alert and very steady, as before a fight, and then all these thoughts fell away and she was left with only instinct: she wanted very much to kiss him. She bit her lip to stop herself saying anything. She did not trust herself to know what it might be.

The afternoon opened up silver with low sunlight as they headed out of London and into the countryside. The motorway was clear enough, but from the slip-roads cars flowed thundering to join them, the dash to leave the city gathering momentum. Isabella avoided looking at him, reminding herself that she was a professional, hoping to be hired for a job. But it was no comfort to think this, because she longed for him to reach across and touch her.

She pushed aside a strand of hair that had fallen on to her cheek and when her fingertips touched her skin she felt the heat rising to the surface and her breath was caught. She was never like this. She was steady and preoccupied, in the best sense, with her work. The phrase 'taken leave of her senses' came into her head and she stifled the nervous gulp that accompanied it. But it was how she felt: her reason had sunk away somewhere out of reach.

She sat on her hands and felt absurd. But she also felt alive. As they drove on further and into Wiltshire, gloomy but voluptuous with springtime starting, she breathed in the fresh-water scent of the turned fields, heard the bare chestnuts dripping on the car roof as they swept by, and when she glanced at him, he was smiling.

Arriving at Eastleigh, the house appeared to Isabella to be full of people, yet the first thing their host, Leo, said to them was, 'I'm sorry, there's no one here yet. Even my wife's disappeared.'

He stepped forward to take her bags from her as she got out of the car. A tall, strong-limbed man, broad-backed, his dark blond hair was curly and flattened in places like a dog's where it has not been brushed – as though it wouldn't occur to him to groom himself. But it suited him. His expectant manner, and his quickness, made his untidiness an aspect of his good looks, as though they were some-thing he was not aware of and so could not therefore be much bothered with. He seemed a little tarnished, too, this effect increased by his being dressed in shades of faded gold: pale yellow cords, tan cashmere sweater, a shirt of overwashed brown check, rusty brogues.

Isabella liked him instantly. He was a perfect match for the house, at least what she could see of it from the outside. Its loveliness, she thought, was in its air of neglect. Solid, it nonetheless suggested the intangible, because its ill repair, in places, gave it a yearnful aspect, as though recalling better days. And, Isabella smiled at her host, like Leo, it seemed to her a place that might have flourished too exuberantly – too bright to be seen – were it better cared for.

He seemed happy to be outside it. Isabella glanced behind him. The place was fluttering with motion, the mood of preparation almost palpable.

Just visible in the dark hallway, a number of figures moved about between the rooms: things were being brought up from the cellar; from the outside, she could see through to the well-lit kitchen, where three women leaned, industrious, over sinks and tables; at the foot of the stairs, she noticed a flash of white that she supposed might mean the children, vanishing upwards. No one there? In that phrase, Leo had wiped out a dozen souls: the staff, his children did not count. But it had not been meant dismissively. His eagerness in hurrying to greet them struck Isabella suddenly as a blind: he was eager for someone else; the person he really wanted was his wife. He felt that no one was there without her.

'She's having lunch in town,' he said, sighing, and Isabella felt a tug of longing – that anyone should mind her own lateness quite so much as that. He glanced up the driveway, rallied and drew himself up at the sight of a car, Celia's, Isabella supposed, turning into the driveway. She followed Will into the house. She had the sense that Leo wished to see his wife alone.

They went up to their rooms. Will carried her bag. They had been placed next door to one another. How had he known? She tried not to think of the other girls he might have come down here with in the past. He strode into her room, placed her bag at the foot of the bed and abruptly instructed that she come straight down to meet their hostess. 'She'll want to see you right away.' Isabella was nervous at the implication that she might have to be vetted before she was allowed to stay. She heard Will drop his bag on the floor next door and go straight back out into the corridor. She ran a brush through her hair and went outside to join him.

But as she approached the top of the stairs she caught, at the end of the landing, the first glimpse of two of her subjects: the girls, nothing as she had imagined – not robust at all, but fragile with an air of definite antiquity – sitting together on the floor in the shadowed semi-darkness, blonde heads bent together over something Isabella could not make out.

They looked up at the sound of her approach, but did not smile. Two tall gilt mirrors reflected their impressions backwards, as though they were the last faint point of light in a long succession of larger brightness.

Suddenly they jumped to their feet, as though called by a third child from another room. They proceeded together through a high white door.

Isabella felt the earlier image she had formed of the place shift and fall away. It had been quite wrong. While from the outside the house's look of neglect had made it – perhaps through its reflection of Leo – appear shabby simply for being lived in, from the inside it spoke of something else. Even full as it was of people, the place felt unnaturally quiet, as though something terrible had just happened and everyone but she knew to behave accordingly, and with reverence. She could hear the spaniels crossing the hallway. They didn't bark. Their claws on marble gave the impression that they were running through it on tiptoe.

Arriving, she had noticed that the carriage clock on the hall table was showing the wrong hour. She had read that error as a consequence of time: it was simply old and had wound down. She had smiled and glanced automatically at her watch to check. But it was more than that: the heart of the place seemed to have frozen.

She went downstairs to say hello to Celia.

part | two

13

The rain stopped around four o'clock that Friday in Wiltshire, but the heavy bank of clouds remained so that the afternoon was dark until dusk, and by then there was no light left to draw back the day: night came on early; with it, a strong frost, and the shock of it gripped the land as though it might be unrelenting. The hedgerows were suddenly still, the trees silent. The only movement was around the damp edges of the woods, and along the gullies and wet ditches where, just perceptible, a faint mist was rising, as though what little heat there had been inside the earth — a distant fire tamped down with layers of soil and stone — was now, finally, being expelled.

It was winter's last stand against spring. The seasons were in the balance. As night came, it seemed impossible that they should move on. The temperature descended. In the park at Sanbourne, by the main gates, a lightning-struck oak tree shrank in the silence, the wood tightening against the cork, moving from the bark; a few more degrees, and it was as though the wasted wood might snap off clattering to the ground. Beneath it, a fine crack froze over on the dew-pond, and the circle of the ice was closed.

Charley Sutton stood indecisive in the doorway of his house. It was almost six and that afternoon's rain had left a gleam of ice also on the flagstones of the terrace. There had been rain in the week, too, and a cold snap on Wednesday had hardened the muddy ground to deep welts where cattle and horses had passed. But he did not like to believe the worst, and he had noticed, by the trout stream, that the willows were already in silver, there were buds on the hazel, and yesterday he had seen snowdrops thick along the short track leading to the kennels from the road.

Sanbourne was just under a mile away from the Royal Fusiliers hunt kennels. Usually he would nip down in the Land Rover. Today he decided to walk across the fields, wanting to check the ground for the next day's meet.

He needed the walk also to clear his head. With Esther gone, he had sat ineffective at his desk and brooded on that evening's dinner: he wanted to see what Dunbar was playing at; and he wanted to see how she behaved. Thinking about it had become intolerable. He had had to get out of the house. His office felt like a cage. Business was good at the moment, but it was no kind of distraction. It was work; this was life; the cage door was open; life was at its strongest. But as fast as it rushed at him, it seemed to be leaving him behind, bereft, and he felt that soon he would be left with nothing. The chase was finally to be over. The thing itself was being killed. He alone was helpless to prevent it. He'd need an army to do it. Thinking this only filled him with greater despair: even Her Majesty's soldiers had been cowed.

So he worked badly, quit what he was doing around lunchtime and went out into the yard, wanting to be busy with something phys-ical, expecting Esther back at any moment. But the hours had passed; it was gloomy by teatime, and still the lights inside the building had not gone on.

He had tried to remember what time Esther had said they were expected at Eastleigh. Was it seven thirty or eight? He decided to phone Celia to check. He went into the office to make the call. The phone rang for an age, and when finally Leo answered, Charley fal-tered: Leo often dished out unwitting misinformation about such things. 'I think your lovely wife said eight, old man, but thought I'd better check.' Leo sounded preoccupied. Before Charley put the phone down – he didn't wish to raise the subject in company that evening – he remembered the papers he'd left that morning with Celia for Leo to sign. 'Did you have a chance to look them over yet? Just need your approval on it, and we can get moving.'

The phone went silent then and Charley thought that Leo's voice, when eventually he answered, sounded distinctly chilly. 'You'll have it. I shouldn't worry, you'll get it.' Then he had hung up.

Charley went back out to the stables. But around six he again found himself staring back at the house from the doorway of the tack room, and, still unlit, the place appeared desolate, as though it had been shut up for the season, or boarded up ready to be sold. He had a pair of stirrup irons in his right hand, the leathers in his left. They had just been restitched and for a moment he drew a blank on which saddle they had come from, where they should go now. His forgetfulness made him feel angry and vengeful, as though he had been taken over, against his will, by a stranger – someone who did not belong here, did not know his way around.

It was this that had decided him: he would go down to the kennels, see that everything was in order there. Leo had said eight o'clock. There was plenty of time. He went back up to the house to fetch his coat, flicking on the lights as he went. Then, with a kind of mad relish, he turned them all off again as he left. If she could so ostentatiously not be at home then he would do the same, but when he tripped, in the unlit gloom, on the edge of a Persian carpet, he ground his teeth and refused to let himself curse out loud.

Leaving, he noticed that the barometer in the kitchen read 'fair'. It was hardly that. He tapped it, sceptical, buttoning his tweed coat, pushing his cap down further on his head. He suspected snow. On foot, it was his habit to carry a gun, and the steel was ice when he took it from the rack.

Now, on the last field before the kennels, crossing the drainage ditch before the gate, he thought that he scented even cooler weather on the way, although the water there had not yet frozen. He hoped that tomorrow would break milder, dampish: a little rain was good for the life of the scent, which lingered, blooming in wet weather. Another serious frost like this would kill it.

None of them knew how the drag might go. It had never been their way. They had only ever done things properly. His great-grandfather had been master of the Royal Fusiliers too. Charley arrived at the kennels and walked briskly across the yard, away from that fact. He felt ashamed: he had let a man down.

Even before he went to them, he could tell that the hounds were nervous. Fed, they were still noisy, when usually they would have settled, their yelp and cry from a distance reminding him of drones busy in a hive. Even caged, their behaviour was a map of industry, their spirits quickening and sharpening, the day before a meet, their instincts fine. What looked like a tumble of dogs to others, Charley could read as a story patterned and purposeful as a book.

He walked past the stables, along the row of stalls. He could smell the linseed and straw, fresh-waxed leather and soapy water, the woolly dampness of the blankets and the high sharp tang of turned manure. It was a well-run place. The feed-room door was ajar; he closed it, flicked the latch. He felt like a retiring general, sleepless on the night before a last parade. There was something overblown about the momentousness of the sentiment: he had done it so many times before. But that was nothing – it faded so fast that he had not even been aware of it – in the light of the anguish he felt at the day's being final.

There were a number of other people at the kennels: one of the whippers-in lived above the stable-block; the three kennelmen roomed in the cottage; they'd taken on a couple of lads for the season to help out in the yard; and that night the terrier-men were expected to arrive from another hunt in Shropshire. Five usually came. Charley wondered if they were here already. He hesitated in the yard. He could see the light on in the kitchen and supposed they were in there having tea or watching television – no one had heard him come through the gate; they would expect him to drop by, but he did not always do so, and without the car he was noiseless.

A horse breathed out once, fast, as he passed the line. The mare recognised him, was quiet. He went round the back of the block to the kennels.

He knew them all by name. His hands clutched the iron bars of the gates, locked. Before he could stop himself he thought of Esther's body held that way in his hands. He shut his eyes. It was a whippet body built for stealth, and he had loved it because he thought that that meant lightness – a vitality that came naturally to her; by contrast it had made him feel strong in his slowness, which otherwise was just itself, a kind of dullness. The hounds surged towards him. Now, gripping the bars, he read his wife's stealth as deception, an attempt to outwit him by being elusive. He thought of James Dunbar. How could she let him fool her? She could not hope to get away with it. It was too great a humiliation compressed into too small a place: everyone here knew everyone else's business.

He watched the bitches scramble to be near him. He touched the ones that came close. A jay, late, was loud suddenly in the hawthorn, and then a blackbird made the hard night liquid. He felt his anguish shift and settle. It thinned out ahead of him to a wilder stream of purpose, as though anything might happen next. He wanted the whole thing to stop, resume, slip back to the pattern that once it so powerfully followed – a fat stream after rain. If things must change, he wanted to be the one to throw the rock that made the difference, to divert the river from its course. He wanted to be the one to do that, and no one else. He couldn't bear the humiliation of standing about on the riverbanks watching some other man – he paused, hatred overwhelmed him. He felt blind.

He turned to look out across the dark fields behind the kennels. Hoping to see something. There was one light, car headlamps, on the road, and the yellow of the nearest house. He could see no people. He felt certain that were he to find Esther and James Dunbar together at this moment he would shoot them both. His right hand touched his gun, the smooth barrel silken now with heat. He was a good shot. He rarely missed.

He glanced back at the hounds and in that second of hatred he hated them, too. Revenges multiplied. He imagined killing them. He saw the heap of dead bodies so clearly in that instant that tears sprang in his eyes. What had he done? The pity of it made his heart shrink, contracting to an organ half dead and not his own. He stepped away from them, towards the night. The hounds cried out. That someone should wish his pack dead, his wife unfaithful, all that had been his now taken from him and laid waste – he staggered on the uneven ground.

The door to the cottage swung open, light slicing through the yard, and he heard the radio, voices and music.

'That you, Charley?' One of the kennelmen calling to him across the yard.

He gripped the splintery wood of the fence. His forehead felt cold. He steadied himself, breathed deeply. The sounds of the cottage gave him confidence. He turned away from the night towards them. 'I'll be through in a moment.'

The man went back inside to join the others. The door remained open, lighting up the yard.

There was time for a quick drink here before he went home to dress for dinner at Eastleigh. It was usual, the day before a meet, for him to put his head round the door, check all was in order, refuse but then retract the refusal of a glass or two of Scotch.

He came away from the block, whistling to himself, as though tonight were an evening like any other, and not the last. He touched the mare's muzzle as he went by; she winnied softly and was still.

As he went inside, the car he had noticed on the hillside approached the kennels, the engine guttering weak with slowness. He wondered if it was the terrier-men, arrived from Shropshire. But the car did not stop. It passed out of sight at the next turn in the road.

14

Ellis had fixed the fuses at Eastleigh and replaced the blown-out bulbs. Celia was in the drawing room having tea with Will and Isabella when the lights went back on, and Leo emerged, cursing, from the cellar. The green baize door slammed behind him. Ellis's footsteps retreated to the kitchen.

Celia had been asking Isabella if she rode. 'Incredibly there's not a horse to be had in the entire south-west of England. Everyone is turning out tomorrow.' Isabella was baffled why this should be so, knowing nothing of the new law, and confessed she had never been on a horse. She remembered a donkey once on Santorini, and a big win last year at the Grand National, but she kept quiet as she didn't think they would count. Celia looked disappointed. She lowered her voice. 'I was going to say that if you're really keen, but don't tell Leo, you might be able to borrow my mare. She'd take care of you, she's very sweet natured.'

Will was astonished. 'But what will you ride? Surely you'll be going out tomorrow?'

Before she had chance to reply, Leo came part of the way into the room and remarked, 'Nothing on earth would stop her.'

Will laughed. 'Quite right.'

Leo turned abruptly and went back out.

Celia felt Leo's remark like a barb, deliberately aimed to wound. He knew what he was saying, in putting it like that, and she rose to her feet. 'I'd better go to Marjorie. You have everything you need?' She left the room. Leo's study door, usually left open, was shut. That, too, struck her as deliberate, and she went upstairs. She would collect herself, and then she would go back down.

As she reached the landing, the hall telephone began to ring. She let it. If it was Henry or Gerald with excuses she would not be able to stand it. She hesitated, her hand on the bedroom door. The phone rang on unanswered. She imagined Leo listening to it, growing more furious, and then she heard his study door open as he went to pick it up. 'Yes, that's right, just as she told you.' His voice was brisk, openly impatient. 'You'll have it. I shouldn't worry, you'll get it.' He hung up without saying goodbye.

Celia heard the study door shut again, and she felt a small bead of tension fall from her, as though an expected disaster had been held off. If someone had called with their excuses, he would have come to tell her. She went into the bedroom and stood for a moment, her back against the door, exhausted. That bell seemed to have been ringing since she arrived back from town. Leo's unfamiliar coldness had killed her pleasure in returning with her news. She dropped her bag on to the ottoman, and the small brown-paper parcel – Leo's cigars – beside it.

The bedroom was icy and she shivered, turning up the heating. Although it was only afternoon and not quite dark, she flicked on all the lights, shut the curtains against what little was left now of the day, and sat at the dressing-table, leaning forwards, covering her face with her hands. How could a person give something that was not wanted? It muddled love to force it on someone who pushed it away. It turned it into a demand, and not a gift.

Leo was wrong in saying that nothing would stop her riding tomorrow because, of course, she had no intention of doing so now. She would have to tell him why, and soon – this evening, it could not wait. But even sitting still she felt a physical, deep rising of dread, almost like the rolling motion of sea-sickness, at the thought even of telling him that she was pregnant, when only a few hours earlier she had stepped out into the cold day as though into brilliant sunlight, her joy at the news blanketing her in warmth, her one thought to get back to him to let him know. I am in heaven, she had thought. After the sorrow of the accident before, now I've been blessed. And the luck of it felt doubly strong for having followed on from something much worse, much further back, for which she had never been able to feel entirely blameless.

Thinking of it now, Celia felt her body shudder with the memory, which she tried to stop in vain. It took her up and held her, and she faced it, because she could not do otherwise, and she waited for it to leave her, her face still covered by her hands.

Today, just when she had been most happy, Esther, and then the woman at the refuge, had appeared as though instalments of that earlier time, returning. Leo knew nothing of it. He knew the out-line, but she had never filled in the picture, and the silence between them had, she thought, meant that eventually it would be obscured. Time would wipe it out; and their not speaking of it would seal the emptiness over, like forgetting. But it had come to her now in echoes of herself unearthed in those two other women, and she felt the memory moving through her as though she would take her hands from her eyes to see another person gazing back at her from the mirror. She kept them there; she did not yet dare look.

It was June, the month of weddings, the air heady with pollen and a warm breeze so that by evening there was thunder. She was twenty-four, and staying in Hampshire for the summer with her aunt Bea. She remembered the pathway and the high banks rising either side, the way ahead hidden, and her happiness blotted out by everything that followed. Like that broken woman this after-noon, she also had a secret map of fractures: hairline cracks to her ribs that showed up even now on X-rays, her hidden motive for

those donations to Frenshaw House of which Leo was also igno-
rant.

With determination, Celia now took her hands from her face,
and told herself to stop being weak. A sudden sound, footsteps on
the upper landing, made her glance up at the door. It must be Will
and Isabella; he was probably showing her the house; she could hear
the children, but far off, and downstairs the cellar door swung shut
as wine was brought up for that evening's dinner. She would have
to go down soon and see that all was in order.

She picked up a silver-backed brush from the dressing-table, set
it down again. She would bathe later. She touched her throat and
hoped she would not cry. Her eyes puffed instantly and, with people
in the house, she doubted she could get away with teabags. She would
be seen; or to request that some were sent up would mean whis-
pers and she could not bear it. She untied her hair.

She forced herself to confront her reflection, but she could not
quite find herself there; she had fallen too far back into the past.
She could still feel the quickness of what followed, all the day's loveliness lost beneath a new world made for her suddenly out of violence.

Drowsy after lunch – they had been outside because of fine weather
– she had wanted to go for a walk. The woods nearby were cool
and pleasant. Bea announced she'd rather take a nap. Celia went
alone, singing to herself. It was less than a mile from the house. The
meadows were crisp with wild barley and thick tufts of rye shuf-
fling in the hot wind. The man had had a couple of dogs with him,
terriers.

She had been afraid throughout that the dogs would bite her face.
They had kept guard around her while it happened. He had been so
much stronger than her, his weight fallen down on her like a punishment already suffered years before. He had smelt strongly of linseed oil and whisky. Afterwards, he vanished. Bea looked after her

when she came out of hospital, and Celia stayed on there for the rest of the year: her mother had not wanted to discuss it. It had been the cause of a decisive and permanent falling-out between the two sisters. It was also the hidden reason, Celia was sure, why Bea had left the estate to her: she had never forgiven herself for letting Celia go off that day alone.

Now she breathed out hard, eyes shut, hands pressed against the walnut of the table in front of her. She heard Leo crossing the hallway and prayed that he would come to her and explain: there had been some mistake, an error on his part, he wasn't thinking clearly, and she had read into his manner a coldness that was not there. But his footsteps retreated to his study.

She looked down at the table and bit her lip hard to stop any sound coming out. She concentrated her gaze, with effort, on the Chinese bowl that was placed in the middle of the dressing-table. It was where she put her jewellery at night before she went to bed. It was bone china, almost translucent in places, and decorated with figures taking tea beside brown pagodas, in the background mountains and a mandarin sun. But for all its colour and gilding, the object was cool-seeming, because although light fell through it, it was also strong.

When she had first met Leo, a year later, she remembered him joking with her about how she had been described to him as 'chilly' when, he said, he thought she was anything but that. He had laughed as he told her this, but she had not, quite, been able to laugh with him.

She knew that he had meant it as a compliment, or as a way of pointing out to her how little he believed it, yet she had been shocked, and had felt his denial almost to be a test: you're not cold hearted, really, are you? It saddened her to see how closely she would have to guard her secret. To have survived, apparently so intact, from that moment seemed to her more like a failing, or an indecent show of strength, as though really she should have been ruined, or at least shown marks of weakness on the surface of herself. She preferred to keep such things concealed. Only now, instead of it feeling like an accomplishment, it felt like a terrible strength to have pulled that off – a strength so un-owned that it was artificial, tantamount to a weakness, as though for all this time she had been merely a fraud, her silence no more than a lie.

A door swung shut further along the landing, and she held her breath. Marjorie. The muted clatter of a brush and dustpan. Celia pressed a fingertip against her brow, trying to rub away the tightness.

Falling in love with Leo, deciding that she would never tell him what had happened, was to prescribe herself the task of carrying around that Chinese bowl for life. By the time they were married, it seemed, mysteriously, that they shared the weight, and because it was also beautiful, the weight was no burden at all. it was a pleasure, something rare. Now danger pressed in on every side, things were changing and uncertain, the ground itself seeming almost to shake as though a convoy of tanks was passing just beyond the window. She might open the curtains and the steel snake would be there, gun-towers twitching. The bowl would break. It was too great a risk to carry around so much love – impossible if she had to carry it alone.

Feet ran along the landing and she heard the children giggle as they thumped downstairs. She picked up the brush again and ran it through her hair, ten swift strokes, crossed to the dressing room and riffled through the row of things hanging on her side, taking down three dresses.

Turning, before she went back to the bedroom, she stepped towards Leo's clothes, the dark line of hanging jackets, and pressed her face into their woolly weight to find him there. The fabric re-assured her. She pulled down the sleeves of the jumper, his, that she was wearing. It was all him. The garden outside was silent; there were no tanks. It was not June but February and tomorrow she would watch the others riding out and it would not be tragic but, for her, lit with joy: she would give Leo a son; she loved him. Something had happened to upset him; she was blameless.

But at this point she always faltered: she could not quite believe in her own innocence, and her doubts were a sly voice, insistent. Everything happened for a reason, and that belief ran both ways: a person did not suffer to no purpose; nor was anyone picked out to suffer without cause. There was always something in them, a failing, a faultline.

The fog rose again across her certainty and what was left was only faith. She loved him. She had to believe that he loved her. She leaned back into the row of her husband's clothes and breathed him in again. The house felt more like home. She heard the front door being knocked, comically – her sister's knock – and Leo answering, more voices raised and a clatter of dogs and children rushing on marble. People were already arriving.

She went through to the bedroom and laid the empty dresses on the bed. She took a tissue from the dressing-table and pressed it to her eyes, blew her nose, tied back her hair. All of this would pass. There would be an explanation. Just as everything, tomorrow, was ending, so much more would take its place. The future, life, was so much stronger than the past, and she held the future now inside herself, and it was the consequence of love. She was wrong to doubt that for a moment.

As Celia turned to leave the room, she remembered: how could she have been so stupid? She had put the Jersey cream in her bag on the ottoman by the radiator. It had been leaning there all this time while the heat had been turned up. She wondered if she should chuck it out and not mention it to Marjorie. She sniffed. Perhaps it would not be ruined.

Her sister, Henry, had indeed arrived, and looked up at Celia as she came out on to the landing. She was laughing at something Leo had said, crouched down on the floor with the two girls dangling from her neck, the dogs whirling about.

Thrilled that her sister was here, for it had been too long, Celia nonetheless faltered: the moment was just behind her; the blonde-haired girl on the ground, the dogs rushing round, guarding. She quickened her step away from it. She was right to keep such things secret from Leo. They were the past; the past could not return. There were only glimpses and she could outrun them. She was safe.

But as she went downstairs, she nonetheless took great care, her posture straight-backed, poised, much as though she carried ahead of her a fragile Chinese bowl.

15

By the time the five terrier-men arrived from Shropshire, Charley Sutton had left the kennels. It was probably as well that he had, for they were already drunk, and he didn't like to see drunkenness the night before a meet. Afterwards they were their own men, but before then he expected some kind of restraint.

Even thinking this, however, made him grimace: they were a bad lot, a law unto themselves. He was aware that he had no control over them. Their passage around the countryside left tales of scandal in its wake and he, by contrast rooted to the spot of the land and house he owned, considered their progress at times almost piratical.

The terrier-men were often migrant workers. The best ones were said to come from Wales. They were paid in cash, or sometimes beer, the free run of a pub for the night. Sometimes, without it being said, they were paid in silence: things they did that afterwards were not mentioned. It was understood that their being so intimately drawn into the portrait of the landscape had, with time, given them a kind of licence that, for being rare, had now made them almost foreign-seeming. It was as though they had travelled so far back into that picture, an island of farmers, that they had come out blackened on the other side: diamond-miners from Africa, dripping strangeness.

But though they were peripatetic, which to an outside eye gave them the appearance of randomness, and of being ungovernable, most had inherited their livelihood from generations before, and for that reason their lives were refined by hierarchy. The ban had offended them: they felt remote from the law, not through wildness but through the privilege of rank. To legislate against them was an outrage: if they were not this country, then who was? To them, the law had favoured the protesters; the mob had won; the hysteric minority, silenced for generations by being ignored, had now been given voice.

A victory had not been won, they were certain. It was a temporary error that, soon enough, would be straightened out. It was almost hilarious, in particular to the older men, that people had become so hot under the collar about something cooked up and now written on to the statute books, all within the space of eight years. Eight years was nothing. Their jobs had been around for almost eight hundred, and hunting was as old as life. Those politicians seemed to them like pipsqueaks, mucking about on the margins of a game that, in the end, would be picked up by time and seen through across a period they could not even look to. They'd be left dithering when the starting-gun went off, wafting about in London, clutching their White Papers, not realising that the chase went on whether their laws allowed it to or not.

The younger men weren't so full of conviction as to think this. But they liked to hear the older ones discuss it: it reassured them; and it pleased them to be able to defer to that authority.

Now, on the night before the Royal Fusiliers' first meet after the ban the five men arrived by Land Rover at the kennels, beer-bottles rattling in the back with emptiness. It was seven thirty. They let the terriers out. The dogs stayed within a narrow radius. Men and dogs had been there often enough before.

Eastleigh was two miles away. The men were expected to be there at nine tomorrow, and to stay with the hunt for its duration. They had discussed the new form: if a scent was drawn, the animal could not be pursued; but they had lingered on this point, and many had amended it to say that it could not be *seen to be* pursued, which was quite different, and made their job all the more important. If a fox went to ground, they would send in the terriers as usual. The hunt would get their scent. The moment of the kill would be unclear. What happened underground, unseen, was as remote as though it took place in a foreign country. It wasn't likely that cops would set up watch around the dens. The whole thing would be concealed by trees and earth. The countryside itself was the supreme disguise.

At the kennels, by the time they arrived, the small kitchen was already thick with steam, the windows white with condensation. A pot, large enough to feed ten, was on the stove: poacher's stew, rabbit and game, cooked up by the stable lad, who was expert in such things and had ambitions to be elsewhere. The men arrived clattering and boisterous, bursting into the bright room that Charley Sutton had left just before, relighting it where he had cast a shadow.

One, however, lingered outside. He wanted to take a cigarette in peace before joining the others. He lit it, and set off, unhurried, down the lane towards the back field. Three horses were out, blanketed. One, a brood mare, the other two not fit for tomorrow's meet. They swung their heads as he passed, weight shifting as they watched him. At the far end of the field, scraggy hawthorns were blacker than the sky, which still bore a bluish tinge, although it was dark, that looked to him like the possibility of snow, and the stars, too, he noticed were vivid, luminous. He knew the place well, and he knew the distance from the kennels to Eastleigh by foot, and the way to take should he wish to get there by night, as, indeed, he had once had reason to do.

He flicked ash, watched it die. A short man, he was the strong output of strong stock, thick-armed, deep-chested, his short neck giving the impression that he could not be bowed. Walking through the lanes, his pace slow, he appeared, among the shifting shadows, almost like a thick tree-trunk, its movement only an illusion. But when he wished to be, he was quick. He could break a hare's neck one-handed; or, impatient, he had a way of tapping its head once, swiftly, very hard, on a flat stone if one was handy, and that would do the trick just as well. Otherwise he used his knife; and it was that skill, as a boy, which had earned him his nickname, 'Cutter'.

He watched the black lip of the horizon: Eastleigh was beyond there. He had been telling himself to stay away, not be a fool. It wasn't even likely, he supposed, that she would be there. She had said she was a house-guest.

He drew on his cigarette, looking out across the fields. He remembered how she had cried out like a caught buck, her body flipped over among the straw, the goosebumps along the backs of her thighs and her arsecheeks rising to meet him. He smiled at the memory, and felt something stronger than fondness, though it was not love. Offering herself to him as she had done – no, he corrected himself, it was more than offering herself, for he remembered her demands – she had given him reason to believe in his entitlement. She had raised him up, and something in him had lodged there now that he could not ignore.

He wanted to reach for it again. He finished his cigarette. He had been so far away, so far down before her, that spying that other place, he coveted it the more strongly for once having strayed there – a secret garden, the gate edging open, one glimpse before it shut. Unworthiness mingled with the memory of pleasure, and together they amounted to a bolt of desire to get inside that place again. It felt like a right; and if it were denied him – his eyes fixed on the distance that contained the house, the stables where she had come to him – he was chill at the intimation, very sure in his mind, that if that were the case, if he were denied entry then, yes, he would be damned.

He thought of her body beneath his, her breeches down like a boy's and her blonde head half hidden in the nest of hot straw pungent with earth smells and the horse in the next stall stamping. He had heard the gelding's breath, which sounded louder even than his own, until, afterwards, he realised that it had been theirs together, and that intermingling had made him lift her up afterwards and drag her round towards him, for the first time kissing her.

Her lips were wet and swollen, as though she had spent all that day in kissing. It was after the hunt; the previous season, just before Christmas; the ground was damp, the scent high and the chase he remembered had been fast, the stubble loamy, slippery; a few had fallen, someone had broken bones, a horse had been shot, the whole day run round with wildness, and at its end a wind picked up so that the wet trees shivered in the lanes and she had arrived back there in darkness, the others already returned – where had she been? He had asked her this. She had wanted to enjoy the evening, or so she said, handing him the reins as though he were the stable lad. He corrected her, it wasn't his job, but took the reins anyway, and she followed him into the stable-block, and stood close behind him in the unlit stall that was steaming with spent horse.

That he had not kissed her sooner reminded him of his former badness, and he wanted to lay those kisses at her feet in an attempt at restitution. 'Forgive me,' he had said to her. She laughed at him, called him crazy, and he had felt the loneliness that always comes with secrets, sharpened by the fact that his, the particular secret he carried with him could not be spoken of. He had dodged punishment; he would take that secret with him to his grave. But having dodged the punishment he had found that he himself had also proved elusive, as though by not bringing his crime to the light he had made a devilish pact of invisibility.

He wanted to be back there. It was where his vitality lay, and without it he feared what might happen to him now. He could not just sink back and disappear. Hoping that she would be there tomorrow – not hoping for a repetition of that time, but for a nod that it had happened; perhaps a little more than a nod, he smiled as he made this adjustment – he felt like a bridegroom, with a bride-groom's pride and hard anxiety. It must all go right.

He looked back to the kennels at the sound of a bottle smashing. From that distance, those men seemed to him like animals, and he felt aloof. He glanced then towards Eastleigh, but there was no sign of it. He lit another cigarette. Reluctant, he turned back towards the smaller house, and able to see in the darkness – for he had been out for perhaps ten minutes now – he felt that he could see into the next day also, and as though brilliant with prophecy, heading towards the light and food, it seemed then also to contain her.

16

'Darling Celia!' Henrietta, Henry, jumped to her feet and went to greet her sister as she came downstairs. She had just arrived from London and was dressed in what appeared to be white silk pyjamas, a large Arran sweater thrown over the top, plimsolls on her feet. Her blonde hair, longer and rather brighter than her sister's, was swept up in an elaborate arrangement, the effect suggesting that the previous night she had been out, formally dressed, and only recently emerged from bed; the size of the pyjamas and the sweater implied the bed might not have been her own.

Leo looked on, sullen. He knocked mud off his wellington boots on to the doormat. It wasn't clear whether he had just come in or was on the point of going out. His hands were deep in the pockets of his heavy tweed coat, a posture Celia recognised only too well: he put them there to conceal them when they were fists; usually she would joke about it, go to him, take his hands out to kiss them, tell him not to be grumpy. Now she did not dare. His expression was black. She was glad of the distraction of her sister's arrival.

'I've got the most terrific favour to ask of you.' Henry glanced behind her at the front door, still open to the evening. 'I've brought my Iraqi with me. I hope you don't mind.'

Celia, knowing nothing of Henry's Iraqi, turned to Leo for help. On another occasion he might have found his wife's sister's behaviour entertaining, but he didn't meet her eye. The dogs had gone outside. He went after them.

'Oh, cheerio!' Henry called after him as he left, fluttering her fingers in his direction, oblivious to his mood. She turned back to Celia. 'I would've phoned,' she went on, 'only my mobile's on the blink.' The two girls, Hettie and Belinda, swung from either of her hands, attempting to drag their aunt away with them. 'And Amir doesn't have one.' She glanced back again at the open door. 'No fixed abode,' she mouthed *sotto voce*, widening her eyes at Celia. Amir, presumably, had been left with the luggage. Celia glanced about for the bell. Where was Ellis now? He was never where you wanted him. The girls were still straining at Henry's arms. She didn't seem to mind.

'Actually, I confess, darling' – saying this, Henry finally shook off the girls, and leaned towards Celia to impart the truth against her sister's ear, and Celia remembered all the other times her younger sister had done this, and all the secrets she had been burdened with over the years: stolen boyfriends and pilfered money from their mother's purse, broken china and whisky decanters topped up with water – 'really, my phone's not on the blink, I lost it last night in the Edgware Road. Completely *borracho* after some dismal charity lark at Frankie's, so went on to Mimi's, and then had to rescue poor Amir from –' She broke off, hearing a sound behind her at the front door. 'There you are, my darling.' She held out her arms now to a young man who emerged smiling from the darkness. He couldn't be more than twenty, Celia judged, and was nervous for that reason in greeting him. Henry was a decade older.

He didn't come forwards, but lingered, smiling, on the threshold. Celia thought he looked a bit simple, but was careful not to raise her voice in speaking to him. Henry's arms fell back to her sides as Gerald appeared behind Amir in the doorway, so close that they appeared briefly to be touching, and then Gerald came round the boy, nudging him off-balance with the quantity of luggage he carried with him. 'There, we're all in.' He set down the bags, smiling. His, Amir's and Henry's.

'Gerald!' Henry flung herself at her brother, her arms around his neck. He had been gone for almost six months. It was the first time either she or Celia had seen him since his return. 'Celia, you didn't say.' She pulled her sister towards her and the three siblings were caught in a haphazard embrace, Hettie and Belinda standing back awestruck. That the adults should behave as they themselves had, seconds earlier, seemed to narrow their childhood by a fraction — what were they to do if the grown-ups were so much like them? They went to stand a little behind their mother.

'I wasn't absolutely sure either of you would manage to come down.' Celia touched her daughters' heads. 'You should've said,' she addressed her brother, 'someone could've met you from the train.'

'I came by car straight from the airport.' Gerald looked at Amir. Egypt had made Gerald's skin match the younger man's, although his hair was a thick pale wave of blond; Amir's, long to his chin, was black rain streaming. Gerald bent to find something in his bag. 'I was right behind you at one point on the motorway but couldn't keep up all the way. Henrietta, you drive like a demon. Didn't you see me on the last stretch?'

He pulled out a bundle wrapped in newspaper, handed it to Celia. 'It's for these two.' He meant the children, who, afraid of their changed uncle, kept their eyes on him and not the present. 'And for you.' He drew out a couple of wide silver bangles, handing one to each of his siblings. The children received their gifts: small white robes, the necks and hems gold-threaded. They slipped them, puzzled, over their heads. Gerald considered them critically. 'I suppose they can wear them in bed or for dressing up perhaps.' He smiled at Henry, and Celia felt the slight exclusion she always experienced when they were together: as though by being in the middle she was less there somehow than the two more definite presences, guarding, either side.

'Amir.' Henry, appearing to remember, drew herself away from her brother and addressed the boy, who now came forward.

'We've met.' Gerald was smiling at him. Celia supposed he must mean just now, in front of the house. It explained the boy's delay in entering. They must have struck up conversation in the drive, and Celia hoped that Gerald did not offend him, mistaking him, as a boy, for someone who worked at the house.

But Amir was happy enough. Celia registered that he was very good looking. Incredibly thin, narrow limbed, dark eyes almond shaped, long lashes making his eyes seem to flash on and off every time he blinked. 'Thank you for letting me —' He waved a slender hand to encompass the house. 'Henrietta has told me much about you.' When he spoke, his voice was soft, humorous, as though, uncertain why he was there, still, the situation amused him. 'They are like little queens.' He smiled at the children, bold now in their costumes.

'Princesses,' Gerald corrected.

Amir did not look to Henry for guidance, Celia noticed, but to Gerald, who, in Leo's absence, took on the role, as elder brother, of their host.

'We'll go to our rooms,' Gerald instructed. 'Chinese Room for Henry, Willow for me?'

'Yes.' Celia hesitated only briefly: if Henry and Amir wanted to hop about between each other's rooms that was their affair, but she could not leave the boy floating, unclaimed, like this. 'And, Amir, Gerald will show you to the Blue Room. It's on the same landing.' It was the best she could do. The room was made up, although there would be no flowers. She would ask Marjorie to go in later when they took drinks downstairs.

Celia glanced at the boy's luggage: a small bag that appeared only half full. She doubted he had black tie. She wondered if, so as not to embarrass him, she should have a quiet word with Gerald to see that he did not wear a dinner jacket, either. She did not wish Amir to feel out of place. But that would mean she should speak to Charlie, and to James Dunbar, and it wasn't certain that she would be able to track down both men in time. She bit her lip. Henry rescued her, unexpectedly, with an announcement: 'Darlings, Amir is a poet, aren't you?' She went to stand beside him, eager, as though claiming her prize. 'He's come into exile here because he was persecuted at home. I've been pulling strings for him at the Refugee Council.'

Amir smiled more broadly, and Celia relaxed. He was an artist. Suddenly, his pennilessness, which until then had simply underlined his foreignness, now took on the gleam of eccentricity: when he was gone, he would become a talking-point. 'Our Iraqi poet, do you remember – the exile?' He was a modern expat. They often fled their homes against their wishes. It had happened in Zimbabwe. They knew a family who had come from there in a hurry.

Celia looked at Henry, grateful. The evening's dinner lifted in importance. Still, in spite of Leo, it might be saved. The world, remote, seemed to draw close, and to have entered the house, which otherwise, to Celia, was so untouched by anything that could be considered 'news'. Here, suddenly, a small piece of the headlines was about to sit down for dinner. Amir wouldn't need to wear a jacket after all. She smiled at him. She would ask Henry, to be sure of avoiding any awkwardness that evening: what did he eat?

Gerald started to lead Henry and Amir upstairs. It was six o'clock. There would be time after all to discuss Bea's will before dinner, as Celia had hoped. She put her hand on her brother's arm. 'Drinks are at eight, but could I have a quick word with you both before then?' His shoulders fell as though in relief.

'Of course.' He glanced at Henry, who also appeared to have expected this. 'Around seven, downstairs?'

'Absolutely.' Henry turned to go. From upstairs, there was the sound of laughter, and she turned back, enquiring.

'Cousin Will,' Celia explained, adding, 'with his friend, Isabella.'

Henry giggled, 'I'm not that bad, darling.'

Gerald paused, remembering. 'By the way, was that Leo outside? Thought I heard someone skulking about but he didn't answer when I hallooed him, so I wondered . . . ?'

Celia forced herself to smile, as though nothing were amiss. 'It will have been him, yes. Do you know, I think shooting's making him a bit deaf, but don't say I said so, will you?' Gerald laughed, and the three went upstairs.

Leo had left the front door ajar. Celia went to look outside but she could not see him. She was quite sure he didn't need to give his attention to the farm at this hour. She heard the dogs barking some way distant, and the high, lone screech of one of the peacocks calling, desolate-sounding, in the darkness; and, nearer by, the restless, moth-like fluttering of agile bats among the cedars.

From the doorway, she could see that the lamps were on at the head of the drive, the windows of James Dunbar's cottage brightly lit between the firs. The rest of the park was in darkness. There was no wind, and the earlier frost, she was convinced, had started to melt, a faint scent of earth returning with the night. It boded well for tomorrow. But there was no sign of Leo.

Her boots were under the coat-rack, and she wondered whether she shouldn't go out after him and try to find him. She could take a torch; he couldn't have gone far. She wrapped her arms round herself briefly: she was still wearing Leo's old navy-blue sweater from that morning. She missed him, an acute, physical sensation as though she had been unearthed and cast aside, her roots pulled up. She wished he would come back. Although the circumstances, at this moment, were utterly remote from what she had wanted, she would tell him her news anyway and hope it might bring him to his senses, return him to her. It was a blackmailer's tactic, but she was pre-pared to use it now. There wasn't much time left.

She went back to fetch her boots. Marjorie appeared at the far end of the hallway, coming from the pantry, a large circle of Stilton in one hand, a brown manila envelope in the other. Celia shut the door.

Finding her alone, the housekeeper gestured to Celia hurriedly, peering upstairs as though not wanting to be overheard. 'Look!' she stage-whispered, and Celia went to see what she had got. 'I was turning down Mr Will's girl's room, and found these.' She opened the envelope and drew out a number of photographs, all of Celia and her daughters.

'And Cook's livid about the puddings. Won't let me use that cream.' She thrust the envelope at Celia. 'You'd better have them.' She headed for the kitchen, grand with revelations. 'It's gone off, or so she says.'

17

'I know Leo wanted to keep the whole thing secret from Celia.' Will was lolling, his legs up on the arm of the day-bed in Isabella's room. 'So better keep quiet about the portrait for now.'

He had gone to her room to ask her if she might like a cup of tea, and see that she had everything she needed. He had misheard her reply when he knocked on the door, and stepped into the room to find her half undressed — at least, she had been wearing a shirt, struggling into, or perhaps out of, a pair of jeans, it was hard to say — which meant that when he opened the door she had begun to topple; he, chivalrous, was therefore obliged to rush towards her and take her arm to steady her. He could hardly have backed away and let her fall.

It broke the glass of formality that had stood between them. It felt appropriate, once they were there, that it should be so: arriving, earlier, they had been taken for lovers, directed to connecting rooms, and as they went upstairs together, Will carrying Isabella's bag, they had seemed complicit in their silence, for neither spoke out in denial of that misunderstanding: to do so would have seemed indelicate, and it was not pressing — they had not been placed in the same bedroom.

It was a mistake that drew them closer: when they returned to their separate rooms after greeting Celia, their thoughts ran towards each other.

Will had crossed to the window, unlatching it and raising the sash – the room, he felt, was overheated. He leaned down to look out into the dusk where little was to be seen, but he could smell the garden: the camellia was in blossom, the earth had just been turned in the beds, and the cypress, damp, reminded him of Italy. He had been in Milan only the previous week and had found himself perplexed with an odd loneliness that had felt like homesickness, although he had only been there for two days. He supposed that he should go to see his parents in Oxfordshire, and tried to connect the smell with that. But he knew it wasn't that entirely. He thought of Isabella.

He turned back to the room, and listened for any sound of her next door, but could hear nothing. Her silence made him see her similarly standing there, and he went quickly to the bathroom, ran the taps for a bath, clattered his dinner jacket on to a noisy hanger in the dressing room.

Isabella, meanwhile, had gone straight to the bed and stretched out full length, staring up at the elaborate knotted arrangement of the four-poster canopy. Her skin felt flushed and at the same time cool, as though grazed with a piece of fresh-cut ice, the water melting along her spine so that she felt it essential to lie down at once. Not to have her back pressed against the bed would leave her unfinished: with that slight mistake over their being together, she had seen Will moving quickly to take her in his arms, and she had bitten her lip with that impression, seeing again how much she craved it. Lying stretched out on the bed was the next best thing to his embrace.

She shut her eyes. She had no idea where the desire had come from. It was so unlike her, and yet so clear, that it made her doubt her understanding of herself: could a person be wrong even about who they were? She felt like crying but a funny strangled laugh came out instead. It was absurd.

Isabella jumped up from the bed. Will's silence next door had meant that she, also, could see him much too clearly, as though he had gone into his room not to be away from her, as politeness dictated, but to offer an invitation: come to me, my silence means only waiting – the request too intimate to be voiced. And then she heard him moving about on the other side of the connecting door, a window being opened, and the gush of water in the bath. She would do likewise.

She went through to the bathroom and turned on the taps, slipping off her jeans, starting to unbutton her shirt, but saw that that would only make things worse: for them to be lying there together, naked, submerged. No, the vision was impossible. She rebuttoned her shirt hurriedly and went back to the other room. Someone knocked at the door, she told them to hang on a minute and had started to get back into her jeans, when there he was, catching her.

Now, that sensation of being co-conspirators was given weight, first, by Isabella's literally having fallen into Will's arms: he caught her easily, set her upright with a 'There you are, girl', and a correct step backwards once she was standing, his gaze averted as she pulled up her jeans; and, second, by their shared secret – the portrait of Celia and the children.

He suddenly remembered – 'Don't go anywhere' – and went back to his room, returning with a brown envelope of photographs: he explained that the idea was for Isabella to make some sketches from life, but otherwise work from snapshots. 'It's important to keep the whole thing under wraps,' Will insisted. 'Probably best not to discuss it with Leo, either.'

Isabella was puzzled. Will explained, 'Best just to deliver the whole thing as a *fait accompli*. If Leo knows it's you who's doing it, he'll only blow his cover. He's terrible at secrets.'

Isabella was glad at the thought of being given free rein just to get on with it, and relieved, too, that she wouldn't have to discuss this weekend how she meant to approach the commission. So far, she hadn't the first idea.

As Celia's daughters had been a surprise to her, Celia, in the flesh, was an even greater revelation. The impression she had had of her from Will's letter was of a sturdy farmer's wife, clomping about in boots, barking commands at dogs, and laughing when no joke had been cracked, someone who would round up her children with a gong or a blast on a hunting horn. Isabella was a little shame faced: it had been no more than prejudice on her part to suppose that Celia might be like that. Will had said nothing to suggest it: simply that she rode horses, and was married to a man who owned land and was a farmer.

Seeing Celia for the first time, Isabella felt completely thrown. She and Will had been waiting for her in the drawing room; they had heard her come downstairs, a quick conversation they could not quite catch had gone on between Celia and Leo, and then Will, impatient, had gone out to her. Isabella had followed.

Celia had been standing in the doorway of the house, one hand resting on the frame, darkness behind her, her body angled in such a way to suggest to Isabella that she was actually posing for a portrait – one of Sargent's society belles, Isabella thought, for Celia astonished her also by being very beautiful, and she couldn't imagine why Will had not mentioned this.

She wasn't sure how else to put it, but Isabella had the vivid sense that Celia was, already, in some way a portrait of herself. Just as people who live in the public eye carry around a personal myth that, with time, becomes the public impression, it struck her that the portrait of Celia was already there in life. Her job would be to attempt to convey that, and she felt unequal to the task. It disconcerted her, because it made her doubt her skill, the mainstay of her character, and in similar measure, she felt the impression of her own self slip.

By contrast, Will was entirely at ease. Indeed, the further they had driven into Wiltshire, the more at ease and self-assured he had become, which was a puzzle to Isabella as he had punctuated the journey with regular cries of 'Bloody countryside, how I hate it! Just look at it! London's the place, don't you agree?' But despite his protestations, he had seemed strangely pleased, she noted, when she had said, emphatically, that she did not prefer London, and that she would leave like a shot if her work allowed it. 'Really? You must be mad. It'd eat you alive!' He had pulled a face as though disgusted; but had also started to hum to himself.

Now Will got up from the day-bed at the sound of knocking on Isabella's door. 'Housekeeping.' Marjorie's voice.

'I was going to suggest tea,' he said, 'but I've got something better in my room.' He glanced at the interconnecting door and back at Isabella. They left by the door that led on to the landing.

Marjorie stepped back to let them out. She had seemed to be leaning into the wood panelling as though listening. 'I've turned yours down,' she told Will, going past them into the room. Isabella wondered what she would make of the already rumpled bed, and knowing what it would be, she saw it then herself, and looked quickly at her hands. She followed Will into his room.

'Brandy.' He rummaged in his bag and pulled out a hip-flask. She did not drink all that often, and hesitated. 'You're terribly pale,' he added. She took the flask and drank, handed it back to him. They could hear Marjorie next door, hanging up Isabella's things in the wardrobe, then the squeak of taps. The forgotten baths. Will, remembering, went through, the opening door sending a billow of steam into the room.

There was a sofa at the end of his bed, and he sat down, holding out the hip-flask to her again. Isabella took it from him, felt a little foolish standing while he half lay there and, warmed with drink, went to sit beside him.

135

'So, the situation here.' He settled himself easily against the cushions. He wondered, and decided instantly against it, if he should mention to her that the middle button of her shirt was undone so that whenever she leaned to take a sip of brandy he could, just, catch a glimpse of naked breast: she was not wearing anything underneath. He did not look away, but smiled at her, and found her lovely. 'The situation,' he went on, lowering his voice as Marjorie could still be heard next door, 'is that Leo wants the painting as a present for Celia's birthday, which isn't until the end of the summer. You know this anyway.' He handed her back the hip-flask; she leaned to take it from him; he looked; he smiled.

'But this weekend I thought might be a good one for you to meet her for the first time, because she'll be in her element.'

Isabella did not entirely understand; she felt slightly daunted by his formal tone. His talking of the reason for her being there − a kind of employment − set her at a distance. She must have shown this uncertainty on her face, because Will frowned, mirroring her. 'You do know the significance of this weekend, don't you?'

Isabella did not. She had been a bit nonplussed earlier when Celia had been so keen to have her ride tomorrow. She had thought her hostess was simply being generous to a fault.

Will tilted his head to one side, and was reminded again of that quality of blankness that, years earlier, had drawn him to her − the excitement of discovering an unmapped area of life. It was underlined by the fact that they seemed very much together now, he felt quite sure − their fingers touched as they passed the small silver flask between them, a rapid series of gifts given, received − and yet where they were he could not say: they had not named the place yet, but he felt sure they were almost there.

Now, with half his mind still in-breathing cypresses and yearning in an unfamiliar way for home, and the other half acutely conscious of her nearness to him, her breasts against her shirt, he reached towards her, his hand quickly buried in her chestnut hair, to draw her to him so that he could kiss her.

Isabella held her breath. His mouth was warm, insistent, and she felt his teeth graze her lips, his touch like a hot sea for her to sink into and have no further need of air. She was conscious of trembling, her body somehow poised and taut on the lowest point of the arc before ascending. It was too much a mirror of everything she had imagined, as though he'd spied her secret thoughts or, worse, that she had come into his bedroom and, brazen, demanded, 'Kiss me, now!' She began to pull away but his hand was still soft and warm against her head and she wanted to stay there or keep descending but she couldn't see how then she might get up, and suddenly she felt clumsy and idiotic. She had no idea how to behave; it was all too awful, like being asked into a man's house for coffee. She managed to duck beneath his arm and jumped up, trembling, the brandy – she blamed it on that – making her stammer. 'I'd better go next door.'

She couldn't look at him, and she felt so much worse now that she was free. She longed for him to reach for her again, but he, too, was standing up, apologising. Her hands flapped at her sides, her heart hammering, and she had a terrible impression that she might start to cry. She felt half wild, as though that had been her first ever kiss: certainly it had blotted out all others, and she didn't want to begin to think what that might mean. But what on earth had she been doing until now?

He backed away; she turned for the door, and suddenly there was the sound of knocking. They looked at one another. He was already smiling, smirking, she described it to herself, and seemed perfectly calm, and she had the urge to punch him for being able to look like that.

It was Celia, her voice lowered, as though she did not wish to be overheard. 'Will, darling, can I have a word?'

Will hesitated. Isabella's cheeks were flushed and he thought that she looked utterly wanton and very delicious, more than merely kissable. He wondered if he should call out to his cousin that they were busy, then take her in his arms again. Next time he would not let her tussle with him, then wriggle away. He would keep tight hold of her until she saw sense and confessed that she enjoyed it. The image came to him – what she reminded him of – a skittish horse, was it that? Or, better, perhaps a well-made boat being run up too close to the wind, the halyards thrumming, the hull making that singular throbbing hum that could be felt most perfectly through the naked soles of the feet.

Will stopped himself, somewhat staggered. He wished he didn't reach for props from the sea or the land at such moments of crisis. He wished he could be himself, alone, and not as he felt – a direct consequence of all that. He shook himself. It was just that he wanted her very much. But it made him feel like a caveman and he certainly kept quiet on that score. He had been educated at Eton, for goodness' sake. Delayed pleasure, he told himself, but took a step towards her anyway and she stood dead still as though he had lassoed her. He leaned towards her and she half shut her eyes as he whispered in her ear, 'Do you know, Isabella, you're all lit up?' She let out a soft cry, almost a sob, then opened her eyes and stared at him with hatred. This, naturally, pleased him a good deal. Yes, delayed pleasure, he told himself, and felt returned once more to modern civilisation.

With his eyes still on Isabella's, he finally spoke up. 'Sure, Cousin C, come in, I'm decent.'

'It's about—' The door swung open. Seeing Isabella, Celia broke off mid-sentence: clearly Isabella's name had been on her lips, and she glanced at Will in mild panic. 'Oh, I'm sorry.'

Will did not rescue either of them with an explanation. He returned more confidently to how he was, and Isabella was furious that he should be able to do so: she felt scattered, half ravaged, and yet he had barely touched her. She started to leave the room. Celia, however, collected herself, and closed the door quietly behind her, effectively shutting the three of them in together.

She had an A4 envelope in her hands: the photographs for the portrait. 'I thought I'd return them straight away. Marjorie found them in your room.' She smiled at Isabella, patient. 'She had no business taking them.' She seemed more embarrassed on that score than curious, but Will broke in, glancing at Isabella with a guarding look, evidently hoping she would not speak.

'Oh, that's my fault, C. I must've scooped up the envelope with Isabella's bags when I brought them upstairs.' He leaned towards Celia, pretending to be nonplussed at what he saw. 'Of you and the girls? They must've been on the chair in the hall, the one outside Leo's study. I'd put the bag down for a bit before we went up.'

Isabella watched him and, astonished, found that at his words she felt a pang of disappointment. Even though it was clearly sensible, a necessary deception – the portrait was supposed to be a secret – it was oddly painful for her to hear him lie. It also cut the thread of her right to be there, and the botched attempt at a kiss suddenly seemed like no more than opportunism: she might have been anyone and he would have attempted it. She felt herself blushing and wished she could stop it. Being aware of it only made it worse.

'But they've been taken from the album. What would Leo want with them?' Celia had grown pale at Will's explanation, and it appeared to bother her more, Isabella thought, than it naturally might have done. Will glanced at Isabella, unperturbed. Evidently he thought he was in the clear.

'I just remembered my bath.' She knew that he must be aware that she was lying too: they had both heard the water being turned off at least ten minutes earlier. But she didn't feel like helping him any further in the deception. She had been drawn into it already: she was here on false pretences, an interloper, neither friend nor hired artist, and certainly not girlfriend. She suddenly wished she had not come.

18

The house was filling now with voices. Celia could hear her siblings talking together in the library – she was on her way to speak to them down there – and Amir was on the telephone in the hallway. Just past seven, and the others would be here by eight.

She hesitated on the unlit landing, the envelope of photographs in her hand. She thought with dread of Leo unsticking them one by one from the album as though to remove her from his life, and it was unfathomable to her why he might have done this unless with that intention; worse, that he also wanted rid of their two girls. She wished Marjorie had not brought them to her. It would have been better not to know. She felt a jolt of anger towards the housekeeper, who really shouldn't take it upon herself to stir up trouble where perhaps none existed. The explanations for these things were always innocent. She remembered the remark about the cream having gone off, and supposed that there were dramas in the kitchen. Marjorie flourished on such things. Celia did not. But she could not imagine what the photographs were for, if not something sinister.

The front door swung loudly open, and Leo came stamping in. He crossed the hall to the coat-rack, kicking off his boots. Noticing her at the top in the darkness, he started. 'What're you doing, Celia?' His voice sounded almost frightened. 'Why're you creeping about like that?' His tone was sharp. 'And shouldn't you be dressed?' He fired those three questions at her as he made his way upstairs and

they clouded her mind with their dislike: a poisonous gas. She heard
Amir lower his voice on the telephone, as though not wishing to be
involved. It was embarrassing to be spoken to like that in front of
a guest. He put down the receiver and went through to the library.

'I have to speak to Henry and Gerald before dinner.' Celia tried
to keep her voice light as he came up towards her. She reached out
to him; he drew back. 'Darling—' She wanted to ask him about the
photographs.

Seeing the brown manila envelope, he took it abruptly from her.
'This doesn't concern you, Celia.' He went past her, tucking it under
his arm, not meeting her eye. But his voice — or had she imagined
it? — was softer as he said that, catching in his throat as though he
were ashamed, and as her heels touched marble at the bottom, the
clicking of leather on stone sounded to her like footsteps in a mau-
soleum, hopeless, retrospective. His remorse felt like a seal on the
end of his affection. Leo disappeared inside their bedroom, shutting
the door with care behind him.

She touched the arum lilies on the hall table, straightening them
when they did not need to be straightened. She thought intensely
about tomorrow: a quick vision of what that day might now contain, an impression of its violence, and her heart sank heavy with
gravity towards it. It was impossible that she should go on like this.
If she and Leo were falling apart, she had no further use for herself
alone. She supposed that he would be well mannered over dinner,
but part of her was indignant that he would when, in private, he
had turned so unjustly against her. But who was ever able to declare
themselves entirely free of blame? She could not. She must have
done something to upset him.

She glanced down at her hands. The yellow pollen had coloured
her fingertips; she drew out her handkerchief from her pocket,
wiping at it. It was as though Leo had found out the earlier shame
in her: he was responding to that. She wanted to wash and be rid

of it. Even the perfume was sickening to her, she supposed because she was pregnant. Before, the girls both born in winter, there had been a number of things she had not been able to bear: lavender, eucalyptus, grass, pine, the fragrances of high summer and her fear – the June day subscribed to nightmares. Instead of giving in, however, she had filled the house with just those flowers, and now they were her favourites. They reminded her of her children, and because of that she loved them.

Henry's laughter carried through to her from the library. Celia could hear her and Gerald talking across each other. She couldn't see how they could make themselves understood. They had always been like that. A third voice, Amir's, was raised to join theirs, and then there was more laughter, and a cork popping from a bottle. She felt incredibly lonely, on the outside even of her own family. After Bea's death she had nowhere else to go but here.

She blew her nose. Leo would come back to her. Wherever he had gone, he had gone in error, through no fault of hers. But she missed him with an anguish so great it was like a physical pressure lifting upwards from her belly, leaning up against her heart and lungs so that she could not breathe.

Amir emerged smiling from the library. He held a key aloft as though in explanation. 'Gerald is lending me a jacket!' He darted upstairs.

Celia went in to see her siblings; they also had not yet dressed for dinner. Henry was by the drinks table, expertly stirring more gin into her martini. Gerald was drinking whisky; a few fingers of it, un-iced, was in a crystal tumbler which he had propped on his chest as he lay heavily against the sofa cushions. The uncorked bottle of malt was beside him on a tray. His red-socked feet were crossed in front of him, on a green silk cushion.

'Top-up!' Henry announced gaily, filling her glass to its brim. It didn't look like Gerald's first drink of the evening either: his hair had sprung from its parting, and fell in a thick clump over his forehead. Celia wished they wouldn't drink quite so much. She shut the door behind her. 'You'd like one?' Henry held up the glass.

Celia shook her head. Henry scrutinised her. 'You're sure – one of my killer martinis?' She held the bottle of gin over an empty glass.

'Perhaps a weak one.' Celia didn't wish to arouse her sister's suspicions about why she might not be drinking.

'I don't do weak.' Henrietta handed her the martini; Celia tasted it, smiling. She would eat the olive and pretend it didn't make her nauseous.

Gerald patted the sofa cushions beside him. Celia sat down, and Henry perched opposite them on the edge of the coffee-table. They knew what she wanted to discuss. She wished that their eagerness didn't show quite so much.

Last month, when Celia had heard the full extent of the estate, she had been jubilant at first: she could buy back some of Leo's land from Charley; safeguard the rest. Certainly she had no use for the money herself. But she had brooded on the possible two reasons why Bea had left the full amount to her. Neither had been spelt out, but both seemed clear enough. The older woman had taken care of her niece after two tragedies: the first, for which she blamed herself; the second, for which she blamed Leo – he should not have let her ride.

Now, over the last few weeks, thinking about how the money might best be divided, Celia had felt that blame implicit in the inheritance, and that it had all been left to her seemed designed to be a goad. Had Bea secretly wished to present Celia with the opportunity to leave Leo? She hadn't had the means to do so, otherwise. Now she had more than enough.

Celia's impulse was naturally the reverse. Riding out with Charley, she had discussed, in confidence – she had not even mentioned the plans to Leo – the ways in which she might see some of the land returned. And there were particular portions she wanted to ensure remained always within Eastleigh's estate.

She thought of this now, watching her siblings' faces turn pale at the extent of the legacy. Henry took a large swig of her martini. 'The cunning devil!' She was momentarily lost for words. 'Gerald, we didn't have the first idea.' She turned to her brother. Clearly they had been speculating on how much might come to them. He dabbed at the corner of his mouth with a handkerchief, discomposed. 'It's astounding.' He laughed. 'How on earth did she do it? You'd better put me in touch with her broker.'

'Did you know, Celia?' Henry's voice was sharp, suspicious, and Celia had the idea that her sister was wondering if in fact the amount was more, and that as executor Celia was keeping the greater sum to herself. She shook her head. It was perfectly true. The first she had known was when the letter arrived that morning a month ago from Bea's solicitors.

'But what'll you do with yours?' Henry persisted, her eyes flashing briefly across the library, implying, Celia felt, that it was a moot point: she had little need of anything else.

Celia had never discussed with her siblings Leo's difficulties. She had no intention of doing so now. 'There's some land we could use for the farm.' She hoped to sound vague.

Henry frowned, clearly sceptical at her sister's choice. 'Really? Not a Porsche then, darling?'

Gerald laughed again, finished his whisky at a gulp and leaned across to refill his glass. He still seemed overwhelmed. 'It really is astounding.' Then he turned to Celia, attentive. 'What land?'

Celia took a quick sip of her drink, glanced at her watch. She should go up and dress. She felt nervous suddenly that she might start to cry in front of them, because she had been thinking of the one particular piece of land that she was most passionate Leo should keep. It was a small beechwood, just beyond the limits of the park. At this time of year the bluebells were starting to show through, though they would not be in flower until April; then they were a mist of blue so beautiful, their time so brief, that they were heart-stopping, the definite mark of spring. The beechwood was useless for the purposes of farming – virtually without value on that count. But it was where Leo had asked her to marry him, and where she had said yes.

She stood up quickly and turned to leave the room. She thought she had heard a car on the driveway. 'You'd really better dress.'

'Don't boss, there's plenty of time,' Henry, petulant, was still in her silk pyjamas. She went to sit on the arm of the sofa facing Gerald, swinging her feet.

'Really, I think you should.' Celia hoped they wouldn't celebrate too precipitately. Gerald had set his glass back down on his chest and was rubbing his hands together. They looked like a pair of con-spirators, exactly as they had when they were children.

'Gerry, I think you should lean on bossy old Celia to give up her share.' Henry tugged at one of Gerald's socks and shot a mischievous look at Celia, who was waiting for them to show signs of going up. 'You hardly need it, do you, darling? Whereas I've got debts like Christmas! You'll only spend it on more horses or dogs or something. It'll just be wasted, with you buried down here in gloomy old Wilts.'

Henry was at her worst, Celia thought, when she was most sure of herself, and she had the urge to tell them the truth, that the inher-itance was hers and they could go to hell. She would see that Eastleigh and the farm were in better shape, then give away the rest. She breathed out sharply and set down her drink.

Gerald came to her rescue. 'Henrietta, you are an actual mon-ster. Ignore her, Celia.'

Henry slapped away his foot, which had been wiggling at her, sig-nalling his disapproval.

'I won't waste it, anyway.' He sighed and turned kindly towards Celia. 'It looks like Devon for me.'

She felt a rush of relief: this at least was exactly as she had hoped. He would return to England and take on the family home. Gerald got to his feet, unsteady, running a hand through his hair. 'It's about time I mended my ways, I suppose.' He set down his whisky glass and rubbed his eyes. 'I'm actually very glad, Celia. There's nowhere left for me, really, after Cairo, and things are winding down there now. I should probably marry.' He waved a hand as though conjuring up a bride. He didn't seem convinced on this point. He repeated, as though for emphasis, 'Yes, I expect I should probably marry, or something,' adding quickly, 'I haven't got anyone in mind, of course, but I should, shouldn't I?' He stood expectantly in front of Celia as though she might confirm this.

The balance between the three siblings seemed to shift by a fraction. Gerald straightened, touching his collar, pulling up his tie. Celia thought he seemed rather forlorn, and her earlier annoyance softened. Henrietta also rose to her feet and glanced from one to the other, deflated. Suddenly she looked very young and lost, all her malice no more than a posture, an attempt at being grown-up. It was she who was now most on the outside of the trio, and Celia went to her but she moved away, finishing off her drink with a flourish. 'You're right, time to dress.' She brushed past Celia.

As Henry was leaving, Celia remembered and called her back. 'I'd appreciate, by the way, if you'd both keep all this secret from Leo, just for now.' Gerald and Henry raised their eyebrows at one another.

'Secrets,' Henry murmured, reassured by the flaw. 'How very exciting.' They went upstairs to dress.

As Celia followed them up, she thought she heard the click of Leo's study door, and turned back, startled: she had supposed he was upstairs. There was no light showing from underneath. She must have been mistaken. But it unnerved her. It was as though an immense pressure was being held off on every side. Suspicion and closing doors. Just as one obstacle was removed, another emerged. Now she might be able to count on Gerald, but Henry was another matter. Her nerves felt tight as a wire set for a trap.

'Cousin C!' Will's voice, calling from the doorway of his bedroom, made her jump. 'D'you think Leo can lend me shirt-studs? Can't believe it but I've forgotten mine.' He came out to join her on the landing, taking her arm.

He was happy, and Celia was relieved that it was so. He appeared to have stepped through from a better-lit place.

'She's very lovely, Will.' Celia pressed his arm.

'I know, C, she is.' Will's voice made her look up at him: it was unfamiliar to her, lower, soft, and curious, as though he had only that moment understood the solution to a complicated puzzle. 'She's the one.'

He glanced down at her as he spoke and she read his surprise there. It was as though a flash-bulb had gone off somewhere further along the corridor, a physical illumination that she might have missed had she not looked up at him at that moment. She felt able to breathe again. His lightness had touched her too. She had just witnessed love.

Downstairs, the front door opened. The others were arriving.

19

When James Dunbar left the army he had re-entered civilian life uneasily: nothing seemed to fit him. He could find no place or situation where he could feel quiet. Even his own self hung ill made upon him. Leaving, he had consciously considered the line about swords being beaten to ploughshares and, turning it over in his mind, he had found that its underbelly was rotten – a maggoty log tipped over in a damp forest. It was simply untrue: he remained a sword, a gun, and all his instincts would lead him to that. It was how he and all the male line of his family had been fashioned; it would take a similar force and stretch of time to beat him to a different purpose; and he could not change the past.

He had fled. He started, idly, in Europe, buying a train ticket that allowed him to range there freely for a month – apart from a stretch in Belize, training, and another in Iraq, he was not well travelled. He did not intend to settle, he merely wished to look. He ended his European trip in Istanbul, and from there took a flight to Cairo, on the recommendation of a friend, who had given him the name of a man who might supply him with introductions. He had a pay-off from the army, and a vague notion that, at some later stage, he might be suited to diplomatic work. But his heart wasn't in it; his heart was not in anything.

Arriving in the city on a May evening, during Moulid an-Nabi, he had been baffled to hear that the festival was religious. For him

God meant a dank cathedral on the granite cliffs in Yorkshire, the only thing moving being the wet-looking incense, rising into a chancery that had always made him think, with the smoke ascending, of an upended boat washed down at rest in winter. There the incense seemed to gather dust with it as it rose. It wasn't religion. It was death. He couldn't understand the intentness, therefore, with which the men flooded towards it. Their hurrying had the appearance of fanatics rushing to suicide.

At his hotel, stepping out of the taxi to smell jasmine and amber, fat blocks of scent on the evening air, he felt released. He wanted rid of himself too. He prayed thanks. He felt at home. He left his bags with the concierge, and went out into the evening, which like a revelation now was night.

He returned to the hotel at around three in the morning, went to his room, but did not sleep. At dawn, with the light, he drew the sheet over his face and slept to the sound of the city restarting outside the window — the noises lightened after the previous day's festival, the litter in the streets made pretty by distance. By mid-morning, the wilted frangipani and white petals of fallen jasmine had the sleety look of English snow.

The connection he had been given was to Gerald Stevenson, Celia's brother, who had told him the address of a café in the Jamaliyya quarter, and instructed by telephone that James should come there at four for tea. As he entered, a young man rose from the cushion beside Gerald and, smiling, left, walking with the weight on his heels so that he tipped back slightly, as though reluctant to be gone.

James shook Gerald's hand. They drank sweet peppermint tea and smoked nargila. Sweat ran along his spine. He sank back into the cushions and was exhausted. His exhaustion was pleasure: without purpose, all his hardness softened, his borders rubbed out, the fight over now, he felt fattened-up and womanish — a prize for men after a war in which he himself had played no part. He reclined, Gerald smiled at him; he felt beautiful and indulged, a pasha. He expected to be handed sweet things dipped in honey, and when, inevitably, the sweet things came, he laughed out loud, and that evening he and Gerald became lovers.

James returned to England a month later, on good terms with Gerald, amicable, but by that stage passionless. Gerald kept a promise, made early on, that he would do what he could for the ex-cavalryman. He gave him an introduction to his sister and brother-in-law's house, Eastleigh.

James travelled down to Wiltshire for the weekend, and found that, yes, he might make a kind of home there. The cottage matched his mood for remaining on the outside of things, set as it was close up against the wall enclosing the estate. His duties would be minimal. He would, almost, be his own man, but not so much that it might come as a shock to his system, for so long run on steady, institutional lines. He noticed winter jasmine, sleeping at that time of year, planted around the window of the bedroom. He liked to believe in signs, and he took this to be one of those: a faint scent of Egypt in rural England.

That jasmine was flowering now, in February, and with the window open, he had caught its perfume as he dressed that night for dinner. The radio was tuned to the eight o'clock news. He had just bathed. The bedroom was warm, dampish. He had raised the sash to let out the steam. The scent unnerved him, however, and did not give him pleasure, because it reminded him of much he had forgotten.

It was over ten years since he was in Egypt. He had only been there for a month. He had not travelled, substantially, since then, and that feeling of being luxurious, a pasha, was transmuted now to a lesser sensation of simply being idle. He worked. But the work was not his own. He was effectively in service. He was not, after all, his own man. He heard about battles on the radio. They no longer involved him. He told himself that he was glad they did not, because in the end he did not believe in their motives, and despised their consequences. But the news reports left him nervous and clumsy, frowning as he knocked things over as though part of him, a secret part of the machine, still ran along that pattern, the bits waiting to engage. He thought of his gun; he still had a licence. He rolled his shoulder, which ached with the memory of the bullet, even now, and he crossed the room to shut the window, cut off the past.

He drank some whisky as he dressed, his hands thoughtful on the crystal tumbler and on the collar of his shirt. He knew that Gerald would be there that night. He had seen him often enough over the years. He liked the man. But he had, since that time in Cairo, always been a little afraid of him: he held a secret in his hands. James did not like that. The remnants of the soldier in him were stirred to think of it – sediment of a dark wine swirled around and rushing full of colour up the glass when water was poured in. To have that secret knowledge of him was to hold him in his power. A subtle grip, but decisive.

He saw himself back in that café in Cairo. Gerald, throughout, had sat on a straight-backed chair, ordering things that his new friend might like to taste. James, already compliant, limbs askew, had reclined on cushions a little lower than Gerald, submissive, sucking naïvely at the nargila.

Sighing, he looked at himself in the mirror, irritated suddenly with the thought that so little had changed. His earlier decision, that soon he would leave Eastleigh, strengthened into a definite inten- tion. He would tell Celia and Leo now, tonight. He picked up the comb, went to the sink, wet it, ran it through his fair hair until the hair gleamed. He tilted his chin up at his reflection, an instinctive flourish that made him feel prepared.

Of course, he had a kind of power over Gerald, too, but James didn't think it counted for much. Gerald's private life was probably of the nature of an open secret – just something the family did not talk about. He supposed it must be understood: it was probably why Gerald, even as the eldest son, had not taken up his duties over the Stevensons' house in Devon. Things would be quite different, he reasoned, if Gerald was worth blackmailing; if he was very wealthy, for example, or meant to marry, or hold public office.

He sighed. Now he really was being fanciful. Gerald was just an old queen who drank too much, going quietly to seed in Cairo.

Leaving the house, he noticed that the jasmine was not, in fact, in flower. It was much too late for that. It was completely over, the petals finished. He frowned as he shut the door behind him, hesitating for a moment on the front step beneath the covering of the veranda. A chill wind had risen, the temperature dropped by a few degrees. He wondered if it would sink still further. The driveway, lined at this point with cedars, was unlit and the darkness, as he paused there, was scattered in a gust with snowflakes – quick, small flakes that would have passed without notice had he not been there just now.

As he left the cottage, setting off down the driveway towards the house, he puzzled over the jasmine. He would have put money on its being in flower. He was certain, beyond all doubt, that he had smelt it just then as he dressed.

The house, when he turned the corner, was brightly lit and his spirits lifted as they always did at the prospect of company, and a party. He did not thrive alone. Apart, yes. But that was quite different.

Going up the steps to the house, he turned at a noise behind him on the driveway. He peered back into the night. 'Who's there?' His voice, sharp, sounded bolder than he felt. There had definitely been footsteps, momentarily, on the driveway, as though someone had followed him downhill through the trees, sticking to the grass where their tracks could not be heard. Why had they made the error of straying on to the gravel? It was as though they wished him to believe in their presence without supplying absolute proof. He waited for someone to step forwards. No one came; the drive was empty. He closed the door behind him as he went inside. His mind was playing tricks.

Marjorie entered the hallway from the kitchen, smiling to see him. If she had ever had a son, she would have wanted him to be like that. She liked him because he was handsome, and deferred to him because he was almost family; but she took the liberty of sharing confidences with him, because he, too, was in the Domeynes' employment, and therefore just like her. Anyway, she would often remind herself, as 'one of them' — or, as she put it, explaining, to her husband, Ellis, who was slow about such things, 'a pansy' — he shouldn't think of putting on airs and graces. Yes, he was very much the kind of boy she'd have liked for a son. (As it was, she had had one daughter and no more, and that girl was a disappointment and lived in London in a place called Shepherd's Market, which, although it was allegedly in Mayfair, had a nasty ring about it all the same.)

She stepped brightly towards him. 'Henry and Gerald are here,' she told him, supplying confidentially, 'though only he's down.' She took his top-coat from him.

He preferred it when she kept her distance. He deliberately moved away from her suggestion that he might, particularly, be interested to hear that Gerald was already there.

'Back from Cairo,' she added, and he wished she wouldn't.

Jasmine, the spook on the driveway, the mention of Egypt. He straightened his lapels and went through. Ellis handed him a glass of champagne as he entered, and he gulped an inch of it in gratitude.

The glass raised, he saw that there was someone here he had never seen before. All those signs he had refused to read suddenly made flesh in the body of a boy, Amir, on the far side of the room, alone, by the fireplace. He forgot all his other motives for being there, and all his desire to leave. He was suddenly very pleased to be exactly where he was.

Amir looked up as James Dunbar entered the room. Instinctively, James went towards him.

20

By eight, the drawing room contained them all: Celia and Leo; Will and Isabella; Charley Sutton and Esther; Henry, Amir, Gerald, and James Dunbar. The children, Hettie and Belinda, were also present, making the number twelve, but they were there as a special treat only, brought out like tricks to delight the adults. They wore Gerald's robes from Cairo, and were allowed to carry round the plates of quails' eggs and smoked-salmon canapés – superfluously, as Ellis was then obliged to linger at one end of the room, hands twitching with redundancy as he watched them.

At a quarter past the hour, Anna came in to take the girls away. They did not protest. They knew their place, and hadn't thought they should be allowed to stay so long. When no one appeared to be looking (Amir, in fact, had noticed her do this, and her eyes had met his, complicit, as it happened) Belinda had popped one of the tiny eggs into her mouth, secretly mashing it before swallowing it almost whole. For her, the evening had been a triumph because of that egg. She went upstairs happy, her younger sister trailing after, Anna shepherding both girls ahead of her.

Ellis stepped forwards, visibly taller by an inch of increased purpose, relieved that, finally, he had the room to himself.

Henry had, of course, entered last. What was the point in making an entrance, she thought, if your audience wasn't at its capacity? To be admired made her feel secure, because only at such moments could she properly see herself: an audience was a mirror. It was why she always endeavoured to look her best.

Tonight, before she went down, she had strayed naked around her room, thinking of Aunt Bea's legacy and everything it would do for her – rather more than get her out of her current tight spot, as she had supposed. Even once her debts were cleared, she'd be left with enough to set herself on a very even keel, and more or less indefinitely, too. To contemplate such a length of time was disconcerting. She thought instead of Gerald. When he had mentioned Devon, the house after all the one she had grown up in, her heart had leaped at the thought, and she blustered with a quip about Celia wasting money on horses, simply to stop herself saying something foolish that she was delighted at that thought of her brother in that house; and might she join him?

She imagined herself there, very quiet, in a wing, and at last coming clean about the fact that she was utterly sick and weary of her life in London. She was no good to anyone there, least of all herself, and she hated not to be useful. This she kept secret from her siblings. Celia, with Leo and the girls, the house, her garden, was just too perfect to understand that a person could be flawed, in conflict with themselves, or find themselves on an unwanted track in life: Celia had everything, even poise; while Gerald, as the only son, was unassailable.

Both of them would have laughed at her, disbelieving, she was sure, had she expressed any such desire to be useful to others. They thought she lived solely for her own pleasure. Yet that was only part of the picture. Her debts were not entirely through cocktails and frocks. Did they really think they were? The greater part came about through her string of pet projects, most of them disastrous. She thought of Amir. She hoped he wouldn't turn out to be one of those, but she was a terrible judge of character. And it wasn't just those projects that half ruined her.

She sighed deeply, and thought also of the many unscrupulous men she had known, who, sometimes with great cunning but always thoroughly, had assessed how much she was worth, and, finding it insufficient, drifted rapidly away. She would find no pleasure in buying any of them back now that she could afford to do so. They were cads. She could do without them. But she wished she didn't enjoy their company so much.

She caught sight of her reflection in the wardrobe mirror and looked critically at her body. Where Celia could not put on an ounce without appearing fuzzy round the edges – and she was a little that way now – it suited Henry's figure to be changeable, her fluctuating weight a kind of barometer, telling the weather in her heart. She was always thinner when she was in love; but when she was not, as now, she softened and grew slightly, and this, she had discovered, made her more desirable to men. Desired, she was made so happy that the happiness often flowered overnight to love, and then her weight descended once again.

It suited her to be thus. It was one of the reasons people could never, quite, pin her down. Everything, even the pallor she took on when she was out of love, added to the effect of no one quite knowing how to catch her. She had been described as careless. But it was not that. She was intent in everything she did. She was merely unreli-able. Passion over, the object of her passion ceased to exist for her. Men rose to the challenge; at heart, she found all of them foolish for doing so; and she loved foolishness, because to make mistakes in her opinion was at the heart of life, and so she found immense camaraderie there – many of those lovers, ceasing to exist for her as such, became great friends. Not the ones who contributed to her debts, or who scarpered when they discovered their enormity, and she frowned again as she remembered them, but the others, cer-tainly.

Tonight she considered: James Dunbar? Although she had never actually met him, she had seen him from a distance, and often heard about his rather fast – at least for Wiltshire – reputation among the county wives. She knew that he was handsome. She had caught sight of him striding around a few times in the stable-yard in long boots and breeches, and for goodness' sake, who wasn't susceptible to that? She held a navy-blue dress against her, discarded it for being demure, chose instead a white silk gown, diaphanous, backless, meaning that it was impossible to wear a bra, which was one step away from being naked, therefore a challenge. She put it on, slipped her feet into high gold shoes, and went down, late.

'They're up from Shropshire, yes.' Charley Sutton had his back to the door when Henry made her entrance. He had meant the terrier-men. Hearing him say this, she faltered in her confidence: Shropshire had been where they had come from last season. Her blushes, as she remembered what had happened after the meet that time, only added to the effect of charm, and she quickly collected herself. She hoped that she wouldn't run into the man tomorrow. She would hate it if he didn't remember her; but she would hate it still more if he did, and worse, if he said something.

She reached for a glass of champagne. Her mind was suddenly back there: the empty stall, the people distantly returning, the horses blanketed at either side, his hands calloused but oddly expressive, she remembered, like a sculptor's. The past. She set him more firmly there. She really ought to fall properly in love.

She glanced at James Dunbar and felt a dart of disappointment. Handsome, yes, very, just as she remembered, but clearly not interested in girls. Why had this not been mentioned? He was talking to Gerald and Amir, standing by the fireplace. She crossed the room, acknowledging, in a disinterested fashion, that Amir presumably preferred boys too, hence the attentive leaning towards Dunbar.

But as she approached to claim Amir, she caught sight of the three men's reflections in the mirror and diverted her course by a fraction to stand beside Leo instead. Of the three men, as they were seen in the mirror, it was apparent that Gerald, and not Amir, was the one leaning closest to Dunbar. But Gerald was her older brother. The house in Devon moved by a degree back into the realm of fantasy; and all his talk of marriage? She downed an inch of champagne, indignant, too astonished yet to be self-righteous.

Leo, meanwhile, had his eye on Celia who, graceful in a heavy pearl choker, her hair pinned up, and a black silk gown, strapless and lean, was moving about the room, attentive to each cluster, her eyes straying occasionally to the clock over the mantelpiece, and not, he noticed with chagrin, lingering unnecessarily on him; nor, and this he noticed with a growing sense of her duplicity – that she could pull off the act so seamlessly! – on Charley Sutton.

Involuntarily, Celia touched the sash of her dress: she had judged that the empire line would hide any possible increment round her waist, although of course it was too soon for any; she wanted to feel the softness there and not be constricted.

She saw that the trio of her brother, Amir and Dunbar needed breaking up, though not for the reason that her sister had alighted on, but simply through three being too many men at once, and since Amir was, for being a poet, almost their guest of honour, she touched him lightly on the elbow and led him towards Charley and Esther, to whom he had not properly been introduced. They looked, to Celia, as though they needed a third person to draw them together; Esther's insinuations were at the front of her mind. She hoped that bringing the boy to them might work as a balm, healing Esther's disquiet with a distraction. They stepped aside to let her bring him in.

For confidence, as she spoke, she addressed Amir. 'So you're a poet, Amir?' Celia thought that Esther was eyeing her with suspicion: her brown chiffon dress floated away from her pale body, giving the uncomfortable suggestion of someone drowning in brackish water, her movements jerky as though weeds might pull her further down.

Charley's manner was tense also: like Henry, he had been aware, though disbelieving, of the trio of other men, and he had blamed the suggestion it presented him with on the fact of the outsider. He thought of all foreigners as somehow being spicy, in the sense of adding unusual flavours to the English. It was often desirable that they should, but it always should be noted. Now, however, he continued to look behind Celia towards Gerald and Dunbar, as though he had a question to ask of them but did not know quite how to frame it. The disquieting effect was still there, even though the supposed cause had been extracted.

Amir held a glass of champagne, just refilled, somewhat askew, and Celia wondered if the boy was used to drinking. Up close, he looked rather younger even than she had supposed, nineteen perhaps, and she decided against asking him if he had had any work published. He seemed too young for that, and she didn't want to imply that he was in any way deficient. It occured to her, also, that it was likely he was a Muslim, and perhaps not used to drinking for that reason. Were they all Muslim in Iraq? Flustered, she changed tack, pressing on in a different direction, hoping to move to safe ground. 'And Iraqi?'

Charley and Esther grew alert at this, and Celia was pleased – she had drawn them together along the same line of interest – until she saw the boy's expression change.

'No.' Amir's voice was raised sharply enough for Leo to glance up from his conversation on the sofa with Isabella – who sat very erect as though trying hard not to wriggle while someone touched the side of her throat with a feather, her lips parted, eyes very wide – and Will who, smiling, was openly contemplating, as he spoke, a point some way below the decency of Isabella's collarbone. Celia did not see Leo glance up: she felt his attention without observing it, and so was unable to discern its quality. Had she turned to him then, she would have seen her husband's suspicion shift aside in instinctive concern for her safety, hearing that angry-sounding 'No.'

Then Amir's voice became gentle again, and he apologised, blustering, Leo thought; and in the same instant his concern shifted aside once more, and when Celia looked towards him – it bothered her that there should be disharmony here, and that she might be its cause struck her like a failing – his expression was as it had been before: she had been too late to see the tenderness.

By then her husband was smiling at Isabella: he raised his eyebrows at Will, the two men were complicit. To Leo, Isabella, with her rapt expression, seemed to belong utterly to Will, and this made him feel bitter and nostalgic; to Celia, the two men seemed merely held in thrall by the girl's prettiness.

'I'm sorry, no,' Amir was nodding with apologies, 'I am a Kurd.' Seeing Celia's anxiety – it was clear to him that she did not know the significance of this – he attempted to change the subject. 'My work has been published in English, though, in a magazine—'

He was mid-sentence, but Charley cut across him, addressing Celia, thinking that he was doing his hostess a service by explaining the significance of the remark. 'Saddam gassed a hundred thousand of them.' He lowered his voice, as though uttering an obscenity. 'His own people.' Charley stared at Amir then, as though having said this, he now slightly disbelieved in the boy's existence: how was such a thing possible? It was against the odds that he should be there.

Amir gazed back at him. The older man, he thought, did not belong in a drawing room. He was better suited to a plain or desert. Unaware that Charley was master of foxhounds, he was nonetheless conscious that he was a hunter: he held his champagne flute like an arrow. But Amir stood his ground, smiling. For his own part, he wished that he had a little pin to hand. He had the urge to run with it round the room and make each one of them spring a tiny drop of blood. He would end with himself. They would not need to say anything. He would not do much damage. They would shed the drop and then they could go in to dinner as equals. Without that drop, they were not quite real to him; they were completely foreign. Apart from Dunbar, who was in his estimation a blond kind of Arab, a bleached Bedouïn tented at the palace gates, he had no idea what he could say to any of them.

Henry, unexpectedly, rescued him. She had noticed the lull in their conversation, and had taken that opportunity to reclaim her gift to Celia, who, she felt, had been ungrateful in not showing more enthusiasm at her having brought him. It couldn't be every week her sister had such people in the house.

Amir was glad that his friend had come, once more, to save him. It was the third time she had done so. The first had been at the Refugee Council. The second time had been only last night, in the Edgware Road.

What she didn't know, however, was that Gerald had been of the party from which Amir had been fleeing when he spotted her. She was drunk, darting with a group of people from bar to taxi. He recognised her, was desperate to get away, tapped her arm, bleated, 'Help!' She sensed an urgency, swept him along with her to the party, where he fell asleep on the sofa. She hadn't liked to move him, hence the pyjamas: her host's. Remembering she had promised Celia about the weekend, she brought him along with her to Eastleigh.

Gerald had not, as he had maintained earlier, arrived back today, but yesterday. He had wanted to reacclimatise himself in stages, and not be press-ganged into coming down to Wiltshire early. So he had looked up some friends in Bayswater, and from there it had been a short step to smoking shisha in the Edgware Road.

Arriving at Eastleigh, he had naturally been shocked to find Amir lifting bags from Henry's car in the darkness outside the house. He felt as though he had finally been run to earth. His siblings knew nothing about his private life. He intended them never to discover it. He could not take things on in Devon if they should, and – although he hadn't realised until that evening quite how soon this might be – he certainly intended to one day, and that meant a wife and sons.

'You disappeared,' Gerald whispered.

'Your sister rescued me,' Amir replied. They shook hands outside in a kind of thrilling truce: if either one decided not to play along, both would be lost. Neither had the desire to ruin their hostess's weekend. There was nothing to be gained by it. Both of them would behave like gentlemen.

Henry led Amir away now, her hand looped through his arm. She had seen Ellis growing restless, which meant that in moments he would strike the gong for dinner. She wanted to go in with her boy. The gong sounded. People stood, or straightened themselves. There had already been a good deal of champagne.

Gerald, unexpectedly, stepped towards Isabella, drawing her away from Will who, openly disgruntled, hung back and, rather rudely, Henry thought, refilled his glass, swigging from it as though to fuel a mood that might turn vicious. This left Dunbar floating. Esther was nearby on the sofa, having sat down after the discomfort over Amir. She appeared limp in her thinness, the brown chiffon still lapping over her as she raised herself up. Her earrings, pendulous, bowed her head. Dunbar stepped forwards, taking her naked arm. Charley, staring at his wife, took hold of Celia, which left only Will, preoccupied with pouring another glass of champagne, discounting himself with that action anyway from politeness; and Leo, looking on at them all, intent.

He finished his glass in one gulp: not fast, but leisurely and savage, as he watched his wife going through to dinner on Charley Sutton's arm. He had seen her strolling around with him that morning; he had imagined her meeting him that lunchtime; and he remembered how she had been going off with that brown manila envelope as they met earlier that evening on the stairs. Had she struck a bargain with the other man already – was he expected to keep the land on those terms? Leo had thrown the envelope on to his desk after dressing; it was unbearable to him to think about it.

Now he wondered how much more it would take, how much more he had to watch, before his certainty would be perfected: she was no longer his wife; her affections had shifted to another man; she did not love him. Here was the picture of her guilt, the way she leaned in to her lover in front of his eyes.

All he needed now to complete his conviction was one last piece of evidence that would add up to proof. He felt certain that any moment now he would find it. He went in to dinner after them. His place was at one end of the table, his wife's at the other. The clock, as he left the drawing room, chimed eight thirty.

21

As the watercress soup was brought in at Eastleigh, Lance Ash, feet
up on the coffee-table at the Lamb and Cross, was treating himself
to a glass of brandy. 'The good stuff,' he had said to the girl behind
the bar, whose hand hesitated uncertainly between Martell and
Napoleon – she had heard of him, and supposed that might make it
better; the man seemed satisfied enough when she poured it into a
wine glass. 'Ice?'

'Good Lord, no, not in this weather.' He made an elaborate show
of being cold, clutching at his arms, lips pursed.

'I'll get the fire turned up.' She nodded through to the other room
where a gas fire imitated coal.

Outside, the snow that had flurried and ceased five miles away
at Eastleigh was gathering, as though sticky, along the beading of
the windowpanes. It had made Lance feel sentimental. He thought
of Christmas. Sentimentality progressed rapidly to anguish. The
drink was necessary. He had no kind of plan, and all maps led to
greater depths of regret. His wife had gone. He had come down
here feeling spiteful, hardened with gloating, but it had all worn
out.

When he arrived, he had sent a message to the man who'd suggested he come, but had heard nothing yet. Perhaps the whole thing
was off. So far he'd seen just a handful of tired-looking farmers, preoccupied, and, when encountered – passing in the narrow lanes, or

stopped for a packet of crisps at a grocer's store – polite, edging away slightly as though to give his grey suit more room. If there were enemies down here they were all in hiding, and he couldn't say he blamed them in this weather.

He settled down with the day's newspapers and his brandy. Dinner had been good, which for him meant it had come in a large helping. He hadn't minded that it was bland. At least it hadn't made him think of Alison. She always cooked things hot. By his second brandy the sadness had begun to lift and he felt the right-eousness stir again inside him. He turned in early, just after ten o'clock. He still had not heard from the man about what time they should meet up for the hunt. He supposed there'd be a note for him the following morning. He was here. It should be easy enough to find.

When he slept, the cars passing on the main road beyond the window thundered through his dreams like horses locked in battle. In sleep, his unconscious desires yearning for the kill, he hoped that he had not come in vain: he hoped that the hunt would go ahead.

Ten o'clock passing at the kennels, and the men there were strag-gling back to the Land Rover to fetch more beer. Cutter had whisky. He had meant to keep it for himself, but while he was out they had rummaged through his bag and found the bottle. 'The sneaky bas-tard,' one of them said, bold. He would not have dared say such a thing had the man been there. When Cutter returned, he did not appear to mind as much as the others had fretted he might. His thoughts were elsewhere. They had not seen him so quiet before.

'You sick, Cutter?' the one who had stolen the whisky asked him, wishing to atone for the theft.

'What?' Cutter was over by the small kitchen window, his hand resting, guarding, on his gun-bag. He turned to the room. Brightly lit, it seemed idyllic: the dogs neat with sleep in the basket by the fire; the men avid and chaotic over the remnants of bread and stew, the playing cards soft with use and red-smudged as though even they were aglow with firelight. 'Sick?' He turned back to the window. 'I'm fine, no. Bit of a head.' Last night they had been drinking. Now he had arrived just too late to be dealt into the hand and his exclusion made him melancholy. He was on the outside of everything.

Earlier, returning to the kennels and dinner, he had stopped, the rope tugging him back to where his thoughts had first led him: her, the big house beyond the trees. He had wanted only to see it. It wasn't far. Less than a couple of miles. Skin tough as seal-hide, he flourished in cold weather. He set out into the night. His vision was good in darkness. If something crossed his path, he'd bag it. Pausing at the sound of thumping on turf, a high whine, doglike and more faint than the breathing that came between it, he pushed aside the sodden bracken just beyond the edge of the park at Eastleigh, to find an old fox dying in a trap. He broke its neck. Cursing it as he went on, downhill now towards where the house lay, the lights inside revealing it in darkness, his voice was tender: the curse was his way of blessing. To catch a creature that way was a shame.

He turned down the driveway, aspiring to the place he'd once been invited to enjoy: her. Much further down, he saw a man's outline on the gravel. He stepped on to the turf at the edges, and carried on. He was quiet. The walk had warmed him and he had swigged from his decanted flask of Scotch at modest intervals, the pewter clinking faintly in his pocket as it touched his knife. He'd left his gun at the kennels.

Unusually careless, angling for a better view, Cutter had stepped on to the gravel, and the figure, reaching the main door, had turned. He had the alert bearing of a soldier, and Cutter recognised him as one of the cavalrymen who had ridden out last season, although he did not know him. When the man spoke, 'Who's there?' Cutter, tipsy, had put a hand to his mouth. Faggot. He half wanted to call out, 'It's me, the fox, beware!' but he kept his silence. He waited until the door closed and then he approached.

The lights he had seen from a way off were coming from the upper floors only, where the windows that led to the landing had not yet been curtained over; all on the ground floor, bar the kitchen, had blinds drawn down. He could see nothing, and he felt cheated, imagining her in there, concealed. He stood on the gravel in front of the house and watched it. He saw a pretty girl in the kitchen, darting about with dishes as though following orders, her dark plait flying as she moved. The plait reminded him. The other had been blonde. It shamed him to remember. A kind of madness had taken hold of him. It was a long time ago. He had been drunk then, too. His breath quickened, as though on the point of conquest, or detection, those two states of peril — both disclosures — momentarily matching in their effect upon him.

He left. He arrived back to find the men content; they didn't comment on his absence. He would have preferred for them, for her, at least to have noticed he was not there. Not to be missed was the worst thing of all; to be forgotten felt to him like death. He thought of the fox. Killing it, he had made it memorial. The trap was no better than a squeezing out of air; amnesia through lack of oxygen.

He thought of the moment tomorrow when he might see her. She would have to give him a sign that what had happened between them had not been in vain. It had happened; it had changed him. He did not want to be forced into making her remember.

'Cutter!' The stable lad's voice was raised, as though he had spoken the older man's name already and yet he had not heard. 'You're in.' The boy held up the cards, just about to deal. He stepped into the light.

*   *   *

At Eastleigh, Ellis waited as Marjorie, his wife, opened the dining-room door. It was his moment. Time to carve, the sharp knives gleaming on the marble sideboard, the white wine glasses abandoned for the red. He brought in the lamb.

22

'Rather like mustard gas.' Charley Sutton was discussing with Celia how foxes might be gassed rather than hunted. 'But I don't set much store by it.'

Charley had a great appetite the night before a hunt, even more so afterwards. He forked a piece of lamb into his mouth, reached for the mint sauce, speared another potato before Ellis took them on their way. He had noticed his favourite brand of cigars, Romeo y Julietas, left out on the side-table as they came in. He was looking forward to those. Leo would have his own stash of Cohibas somewhere, no doubt. Celia was an excellent hostess, and always kept a good table, if, at times, a little exotic for his tastes. He glanced on instinct at Amir, placed opposite.

Dunbar and Esther had been seated next to one another, further down the table, but Dunbar appeared not to have said a word to her yet. Her flamboyance was provoking because he held it so well in check. Charley had them in his sights, but his focus was on tomorrow now. If Dunbar tried anything funny, he would bring him down. He glanced down the table: the *placement* must have been tricky – they were a couple of men too many.

Overhearing his tone, Isabella smiled. She half expected him to add, 'And it's hardly cricket.' The thought sounded incomplete without it. She had only just discovered, over drinks, the significance of the weekend here in Wiltshire, and she felt a combination of nerves and tenderness – as though, unexpectedly, an acquaintance had invited her to a close friend's funeral.

She cut another corner of lamb and followed it quickly with a piece of cabbage: her own fault not to have mentioned she was a vegetarian.

When, over drinks, Leo had spoken to her about the ban on hunting, he had clearly been torn: since she was from the town, she would be against hunting; but because she was, he supposed, Will's girlfriend, she must be for it. She confessed that honestly she had never given it much thought. She had always admired Stubbs, her favourite painting was Ucello's *A Hunt in the Forest* in the Ashmolean, though mainly for the perspective, and it struck her as a peculiarly inappropriate way to end all that – like ugly neon streetlighting turned on across an evening under stars. Banal, in aesthetic terms, but also simply excessive: what were the lights hoping to illuminate? It was all rather muddled, and she wondered if, also, it made her a snob to think that such a ban was depressingly suburban: the edges of the nation's cities bloating out across the land.

Of course, she didn't say any of this. She didn't know how to put it without sounding too much like an artist, so she left it at that: 'I'm not really for or against it, just interested in all things equally, I suppose.'

This satisfied Leo, not as a good argument, but because he took it as proof positive that the girl was hopelessly in love with his wife's cousin. Her judgement was completely off kilter, and he raised his eyebrows at Will, implying as much. Will was happily preoccupied with trying not to look at her breasts, so did not notice.

Now Isabella wondered if she should mention to Charley, who was still frowning over the unsatisfactory business of gassing foxes, that London was inundated with them: they had all moved there. She often saw them strolling about in Regent's Park. They'd become a menace, and very bold. People were always complaining and plotting against them. She supposed that now they'd migrate back. The country would be safer than the cities.

There was a large log fire behind her; above it, a high gilt-framed mirror, wreathed around the top with early blossom from the greenhouse. The scent of it drifted down to her. The blinds were drawn across the night. The dining room felt like a gilded box. Candle- and fire-light made the people precious. The doors were backed with dark green baize. The house around them felt to her like velvet.

She was awestruck to see how much was also muffled by sheer good manners: that no one remarked on the strange trio of James, Gerald and Amir, their languid complicity reminding her of a trip taken as a girl with her parents to Tunis, passing the baths where the men emerged in pleasured clusters, arms draped round one another's shoulders as naturally as damp towels after a swim.

Her parents, she imagined, would have approached this dinner as more literally a last hurrah. There would have been fights by now over the pros and cons, hilarity and uproar; later, things would have been broken. Theirs was the spoken version of this evening's play of silence. It was everything in reverse. In both cases, Isabella felt herself an observer. She could not take part in her parents' wildness; nor was she part of this evening, although she admired it, from a technical point of view, because it seemed immaculate. It was like being shown a gold statue behind glass at the V&A. She felt that she was peering to make out the secret of its loveliness, and to see how it was done.

She had already made a few swift, furtive sketches of Celia and the girls: ideas about how she might arrange them more than actual drawings. She was looking forward to starting proper work. She thought that Leo was wonderful for wanting to keep the whole thing secret. Often, in such situations, it became a tug of status, 'our artist', and she was made to feel like a hermit brought in to take up residence in poor quarters, the family's latest fad, or a superfluous servant on hand to entertain. The fact that, according to Will, he would trust her absolutely to come up trumps, simply deliver the portrait when it was ready, pleased her greatly. It flattered her and gave her confidence: she would not disappoint.

Coming down to dinner, Isabella had found the portraits on the top landing familiar, and leaned in to read the artists' signatures. But it had not been the work in general that had reminded her of something: it was each portrait in particular. The family line was still strong: pieces of it had been evenly distributed among many of the people here tonight. The two girls, their faces so far unbrushed by the present, were the family's best print of the past.

'Let me take you down.' Will had emerged from his room and walked briskly towards her, giving her his arm. Not meeting her eye, he added, 'You look lovely, by the way, and I'm sorry about earlier.' His manner had changed, and she felt rebuffed.

She was wearing a violet silk dress, low-cut, narrow-sleeved, the hem skimming the floor – a dress she had bought on a whim and never worn before: there hadn't been the occasion.

She tried to make her tone of voice sound self-mocking – 'This old thing' – but she only sounded forlorn, and he took her remark as seriously meant.

'No, I am, and you do, don't worry.'

She had the urge to pull him by the arm back to her room, flick open the hook of her dress and demand that he be as he was before and simply kiss her. It was too great a strain – that lunge, her retreat, their formal manner faintly conjugal as they descended. But she feared that, for him, their behaviour was so well worn a track, that now she had jumped off the train he had meant for them, he had ceased to notice her. She looked lovely, but she was in the past. It made her want to pinch him. Or, she thought, and swallowed hard, better still to bite him.

As they crossed the hallway, Will had glanced at her, as though feeling that thought of hers come to him through the light pressure of her arm on his. He looked away quickly. Her neck, exposed, was too much for him. He wanted to kiss it. As soon as they were in the drawing room, he let go of her arm. Had he stayed touching her a moment longer he knew what he would have done.

Now Celia was discussing a house in Devon with her brother. The ha-ha wanted attention apparently, Wilmot was threatening notice, and the bats had become a menace in the tower.

'Oh, Wilmot!' Gerald threw up both hands in despair.

'There are no field mice left!' Henry, calling down the table, added this piece of information, which, she said, had come to her via a cousin whom she was worried 'really might not budge without some welly'.

Celia closed the matter with 'You'll be happier married.' All three siblings, satisfied with this diagnosis, turned their attention instantly back to the lamb.

'One of yours?' Henry enquired, leaning forwards to address Leo, who nodded.

Aside from the mode of conversation, which, bringing as it did such things as bats and marriage together so – to the speakers, at least – coherently, their remarks had startled Isabella: was Gerald really expected to marry? He seemed happy enough at the prospect, she thought, if perhaps a bit subdued, as though he'd glimpsed a clear way through the fog to find not the gentle hill he'd been expecting but a mountain.

Charley had heard the mention of Devon, and spoke up. 'Isn't Anscombe about to fall off his twig?'

Gerald appeared to brace himself. 'Well, I had heard something of that kind.' He set down his knife and fork but kept his hands poised over them as though thinking he might need them suddenly as a weapon. 'But I think he's been about to drop off for years.'

'That would mean a by-election?' Celia addressed Charley, but turned to smile at her brother.

'It's your neck of the woods, you should give it a pop.' Charley drained his glass of claret decisively. It sounded less like a suggestion than an order, and Isabella changed her impression of the room: not a jewel box, but a box of dice; each throw was a manoeuvre. Gerald looked glum for a second, but then he rallied. It was the life he was cut out for.

'Certainly time you stopped buggering about in Cairo.' Charley laughed, but turned back quickly to Celia. Bothered by his choice of words, he changed the subject. 'So, tomorrow.' He and Celia began to discuss the next day's meet.

Gerald picked up his knife and fork and, aloof, started to work again on the meat. He, too, had turned his thoughts already to tomorrow. He hadn't given the day much attention: he had travelled here for Celia and the will. But now he felt himself caught up in something momentous. He was by nature a narcissist and, insecure, he had sought himself in remote pools all his adult life. Now, thinking about hunting in spite of the ban tomorrow, he felt an almost breathless rapture. For him, it was not hunting, but himself that seemed to have been made illegal, and this he found thrilling. He would come home, but home now seemed far more complicated and exciting than he had imagined. He hoped he had been given a fast horse. He was in the mood for a damn good gallop.

Isabella took a sip of wine. She met Will's gaze further down the table. She wanted to be back on the sofa and, instead of jumping away, she wanted to move towards that kiss. She did not wish to be frozen. The wine warmed her and, smiling at him, she noticed his look of surprise. Had she really been so cold? She wished that she had not. She took another sip of wine, and with the glass at her lips she thought of the touch of his lips that might replace it. She set down the glass; her hands were trembling. She pressed her palms, to steady them, against her thighs beneath the cloth.

'You'll be out tomorrow?' Henry addressed Esther, who sat slightly more upright.

'Of course. We all will.' Esther had hoped to set Celia's sister, in her voluptuous good health and outrageously suggestive gown, at a distance with that 'we', but it only drew her in.

'Absolutely!' Henry raised her glass. 'Won't we just. Can't wait. The forecast looks fair, too. I read they're expecting three hundred out, up and down the country. I wouldn't miss it for the world. Damn good gallop!'

Gerald looked up, startled: his younger sister often spoke his private thoughts aloud like that; he grinned at her.

Charley, overhearing, was disarmed by her enthusiasm. He liked Henrietta but found her generally most unnerving. She was like a turned-out version of Celia, with everything that should be secret openly on display. Leo's wife was a fine woman in part for being mysterious. Even though he counted her, now, as a close friend, he had always thought of her in such terms – like a pale statue glimpsed at a distance through the trees. He was very glad not to have married her. It would have brought her up too close. To have her so near would have stifled his affection.

Thinking this about Celia, he felt a stir of disloyalty, as though he had criticised another man's property. But in some ways he admired her most for being his one-time rival's wife. Looking up on instinct as he thought this, at Leo, he saw that he was being closely scrutinised.

'You say you haven't an opinion about it, but don't you think' – Leo had raised his voice: looking at Charley, he was addressing Isabella, who nervously sipped her wine – 'it'll be better when it's over and done with?'

Leo finished his wine and held up his glass to be refilled. He had returned to the subject of hunting, and seemed intent on making her take sides. Isabella felt that she could hear Celia's alarm in the increased gentleness of her laugh, as though she hoped to soothe her husband's sharp tone with that sound, directed at him from the far end of the table.

'I mean, coming from town, you must think it's absurd. The knickers' – he took the bottle of Cheval Blanc from Ellis's grasp; the man stepped back, dismissed. 'I'll take it.' He refilled his glass; then remembered: 'Oh, you'll want some,' and filled Isabella's glass also, spilling red wine as he did so on the cloth – 'the knickers in a twist, and over what? Bloody animals.'

Leo had transferred his scrutiny now to Celia, and was staring directly at her, as though willing her to tell him to shut up, but she had turned to Amir, sitting on her other side. Charley was the only one looking directly at Leo. The rest of the table was complicit: such behaviour did not exist if it went unacknowledged.

'You're better off away from here, in town, I'd say.' Leo drained his glass, poured another.

Isabella, alarmed, noticed Will watching her in sympathy. He shook his head at her, and raised his eyebrows as he touched the stem of his wine glass lightly, with his fork, signalling to her not to worry: Leo was only drunk. She thought Will was like someone grimacing over rain at Wimbledon: if not today, then tomorrow there would again be tennis; it wasn't serious. She thought it was. She wished he would do something.

'You are though, really.' Leo turned to her, as though she had spoken in denial. 'At least there everything's out in the open. All the talk' – he picked up the butter knife from his plate; Ellis was at Celia's end, clearing – 'all the cut and thrust,' he went on, aggressive, swiping at the air in front of him.

Isabella looked directly ahead to Esther for help. That woman's face, however, was sullen with a kind of delight, like perfect malice, as though she had longed for just such a scene to transpire; her silence was a goad, spurring Leo on. She might have said something, Isabella thought, annoyed. Leo was Esther's friend, not hers.

Isabella drew breath. 'If I had to take sides' – she noticed that Celia was making a show of being locked in conversation with Amir, who was leaning away from her, his smiles sent openly across Will and Esther towards James Dunbar – 'I'd say that I certainly think it's a shame so much will be forgotten.'

She had hoped to keep her tone calm and then change the subject, but at the word 'forgotten' Leo laughed angrily. 'Celia's good at that. It's her speciality. She couldn't care less if I hunt with her tomorrow.'

Celia flinched at this but did not look up. Isabella thought Leo incredibly rude; she was shocked; she pressed on. 'But Will tells me that your and Celia's families have always hunted, and your children ride, don't they? and I can certainly imagine being sorry on that score, for my family and friends.'

She had meant, with that remark, to include everyone that night at his table, and by including them she had hoped that their presence – each person like pieces of an argument – might win the day and silence him. She herself brought no weight to the case: she was impartial, it was simply not her thing. But her words seemed to land like a match to dynamite in his mind. In one smooth gesture, steady and relentless as a spark running up a fuse, Leo raised his glass, re-filled it and stood up.

The table was silent. Noises carried from the kitchen: where their food came from had been mysterious until that moment. There was the clatter of a pan, a cheerful curse, the methodical, muted crack of china being stacked.

'Do you want me to show you what family and friends are like? Do you want to see some proof?' Leo strode from the room and returned, moments later, with a brown manila envelope. He dropped it on Isabella's plate in front of her. She stared down at it: the photographs for the portrait?

'Go on,' Leo told her, 'open it, and tell me what you make of that.'

Waiting for her to do this, he took another deep gulp of wine. Isabella felt horribly implicated in something she did not understand. She shook her head. Leo snatched up the envelope and held it aloft. 'I'll tell you.' His voice was tight with menace, his eyes fixed on Celia who, with equal concentration now was staring at her hands clasped on the cloth in front of her. It was clear she was trying desperately not to cry.

'Yes,' Leo went on, 'I'll tell you. They take everything from you, bit by bit.' He snapped his fingers as though that gesture of obliteration proved his point. 'I've heard you all. *Don't tell Leo. Keep it secret from Leo.*' He steadied himself against the table. 'They take your land, your wife. That's what family and friends do.' His voice lowered, and was broken, full of anguish. 'And when they've taken everything of value, they expect you to sign over even the place where you gave away your soul.'

Celia was staring up at Leo now in horror. He seemed very far away, a nightmare running on uncontrollably.

Suddenly he crossed to the fireplace and threw the envelope on to the flames. 'But I will not sign away my soul to you, Charley Sutton.' The sparks rose up, furious, a log dislodged into the grating and he kicked it twice until it settled.

Ellis came into the room but stepped backwards as though he had not been there. The kitchen fell silent shortly after.

Charley began to stand up. There was no rush in his manner. Setting down his napkin, he seemed to collect himself. 'Leo, outside, my friend. This is preposterous. I am sorry.' He leaned very slightly towards Celia, addressing his apology to her.

Gerald coughed and swallowed: he had stopped chewing. Henry

drained her glass. They had been singled out more than the others. Esther seemed almost to have been revived by Leo's outburst. She sat bolt upright, bright-eyed; the waters had subsided. Will drummed his fingers on his thigh and waited. Amir and Dunbar were together in appearing almost to smile, teeth slightly bared, defensive.

Charley had not yet moved towards Leo, but he held out his arm, indicating the way outside, hoping to pacify him. Leo stared at him for a moment, then, as though he might be going to ignore him, the crisis averted, the worst over, he crossed to the side-table where more wine had been left out. He poked at some of the bottles as though Charley's manner had undermined him. He was straying on to less certain ground. He ran his hands wildly through his hair, whirling round, remembering. 'And where the hell is Frenshaw House, Celia? Charley?'

Celia was visibly trembling. 'Don't make me explain that now.' She seemed almost to be praying as she said this, her voice almost a whisper as she shut her eyes.

'Is that where you go?' Leo demanded. 'Is that why you didn't want me to ride tomorrow, because it's so well known now what you're up to?'

'Come on, outside.' Charley was somewhat reassured by having no idea now what he was talking about. He had never heard of Frenshaw House. 'Come on, cool off.'

Leo ignored him, took up another bottle, refilled his glass. His hands were shaking. He began to move back to the head of the table when suddenly he stopped, picking up a small decorated box: Romeo y Julieta cigars. Celia's gift for him.

They were not his favourite brand but Charley's. Unwittingly, for she had been distracted by her good news, she had bought the wrong kind.

Leo stared at the box for a second, then at Celia. He placed the box very carefully back on the side, his voice now full of venom.

'You have mistaken me, dear wife, for another man.' Then he hurled his red-wine glass at her. It smashed against the far wall, just missing her head.

Charley rushed round the table, taking Leo off-balance, wresting his arms behind him and pushing him to the door. Leo staggered as he went forwards and, tussling, they were half out of the room before Leo struggled round, his words fired out at Celia's back. 'How can you be so cold? Look at you. Do you think you can get away with this? You were supposed to be my wife. Go hunting with your lover tomorrow and then see what happens.'

Charley pushed Leo backwards hard, out into the hallway, not speaking but roaring in anger. Then the front door could be heard to open and slam shut and there was the sound of gravel being kicked around as the men fought, moving distant from the house into the night.

No one dared look at Celia. It could be felt that she was motionless. Esther was the first to stir. Only seconds had passed, but with her movement the crisis inched from dead centre, and as she stood up, hurrying towards Celia, the others were able to breathe again and, finally, turn to her.

Esther's manner was a revelation. With her arms swift round her friend's body, her thinness was suddenly like strength, a tautness in her gestures that was a determination to get across what had happened. Seeing her own suspicions enacted had brought her fast to her own senses. She was glad they had gone no further. She said something close against Celia's ear that no one else could hear, and kissed her cheek. At last Celia moved, seeming to draw back, and her left hand shot up to her face, covering her eyes.

Esther held her closer and, addressing the room, spoke on behalf of everyone left at the table. 'Darling, he's mad. None of us believes a word of it. It's too ridiculous. You're nothing of the kind.'

Celia's hand remained across her face. Gerald had stood up, and Henry, too, had gone to stand beside her. Esther withdrew in the presence of the siblings, but they looked uncertain, either side of Celia, still seated.

'Charley will sort him out.' Esther glanced nervously at the window. The blinds were drawn down across it. Nothing could be seen. The night outside was noiseless. She edged towards the window as though wanting to see what was happening: a ringside seat. She rushed out into the hallway suddenly, undignified.

As she left, Amir began also to stand, but slowly, and, as though Celia's body responded with habit through being a hostess, the host now gone from the table who else might give the lead? – she moved at last, her hand falling from her face, her slim back very straight.

'Thank you,' she addressed the boy, who was alone in not attempting to meet her eye: everyone else was staring; it was unbearable. He put out his arm, she rose, took it, and they left the room together. She could be heard to ascend the stairs unaccompanied.

Amir's footsteps, uncertain on the marble outside, recrossed, and he came back into the room. He put his hands into his pockets, like a child, defiant. 'It's better.' He turned again and left, going into the drawing room.

Gerald, his face drawn, pressed his mouth once, hard, with his napkin, half stopping something that sounded, when it emerged, like a cough, his in-breath afterwards a kind of strangled whimper, caught.

He looked around the room at those remaining. 'It's over now.'

23

Isabella left the door to her bedroom ajar in the hope of hearing some sign of what might be going on. There was nothing. The house was silent.

When Charley and Leo had rushed struggling outside, the others closed ranks; she left them to it. James Dunbar went through to the drawing room to join Amir. Cigar smoke already drifted into the hall as she went out. Men ahead, the family behind, she thought of the kitchen: perhaps she might have a cup of tea. But that room's quiet told her she was not wanted there either – they had their own business to attend to.

So she darted up to her bedroom. She supposed she should leave early the next morning. Someone could give her a lift to the railway station in the town. She didn't have much to pack. She put a few things into her bag.

The evening had grown chilly. She touched the iron radiator. It was lukewarm. She turned the tap at the side and a loud clunk of air sounded in the pipes. She felt overdressed and cold. She rummaged in her bag for a sweater, found a large, pale blue cashmere one, and quickly put it on. Crossing to the window, she peered out through the curtains, could see nothing on the back lawn, so drew them wide open, raised the sash and leaned out in relief. She bit her nails and wished she had brought a glass of brandy upstairs: she felt both sick and sober, and her nerves were ragged.

It was as though she had been hijacked, her impartiality used like solid blocks for Leo to run up and then crash down from. She had not agreed to collude in that. It was treacherous. She had been involved because she had watched, and now it felt as if that was all she ever did: made sense of things afterwards; by which time it was too late. Whoever had said this was right: art really did make nothing happen. She just mucked about with paint.

The air was so cold that the scents of the garden would be dead until the morning. The year seemed very far away from spring, liable to tip back to winter – a pendulum that might get stuck at that lower point and not swing back. It would take too much heat, and there was none here now.

She wrapped her arms round herself and shivered, turning back to the room. Her drawing book was on the chest of drawers. She went to pack it away, glancing through it as she did. They were just rough sketches, marginal notes, of Celia and the children. It had been tricky to catch the girls, who flitted and were never still. Isabella thought they were like tiny native birds, elusive by an instinct that they were rare: they belonged here, yet they were almost, now, extinct.

She thought of tearing the drawings up. The commission was macabre: what had Leo wanted a portrait of his wife for, if that was how he felt? She would have no further part in it. It was as though Leo wanted to fix Celia in paint, not as an act of love but to snare her there, so that she could not escape, hold up the cold image to show how far she had fallen short of that perfection.

Arriving, Isabella had noticed the visitors' book on the hall table, a heavy black pigskin volume two inches thick. It was open at the present day, but the page was near the end. The years were all behind. Isabella wanted to avoid signing that book. She did not wish to put her name to this weekend.

Isabella went back to the window. She found the silence chilling.

She had thought the house immortal for being antique. Now, without love, it just seemed dead. The door ajar, she wanted to hear signs of life, evidence that the life inside went on. She needed proof or she couldn't quite believe it. Leo's anger, breaking over Celia, had wiped it out. But the house was silent. Gerald had been right. It was all over.

Isabella shut her eyes and prayed that Celia would somehow rise up as she was, and that this would not harm her beyond repair. It felt vital to her that Celia should be able to do this, because it was everything she herself feared: to step down warmly into life, to love, and yet to be cast out. To risk so much, to be rejected, could be enough to kill a person, to strike at their heart and turn them to stone. It was a place from which you could not return.

When she opened her eyes, she saw that snow was falling. Her breath steadied, she felt a wind run through the cypresses towards her, and she heard a car far distant on the road.

Her bedroom door clicked shut, very softly. She turned back to see that it was Will. She went to him.

Crossing the distance of the room felt to Isabella like a kind of falling – a release of effort that left the rest to gravity. His arms went quickly round her in a fierce embrace that in its necessity felt more like a kind of cushioning. She landed but went no further. She was safe. He held her tight and they swayed, and then gravity weighed on them equally, and she clung to him as they sank to the floor together.

On their knees, facing, Will took Isabella's head in his hands but did not yet kiss her. He had come straight up from downstairs, walking fast, then breaking almost into a run as he took the last stretch to her room. He had not noticed her leave the dining room, and in her disappearance – he had looked round and she was gone – he had had an intimation of losing her. His family had clouded his vision. It had struck at him and he had felt that he might almost cry out. He made his excuses and dashed after her. To delay a second longer was a waste of time. He had glimpsed love, and it was her, and he had done nothing about it. He had to begin life now. He pulled her back towards him and held her close. He would not let her go.

The sash window rattled with a flurry of snow that sent the heavy curtains billowing inwards. He looked up and, standing, drew Isabella, staggering, to her feet beside him. It was as though they had just risen from prayer in the middle of a hurricane. Surviving it, he felt almost married. The sensation understandably alarmed him. He had the unfinished thought – If we can get through this . . . The open window gave him an idea.

'Come on.' He began almost to drag her from the room, was checked by chivalry, and turned back with tenderness to her. She, too, was now collected, and with her other hand straightened her hair, which was sticking up, mussed and dishevelled. He paused, watching her, which felt to him like the closest thing actually to helping her. Groomed, she became almost as she had been, and he took a step back towards her, wanting to mess her up again. This time, fractionally, she retreated, and in her retreat, again, he felt a nuptial thrill of agreement: that spot, moving, felt like a place that they could stay for ever.

He picked up a white wool throw from the bed. 'Take this.' Handing it to her, it was as though he presented her with a gift, and she accepted it with just that look of pleasure and consideration. It was thoughtful of him. But not knowing yet what he had in mind for her, she simply stood there holding the blanket, perplexed, enjoying the gift's mysteriousness: it was the first thing he had ever given her; she felt happy in part because it was negligible, just a blanket from the bed, and therefore its significance was a secret from him. She held on to it.

'Air, come on.' He looped an arm round her waist, liking it for the inexactness of its fit. There were so many new places he wished to discover. She was not like him. He felt exploratory where before he had felt inevitable: whatever strange thing he did, it would have been done before; having so much of himself in common with the past, his life already so well mapped, it had not been his own. Now the map was covered with spilt red wine and a smashed glass, the terrific force of Leo's rage. If that kind of thing went on, he could certainly do as he pleased. He had licence.

Leaving the room, they seemed washed up on the brink of this new territory, many miles still from being safe, but with their eye on a horizon that did not yet contain them. They could make their own way now. They went quickly downstairs together.

Instead of going out through the front door, after Leo and Charley, he led her through the library to the back, where french windows opened out on to a terrace, with steps down into the garden. He drew aside the heavy curtains, turned the key, and they went out into the night.

Across the empty lawn they stumbled, half running, in their escape, cutting a wide, arcing path like a new boat bent against the wind, sails inexpertly trimmed, the design not yet perfected. She wore the white blanket he had given her like a cloak, and snow was falling. At the far edge of the grass, where the red-brick wall rose up and the trees began, they turned back to the house. They had shut the door, and the curtains had fallen across, closing the place up in darkness. But there was a half-moon, and stars bright because of frost. They could see their way. He led her along the wall to where a wooden door, standing open, led out into the next part of the garden.

Fruit trees were espaliered there in elegant, empty rows; leafless, they appeared to have been cast from thin-wrought beams of iron. Shutting the door behind them was like entering a different house, one where they could be together. On the opposite side of this garden, a further room, as though approaching the last part of an enchanted box, was a small summer-house, set into the corner, its lead roof spiralling upwards, as ambitious in its beauty, though on a tiny scale, as a pale church spire.

'This way.' He looked back at her. She followed. They went inside.

24

Leo was stronger than Charley had bargained for, and when they burst outside, their joint anger sent them stumbling, locked, across the gravel. They fell together at the edge of the lawn, and Leo's head struck a stone, giving him a permanent scar in the middle of his forehead: for a second time he had been blooded.

They rolled a short distance on the cold grass, neither speaking, the fight their argument, until, finally, Charley had Leo subdued, his face pressed down into the lawn. Leo wriggled in protest, and then was still. Charley let him go and lay panting beside him, staring upwards, his body cooling. Eventually, Charley spoke, 'How could you?' And the fact that he received no answer, he took for shame: Leo had seen sense.

They both heard the front door of Eastleigh swing back fast against the frame, the light from inside making the scene outside seem secret: what were they doing in the dark?

Charley turned to Leo. 'You should go to her, quickly.'

Leo began to move, pushing himself around and upwards so that Charley could see his face.

'Why would I?' Leo's voice contained all the poison of his madness: he was still convinced. 'It's you who should go to her.'

It was too much. Charley sprang, violent, to his feet and with the same force of that gesture kicked Leo twice, hard, in the belly. He had never done such a thing in his life. He stepped backwards quickly.

He wanted Leo up so that he could fight him square. But he also wanted him where he was, with that appearance of being half dead on the ground at his feet, because that was where he belonged. Charley moved further backwards. It was a huge effort to force himself to go away. The scene transfixed him. It was as though he backed away from a fallen king, the sight too horrible to look at, too great to turn from.

'It's you who should go to *her*,' Leo repeated, and his voice now was diabolical with laughter, a cackle at the end of the sentence that terrified Charley, as though Leo's madness were an infection he would be left with. 'It's your wife, I mean.'

Charley swung round, and saw the reason for the light: Esther, coming towards them across the lawn. He left Leo where he was and went to her. She must have seen what he had just done and he was ashamed. He didn't want her to get any closer.

'Come away.' He turned her fast and herded her towards the house. He was conscious, as he moved her, that to touch her felt like chivvying along an unfed horse. The life in her body seemed latent: it was there, but neglected until it had almost gone. It redoubled his feeling of brutishness – to Leo, and now to her. He had given her expectations he had not seen through. He felt huge, his arms overstrong and clumsy with health, as though he had too much of it when she had so little. He got her to the driveway but she was dragging back and he felt cruel too, as though he were pushing her inside against her wish.

He slowed down: she had come to an absolute stop. He saw that she was crying. He folded his arms round her and held her tight. She appeared to be suffering in a way that made him stricken with remorse. How had he not noticed? He held her more gently. He could feel her shoulder-blades through her dress, and her torso bending weakly against him. She was barely any longer with him, as though she had chipped away at the woman he had married because that statuesque vision of happiness had seemed to her untrue.

She was right. They had not been as he had wished, either. He had been worse than inattentive. He had been somewhere else entirely; his heart had not been in his marriage. He had had his eyes always elsewhere: on his work, on the hunt. He held her more closely. She clung to him. He buried his face in her red hair, which often, in the past, he had joked was what he most loved because it was foxlike, and he had caught her, his trophy brought home.

Now it grieved him. He had caught her, yes, but he had not considered that what he loved about her was the red rush of her darting swiftly ahead of him, her separateness thrilling for being set at a constant distance – he had only to reach out his hand and she would be there, coming to him. But how long had it been since he reached out his hand to her? He had not done that for a very long time. She had slipped away, gone to earth and almost died there before he came to find her.

He had come now, but he feared she might already have gone from him for ever. His body shuddered with sadness as he held her. They were in the light. He could not believe his foolishness in suspecting her and James Dunbar. That man had a lot to answer for. It was abhorrent. He had fooled them all. Esther was saying something against his shirt-front, he couldn't quite catch what it was, and then he realised she was saying sorry.

He drew back, groaning. It was too much. 'Darling Esther, it's me who's sorry. How can you be, darling?' He held her more tightly again, but she pressed him away.

'No.' She reached a hand up to her face, wiped away tears; her skin was very pale, her eyes hollow and blackened, the skin thin over her cheekbones. 'No,' she said again, 'I am sorry. I thought you and Celia – I'm just like Leo.'

He kissed her forehead. 'My darling, you're hardly that.' He started to take off his jacket. She was shivering. He put it round her.

They would go home now. He was thinking of that, of getting home with her and being in bed where it was warm and they might begin again. He desired her. He straightened his jacket round her. Suddenly, in her thinness, she looked like the girl he had first met. Her slenderness then had been a form of reserve: a way of always being collected, which he had liked because it made him free to pursue his own life, one pace aside from her. His error had been to let her get away too far. He smiled at her. He would make amends. It was Leo and Celia they should worry for.

'No.' Esther's voice was strangled. She looked beyond Charley out across the lawn. Leo was weaving back towards the house. 'I'm just like Leo. Everything he's done I understand. He was wrong about you.' She stared up, anguished, at Charley. 'And you're wrong about me.'

He tried to take hold of her and she stepped back, half turning to the house, as though on the point of flight. He moved towards her and did take hold of her then, a hand strong on her upper arm. He heard Leo behind him, slow, on the gravel.

Esther was shaking her head. 'I'm just like Leo. I love Celia just like that too. She has too much—'

Charley stepped quickly towards her. He stopped what she was saying by kissing her, his mouth hard on hers, and passionless in its violence. He would not let her get away that far from him now. This was where all that stopped, at this point, now that Leo had been brought down. The day was over.

A flurry of snow rose up round them, and to Esther it felt as though the circle of the moment had been shaken, suddenly and very hard, a swift gesture to reset a bone.

She felt his teeth crack against hers. It was not a kiss. It was painful, a kind of cannibalism, as though he were prepared to eat her, if that was what it took to make her his.

She resisted. She could not return. She was too weak. She felt that he wanted to bite into her face to eat the words as they came out, make them disappear. But the emotion was there, without the words. He could not kill something that was still silence. It was futile. He was trying to drag her along with him as though he hoped to push her back into the past before these days came out. But they were here now, and they were not together.

Esther's body was shaking, racked with tears. It was as though Charley was trying to claw her back from the dead. The strain of returning was too great for her. She had wanted, just then, to tell him: Celia has too much strength.

Before tonight, she had thought only of all that Celia had: the children Esther craved, that Charley had wanted to postpone; a beauty unchanging since Esther had first known her; Leo's evident devotion. But now the glass had shattered and Celia had left the room afterwards still not broken. The vision of her doing this had been horrifying to Esther. She had had to get away outside to breathe.

When she had leaned down to take Celia in her arms, kissing her cheek, Celia's body had indeed felt frozen and her cheek was cold. Her beauty, and with it everything she had, suddenly seemed less a physical aspect than a decision taken a long time ago and stuck to. It was a terrible strength. A pretence of perfection. It was not life. It was refusal. She had tricked them all with her appearance of vitality. She was not to be admired. She was a warning.

Esther felt Charley all around her, covering her with himself, but it was too late. It was retrospective. He was kissing a wife who had already gone. Celia's chill had touched Esther, too, because she had loved her. Love was a sickness, infectious, and it had brought her close to death: wanting to become her, the love was a form of envy that had almost wiped her own self out.

Charley pushed Esther forwards, then began to steer her off to the right, and she was glad. She was aware of Leo like a black star passing somewhere behind them on the driveway going back into the house. She did not want to go inside. She heard the front door closing, and with the blinds down and a high mist like a cast across the moon, finally they were alone in darkness.

He grappled her against him. She felt that he might snap her he had her so tight, his nails pressed to her skin hard enough to draw blood and she wanted that, too. She felt like a savage. She tugged at his hair and his head fell back and she bit his neck, the bite becoming a kiss as they found the wall of the building and he lifted her up on to the window-ledge, the sandstone rough against her bare legs as he pulled up her dress. Her arms were round his neck, and his round her back, and she felt the kindled suddenness as he entered her, and she fell in love with him squarely again. Her husband. She felt no other love. She was his wife. Everything else had been burnt out. He blew himself into her and she came alive round him, and it was the purpose of him being a man. It filled him with gratitude. Neither could say how, after everything, they should be blessed with so much luck. They did not question it. They took it.

Staggering as they held each other, at last they moved away from the house. They turned at the sound of a blind being run up fast in the drawing-room window they had just left. They were in the dark, concealed, but turning back, they saw James Dunbar and Amir, standing very close together, peering out into the darkness. Perhaps they had heard something.

Charley and Esther looked back. The two figures were gilded by candlelight. To Charley, it gave them an aspect both ancient and terribly young, and, because they were behind glass, it also seemed to him that they were trapped.

James reached across to Amir, turning to him, saying something that, of course, they could not hear. But the light in the room showed plainly enough that both men were smiling, as James, very softly, touched Amir's face.

Charley turned his wife round and strode away with her into the night. He was glad to escape, to be with her, and tomorrow she would come with him, and they would go hunting.

part | three

25

Marjorie and her husband, Ellis, were listening to the news on the radio in the back kitchen at Eastleigh. It was eight in the morning on Saturday, 19 February. When hunting was mentioned, Marjorie bent more avidly over a piece of silver – a sauce dish – that had wanted polishing, rubbing at it hard with a soft yellow cloth.

Ellis said, 'Tea, I think,' talking across the radio. He didn't want to listen.

His wife, nodding, replied, 'Ah!' as though it had been exactly, and the only thing, she had been thinking.

Cook would be here at eight thirty. She would have help from two other women from the village. They should be here at nine. Eastleigh, hosting the meet, due to gather at ten in front of the house, would provide sandwiches and sloe gin, whisky, if it was asked for. First-timers always asked for whisky, for their nerves.

Last night, Ellis had been discreet. Exiting the dining room backwards, sensing, rather than seeing or hearing, that something in the room was terribly wrong, he had retreated into the hallway and found that his heart was hammering in his chest. He had stopped, a bottle of Sauterne in one hand, white linen napkin in the other, and had given himself a fright by not entirely recognising himself in the dark mirror that hung to one side of the empty fireplace. He felt spooked.

The paintings, gloomy portraits and sullen landscapes he had always avoided looking at, now pressed in on him like emblems of death. Specifically, he thought of those black wreaths the Victorians used to decorate the cortège, revelling in the business of mourning, black plumes elegant on the heads of the horses, only making them act more prancy, he thought, cowering a little beneath the paintings. Inside that room was life. This art was death. Opening the dining-room door had been like opening the door of a fast-moving train in error – vague-eyed in search of the loo, finding the earth rushing by instead. It was why he had jumped back. Life and death were all brimmed over. He felt like a witness to a murder, and he wasn't sure whose side he should be on.

He did not like to lose his composure. It had only happened on a very few occasions before. Marjorie had been the cause of most of those, he thought, which meant that they had occurred in private, no one else's business. He was hesitant about returning directly to the kitchen. On instinct he patted his breast pocket: tobacco. But he had given up his pipe almost ten years ago. He took this as a sign that he had indeed had a terrific shock. His memory was muddled. He glanced, longingly, at the front door. He would have liked a breather, but didn't want to be caught acting peculiar while he was meant to be in attendance. Should he attempt to go back in? He heard Sir Leo's voice raised in the dining room, and headed for the kitchen.

'What on earth?' Marjorie had been at the table, stitching a fallen button on to Lady Domeyne's black hunting jacket. The thread was poor quality – the haberdasher's in the village had been replaced by a Greek takeaway shop; she had bought it from the new supermarket across town. She had been sighing as she worked with it: it had broken twice already.

She half rose. 'Jack, are you—'

He had held up a hand to silence her. He crossed to the stove and poured a short glass of cooking brandy. Marjorie did not comment. He went to sit at the opposite end of the table, facing his wife. He

drank, straightening his back. Cook had not noticed. She was rattling china for next door's coffee. Marjorie, bent again over her
sewing, went 'There!' She gave Ellis a searching look, leaning towards
him, mouthing, 'You all right?' He nodded, slowly. She was not convinced. He had alarmed her, coming in pale like that, his thin white
hair stuck up. He angled his head towards the wall, meaning, 'Next
door, not me,' and she breathed in relief. She had feared he was ill.
But it was just them.

Marjorie took the jacket to where she'd put the hanger on the
back of the pantry door, hung it up, and then, as though it were
entirely inconsequential, recrossed the kitchen to her husband,
standing behind him, and quickly – they did not like to do such
things in public – bent down to kiss the top of his head, smoothing
his hair, whispering, 'You had me worried, love. I thought it was you
that was wrong.' He reached his left hand back to her, touching her
thigh for reassurance, both his and hers, then reached higher up,
squeezing the tips of her fingers, which she stretched down.

When, from the hallway, there was the sudden, swift, racketing
sound of the dining-room door thrown back, footsteps chaotic on
the marble, then the front door going, the glass rattling in the frame,
both Marjorie and Ellis were prepared.

Cook was in a panic. She held a dish of meringue and drew it to
herself at the noise. Its soft Jersey cream middle wobbled but did
not collapse. Her hands were stained blackcurrant. She was sweating,
and alarm had made her unkempt. Marjorie, shaken, was nonetheless victorious: she had given in over the puddings, but look, there
was the cream. Jack had settled that, also.

Ellis rose to his feet, magisterial. 'I should wait with that, if I were
you.'

Cook stared, agog. What on earth was going on?

Ellis continued, as though intuitive, his expression calm, his face
its usual colour now. 'I think coffee in the drawing room might be

more appropriate tonight. But we should wait on the call. I think that's best.'

He took out that day's *Financial Times*, wrinkled, from the basket by the door, and spread it calmly on the table, leaning over it, turning the pages very slowly, lingering in the back section so that he could see how his nest-egg was coming along. This always cheered him. He had invested in Vodafone, and when he retired in five years' time, as long as he played his cards right, he would be a rich man.

Marjorie watched him, impressed. He was cool as cucumber. But he had given her a shock. She depended on him. They had come along too far now for her to do without him. It was like she had been born to a life that meant only him. She knew no other. Her good fortune felt more accurately like her right. The clock whirred and settled. She was relieved he didn't tell her what he'd seen next door. If he had judged she didn't need to know about it, then that was good enough for her. It would mend itself by morning. She was content.

But now that it was the following morning, Marjorie's contentment had vanished, and she felt that Jack should have warned her. Both had caught glimpses of the same event. His had been the heat of it, burning off – he'd caught its smoky whiff, and retreated at the thought of flames. She had seen the morning version, the embers smouldering. Now they were party to different things and, as though carrying a terrible secret, she felt apart from him, therefore alone.

She had been taking Celia and Leo their tea as she always did on Saturdays – going into the room to open the curtains, putting the tray on the side-table. Her pace was uninterrupted: she swept in and out as usual, shut the door behind her, wordless, with a discreet click. She had stepped back out on to the landing already startled at what she had seen, and then the door at the far end opened, and there was Leo, half clothed, his face like murder.

Marjorie went quickly downstairs. Celia had appeared distraught, even in sleep – and the fact that she *was* asleep indicated something badly out of whack: she was usually sitting up in bed by the time Marjorie went in, blonde hair prettily brushed back, a book in one hand, the other resting on Leo's head as he dozed on beside her. Celia would glance up, smiling, and Marjorie would go downstairs and count her blessings: she was glad that there were other people as happy as she and her Jack.

Seeing that happiness now in disarray felt to Marjorie like a portent of some wicked thing at work, an evil yet to come. It was all wrong. The order was upset. Bursting out of the tapestry bedroom, Leo had looked fit to kill, and when Marjorie went into the kitchen, panting, she listened out consciously for the sound of shrieking, and china smashing overhead. Nothing came. Ellis stared at her. He would know what was in her mind. She stared back at him. They could not speak of this. It was too much.

They seemed to hang suspended there together, listening. Then there were footsteps in the hallway, quick across the marble, and suddenly – but how had she collected herself so fast? – there was Celia, immaculate. Her manner was hurried, but it was not flustered: it had purpose. Later, Ellis would describe her as being 'like an arrow', and Marjorie had agreed, 'Yes, die straight. Perfect.'

She was half dressed for the hunt, in white breeches and shirt, but no stock yet or jacket. That was what she was looking for. 'Bless you, Marjorie.' She had noticed the mended button, and took the jacket from the hanger. 'Cook's due at eight thirty?' She checked her watch. They had discussed it already; her two women from the village would be here at nine and get straight down to the catering. It was eight twenty-five.

Celia, smiling, went over to the window, looking out and upwards. 'What luck!' She turned back to them both.

Could they tell that something terrible had happened? It was not apparent to anyone but an expert witness, and that meant them. But her appearance, the surface unbroken, was pristine in its conceal-ment. Had they not seen the two earlier bits of evidence, those two spots of residue after the event, they were quite sure that, no, they would not have been able to tell that anything was wrong.

'What luck, really,' she smiled at them both, 'that we should have such fine weather for today.'

'God must be a huntsman.' Ellis, amazed at Celia and, in addressing her, omitting to use her title, was more familiar in this remark than he had ever been. Marjorie allowed it: she was glad; it was appro-priate.

'We really are very fortunate.' Celia slipped into her jacket. She allowed it too. It was her sign to them: thank you. 'Ah, good.' She had seen Cook crossing the driveway to the kitchen door. 'It should be a wonderful day.' She left the room.

Ellis and Marjorie stared at one another. Celia had seemed tri-umphant. Clearly if there was trouble, they would not be required to think of it. And without hard evidence that anything remiss had occurred, they could already start to forget it. That was Celia's plan. They would follow. She had drawn them back in. The day would go ahead. The thread would hold.

26

Coming in from the garden the previous night, Will and Isabella had caught sight of the lights of Charley and Esther's car, turning out of the driveway. The drawing-room blinds were raised and, although they could see no one from outside, when they crossed the hall they could hear voices, lowered to a murmur as though not wishing to be overheard. They did not wish to be heard, either; shoeless, they went up to bed.

Cigar smoke drifted out: Gerald had come back down to join James and Amir. He had not meant to break them up, but his presence worked as a delay, and a sponge, too, soaking up the static that had come off around Leo's outburst, sending the electricity back to earth. He made sure that they did not discuss it.

Around twelve thirty, the three men rose to turn in, and it was James who left the house, heading back alone to his cottage by the north gate. Gerald and Amir went upstairs to their rooms, on opposite sides of the landing.

Leo having made himself unmentionable, Gerald had assumed the position of authority. There would be no further upset. He restored order. He had seen the way ahead to Devon and, more than that, the urgency of his assuming tenure there: if this kind of thing went on at Eastleigh, Celia would need him closer at hand than Cairo. He had never felt so much like her older brother. He felt chastened and ashamed at not having felt it sooner. His instinct was to take a whip to Leo. But it was his house; she was his wife. That made things complicated, and his revenge stopped there. He would think of something else by morning. He would have his dish served cold.

He went up to bed, climbed decisive into striped flannel pyjamas, tying the belt in a solid knot, and fell fast and heavily asleep.

Henry, next door to Gerald, slept badly. She went upstairs shortly after Celia, sobered and exhausted. She crept along the corridor to Celia's room but could hear nothing. She didn't know whether Leo had come back inside and, fearing him, carried on along the corridor to her room. At the sound of her brother's door shutting, she woke from a shallow sleep where her dreams had been a broken repeat of everything that had just happened.

She felt very cold. She drew the blankets tightly round her and wriggled further down. The house was again noiseless. But she felt anything but empty, and she did not want to be full of so much that did not concern her. She hated life to impinge. She wanted it to open and let her just sail through. Her sister's life had always been, for her, a smooth river in which occasionally she could float: the house was always open to her; when, in the past, she had been in difficulties – men, debts – she had often dropped in without warning and was swept along. She had not needed to concern herself with what might lie ahead.

Now she felt that she had been caught, snagged on a rock in the stream, and was angry with her sister for what she perceived as a deception. Why had Celia concealed that she was in difficulty with Leo? It was as though the river had not been fast-moving, after all, but frozen. Henry had been skating, not swimming; no part of herself had been dipped into her sister's life. Now the river had melted, the rocks were there, and she had foundered where she might have avoided doing so. Celia had brought her down.

Edging back towards sleep, weary with irritation and drink, Henry wondered if she should leave early the next morning, hop into her car and bolt back to London as she had often enough in the past. Amir could fend for himself. Gerald or Dunbar would take care of him. She turned over angrily as she thought this.

Her indignation at having been kept in the dark about her siblings' lives needled her and became, with dwelling on it, a kind of priggishness: they had no right to steal her place with their surprises. She felt very much like the youngest child again. She wanted to ruin their games and with that wreckage be returned to the light of everyone's attention.

She turned on the bedside lamp, went through to the bathroom for a pill, which she glugged down. She felt frowsy and left behind. She read the ingredients on the bottle. It was a miracle she hadn't had the most terrific breakdown. She punched the pillow as she got back into bed.

When at last she fell asleep, she was full of hatred for them all, and self-righteous with the sense that people could hardly expect her to behave well if their lives were going to be so ruinous. She would find a way to go one better, which, she thought with relish, would be pretty bad indeed.

By morning, her hatred had levelled out into a kind of furious concentration. It was eight thirty, and therefore too late for her to dash unseen to London, and she held back from the idea of causing a scene by doing so openly. But waking late meant that at least she had had a decent sleep, and would look fresh for the meet.

She leaped out of bed and considered this as she assessed her appearance in the bathroom mirror. She showered, brushed her hair, and dressed meticulously, with savage precision, spearing her stock with its gold and diamond pin, standing back to admire the fit of her pressed white breeches, buttoning her tailored black jacket, flicking a speck from her lapel. She swept her blonde hair into its net, tied it with a green velvet ribbon, and considered that Celia would probably look dreadful. She couldn't have slept a wink. Henry smiled at her reflection before she went downstairs. She would see if someone was free to clean her boots.

Her sister was in the hall, by the front door, on the point of going out. Henry went across to her, intending to be magnanimous in carrying off her concern, seeing what she supposed would be her sister's distress. Celia turned, touched her absentmindedly on the arm. 'You look wonderful, darling. There's breakfast if you hurry.' Henry was the youngest sibling still. Celia was already moving from her, her attention elsewhere, her face untroubled and lovely.

Then, as though just remembering, she glanced back. 'And there'll be Gerald and Will, too. I'm so glad we'll be able to show a united front like this. It's so important today.'

To Henry, this sounded like both an explanation and a command, shutting her out, putting her in her place: you might not quite understand why, but you had better stay in line. She felt belittled, and she knew that Celia's having said it was important, on this day in particular it had nothing whatever to do with Leo's outburst. It was the politics she meant, the public law, and nothing to do with her heart, which, Henry judged, should surely be a little cracked, if not actually broken.

Henry hesitated in the hallway, holding her boots, uncertain what to do next. All malice had left her. She found her sister's composure chilling. Although for that reason she was able to feel superior, momentarily – at least she herself felt things deeply – watching Celia go outside, she felt frightened for her. It was like watching a ghost, something untouched by life, its progress unbroken even by solid walls. Henry had the impression she could throw something at Celia, much as Leo had done last night, and she would not even flinch. She recoiled at the thought that he might in any way be right.

She went in search of toast. She would see if Marjorie could dig her out some wax and a soft cloth. She had better clean her boots herself.

27

Footsteps drumming along the landing had been what woke Isabella, and when the bedroom door opened, Will whispered in her ear, 'Don't mind them, they're our alarm clock,' and the two girls, Hettie and Belinda, crept in round the door and crossed to the window.

It was nine thirty, and the room was dusky with the heavy brocade curtains tightly drawn; these the children threw open, the wooden hoops rattling on the poles, flooding the room with brightness. They approached the high bed, curious and giggling, dressed in Gerald's Egyptian robes.

'Is it very late, brats?' Will drew the covers closer round Isabella's bare shoulders. He kissed her face.

'You're going to be punished!' They were ecstatic at the thought of his being in the wrong. They had not shut the bedroom door, and from downstairs came the sounds of boots on marble, the gravel crunching as horse-boxes arrived, doors swinging briskly shut, voices carrying upwards. The house was being shaken into life, the light from the garden, the tall pines nearby, greening the bedroom with a sense of springtime waking. The sunlight, warm across the bedclothes, was lucid and dustless, as though it had been washed, then carried inside on a quick, fresh breeze.

The girls scampered back on to the landing. Will turned Isabella to face him in his arms. She was smiling. She felt very wide awake, her sight clear, but inside her everything seemed to have melted and dissolved, as though she had been picked up and held over a bright flame until the impression of herself, waxen, had liquefied, running clear and warm. It had happened so easily. Her eyes shone. He kissed her face, her neck, moving close against her.

'Darling,' he drew away, came back close, kissed her again, 'Cousin C will kill me if I'm not on time.'

She kissed him back. Her limbs were soft with sleep but her life quickened and raced inside her, opening up a wide green field ahead, the vista huge, the landscape at once familiar yet more thrilling than she had thought possible: a beloved face, re-encountered after separation.

More footsteps could be heard downstairs; and doors were shutting smartly along the landing. Everything appeared to be going ahead as planned. They heard Gerald calling, 'These your gloves, Henry?' There was no reply. Gerald's voice again as he came back upstairs: he appeared to have forgotten something, too. 'Oh, bother!'

Then Marjorie's voice, stern: 'Fingers, not doorstops, and, Anna, you really should rein in those children if you can't keep them to heel.'

The baize door to the dining room, hinged to swing both ways from the hall, could be heard to do so now, as though someone had rushed through at full speed. The house was being turned out of doors; more boxes were being driven along the drive, and they could hear the horses as they were expelled down the ramps. The peacocks were loud in protest, drifting imperial and raucous towards the lake to join the geese where, apparently, it was safest. The dogs, already confined to a room where they would not get out and be a nuisance when the pack arrived, were protesting also, and, finally, making themselves known with barking: even from upstairs, they could be heard to throw themselves against Leo's study door, a regular, violent thump and shuffle, that room their chrysalis, which they were doing their utmost to slough off.

Will moved back from Isabella, holding her soft but away from him as he remembered. 'A confession.' He smiled, for he thought that it would please her, now.

She nibbled his fingertips where he held her.

'The portrait.'

She rolled her eyes. 'Don't tell me it was really of the dogs. I don't do canine art, I'm afraid.' She tried to pull him back towards her. 'I can't see how it'll be wanted now, so I shouldn't worry. I haven't been let down.'

His hand strayed downwards to her hip, and he drew her in. 'The point is,' he whispered against her ear, 'Leo didn't ask me to find someone to do a portrait at all.'

He felt her move back a little, not understanding.

'Don't be cross, darling, it was just a ruse. I had to think of something, some lure to trap you. They probably will want a portrait at some point, when all this has blown over. I might commission you myself.'

'But the photographs?'

He blushed. 'I nabbed them. Album's in the library.'

He leaned away from her to gauge her reaction. He had thought she might take it lightly, and be pleased that he had been plotting ways to snare her. But she had been thinking of Leo dropping that envelope in front of her last night, and she balked at the suggestion that a lover's game might have added to the tangle. She had been caught, and she had never in her life been happier. She smiled at him. He took this as sign that all was well. The result was this, and it was good. If his methods had been perhaps a little less than honourable, they had been forgiven and were past.

'You stay in bed, sleep more. I have to get up.' He started to slip out of bed. She kissed him again, and watched him walk naked to the bathroom. She thought, My love, naked as a fish, and wanted him again, and when he turned back to her, as though she had spoken the thought out loud, she felt the foreboding lift. Who had caught whom? It was impossible to say. She adored him.

'I can't sleep now, no chance.' She smiled. 'I'll come on foot to watch.'

They washed, dressed and went downstairs together. Many of the horses were already gathered outside, although the pack had not arrived.

Dunbar had been waiting for Will and, seeing him, brought his horse round from the stables. It was one of Celia's, a thoroughbred gelding, dark bay, almost black in places, throwing its head back against its martingale, its nostrils wide with life. Will held out his hand to it and the animal bent its neck to lick the palm, growing steady as he whispered against its neck.

Isabella stood back: to her it was a vast and dangerous beast, and not at all in the same category as that donkey of hers on Santorini. She was glad to be a spectator and not riding.

He jumped up lightly and blew her a kiss. He had dressed in a hurry; he finished the job now, in the saddle, straightening his stock, tucking in his shirt, his legs dangling at ease out of the stirrups, the reins long as the animal got used to him.

He patted its neck and moved away. He was very happy. It felt good to him to be in the countryside and in love. The two were suddenly, and for the first time, intermingled in his heart.

It was a clear day, the air dampish and fresh, the hedgerows sparkling with water that last night had been snow. It was a perfect day for hunting.

28

After his full English, Lance Ash asked the proprietor of the Lamb and Cross if there were any messages for him, and was annoyed to hear that there were not. 'Why's he playing silly buggers?' he asked, under his breath, meaning the friend who had invited him down, then left him in the lurch without word about when or where they should meet.

He went outside to inspect the weather. The car park was half full, which meant five cars. He had parked his black Cavalier under a tree – he hadn't noticed it the previous night – and now the roof was covered with white bird-droppings. He looked angrily at the sky, which was cloudless, blue. There was little chance of the rain he needed to get rid of that muck.

He took out his mobile phone. No signal. He sighed. He disliked waking in a place he had arrived at in the dark. It made him think of returning home to discover that everyone had remembered your birthday – the way they jumped out at you from behind the sofas bearing gifts. He hated that. It had never happened to him, but the thought of it filled him with dread. He did not like the whole business of presents. It felt like that now. The day, with its insistent loveliness, had ambushed him and he felt disarmed. It was beautiful, but he wasn't sure what to do with it next, as though he'd lost the instructions.

The lanes were empty. He leaned forwards, gladdened at the

sound of a distant car, but none came, and he went back inside, up to his bedroom, despondent. How could he cause a rumpus if he didn't know where to go?

He ran the taps to have a shave. He might as well be prepared. He took out his can of foam and the razor his wife had bought him at Boots. He stared down at it in his hand. He hadn't asked her to get it for him. She must have noticed that his old one was done in. Why had she always been bringing him those little presents? He put it back on the glass shelf over the sink and turned off the taps. He thought he would cry if he tried to shave. He would think of Alison coming up behind him in the bathroom at home. It had irritated him, the way she danced behind him, distracting him. It put him off his stride and often made him nick himself with the blade. 'Look what you made me do!' He imagined her arms looping round him and the way he'd push her off – he must have been mad to do that. He shut his eyes, steadied his breath and pulled out the plug so that the warm water drained away.

He crossed the room to try the radio, went past the BBC and found a local station, listened for a moment, let his indignation take hold again. Hicks. He turned it off. No, he did not feel safe in the countryside. There was too much of it. Its excessiveness indicated a kind of richness that could be matched only by those of equal privilege: it was something you had to be born to; you couldn't take it up in later life, like a hobby, and hope to belong there. People who attempted it were naïve. He thought of barn conversions and chapels turned into expensive homes for stockbrokers, and scowled. The countryside should be made accessible to everyone or it should be stopped. He remembered the opposition a couple of years earlier to the deputy prime minister's road-building proposals. People were sentimental about fields, as though they were untouchable. It was muddle-headed and, these days, made little economic sense. Whatever grew there could be grown much cheaper somewhere else. Farmers were a burden on the economy. He had been in support of the legislation.

But it was too late now, he always argued, to start imagining that the countryside would change of its own accord. It was stuck in its ways, and those ways were in the past. If it refused to modernise then, like everything else, it would soon become obsolete, by force if necessary. It had happened to the miners and the fishermen. The farmers would be next. His grandfather had gone down the pit in Selby. It was no life.

He remembered a trip he had taken with Alison some years back. He thought of it as a 'trip', but really they'd gone up there for his gran's funeral. They had decided to make a long weekend of it. They hadn't been getting away much at the time. Alison had been sceptical, Lance remembered, when he had pointed out the place where his grandfather had worked as a lad. 'Looks quite nice,' she had said, cautious. The pit, of course, was long since shut. The factory that had gone with it had been converted to a waterside restaurant, with bars and a nightclub. 'Quite chi-chi,' she had added, and he had tried to explain what had been there. But perhaps it was sometimes best that certain things were lost. His grandfather had died of emphysema at the age of fifty-five. Lance hadn't known him. His gran had been a widow for thirty years.

Now he sat on the edge of the bed and wondered what to do. He glanced at the window. He had heard the sound of hoofs on Tarmac, a number of horses, by the sound of it, going by. He went to look out.

The view from his room was of open fields, stubbly and bare, but beneath a blue sky they were glistening and he thought of the sea. Directly below his window – the room was on the first floor, and it was not a tall building – rosebushes, cut back, had already started sprouting, and their shoots, reaching upwards, reminded him of Jack and the beanstalk, the shame of the undersold cow, the riches at the top of the tree. There were diamonds depending from the cobwebby hawthorns, too, and although the scene sparkled it was also soft, and he thought of the word 'bosomy' when he looked out at the hills, which seemed breast-like, fertile, somewhere he might like to rest.

He undid the window-latch. It was double-glazed, so he undid the next one too, throwing it open so he could lean out. The downs rose greenly at the horizon and the far-off pinewoods were like a seam of coal, glittering dark in the early light. There were more horses, and the clip of metal on stone sounded like water dripping in a cavern underground, something that might have gone on for ever without him having heard it.

He craned to see, but he was at the wrong angle. He would have to go outside. He started to throw his things into his bag. He hadn't come with much. His hands were clumsy in the excitement of his haste. It was like a carnival going by. He didn't want to miss it. He'd find his way without that connection's help. It should be easy enough, he thought, hurrying downstairs. He'd follow the trail of sound.

He had already paid for his room. He threw his bag into the back of the car. The horses were out of sight but he could hear more in the distance, approaching on the road.

The hunt was going ahead, and that he had anticipated their defiance reassured him, for he had never doubted that they would.

He gunned the engine and set off. He wound down the window and his mind raced. The reassurance of being right was mingled with another sensation, which was stronger. It was like the moment he most loved in politics: crowding out through different doors, voting with your feet. It was so much more than talk. It was physically to put yourself across a line. The sword-length that separated one side from the other could be felt most keenly at that moment: you moved along the blade's edge and you took the consequences; there was nowhere to hide; it was the starkest way of revealing your intentions, and therefore saying who you were, and he loved it for that reason, too. Democracy was a great leveller. Your past fell away from you, unimportant. He often found himself followed out by toffs.

Driving along blind, it felt like that right now. He hadn't the first clue where he was, beyond the county of Wiltshire. But he was eager to see what the scene looked like – these people rising to vote with their feet. He had already gone out through one door and made his choice: the Act was law. But now he wanted to see through the other door too – to see what went on there.

With the window down so that he could hear which direction he should take, the morning felt wonderful on his face, the clean air sharpening his instincts and giving him confidence. He thought of Alison in their house, collecting her things, and he missed her acutely, with a pain that confused him so much that he made himself turn from the thought of her. He did not want her with him at this moment, which felt private, and he felt stronger by one shade for being remote from her.

He noticed a bird hovering above the hedgerow at the crest of the hill as he approached. A kestrel. He named it to himself, pleased to have recognised it. There had been kestrels where he had grown up in Wetherby.

Suddenly it swooped down. It was purpose and oblivion all at once. Its descent had the necessity of gravity about it, and his breath quickened as he watched it fall, vanished in the kill.

29

The dogs jumped up at him but Leo held them back, growling at them until they whimpered and were silent. He went round to his desk and sat down. From there he could see the hunters gathering outside the house. Many were laughing. Marjorie and two women he didn't recognise were handing round the stirrup cup. No wonder there were accidents. He leaned over and pulled the curtains across so that he did not have to see them.

The dogs were throwing themselves again at the thick oak door and now he let them. If they were trying to get away from him they would fail. All the running and dodging had been done. All that was over. He had a clear view now, and when punishment came, he would be exact. He felt lucid and more rational than he had ever been. He felt that finally he could see, where before he had been blind. They had all tricked him, and at the eleventh hour they had been rumbled.

In the gloomy light he took down his guns and laid them out. He heard his wife speak in the hallway. 'I'm so glad we'll be able to show a united front like this.' His hand hesitated over the metal. He could hear her, and knew it was his wife, but somehow he could not recognise her voice. A united front — how could she? He heard her walk away, going outside, and he jumped to the window to see her going round towards the stables. She looked the same, but she was now quite different. He felt that she had publicly denounced him. Her silence spelt out her guilt so powerfully to him that it amounted to an accusation: you have failed me.

He chose the gun, a single-bore rifle, good for deer or, where necessary, horses, and locked the others away. He had only had cause to shoot a horse once, and he had hated to do it, for more reasons than he had ever explained, but that time it had been a mercy: it had broken both back legs. It was when it had fallen with Celia. It wasn't with this gun but with a pistol. The vet's lad had been riding with them, and had been called to do it, but he was eighteen and afraid. Leo had thought the boy might shoot one of them by accident, his finger sweating on the trigger. He had grabbed the gun from him and shot the horse himself, one bullet to the head, and then he'd been off to hospital for Celia. He had had to be reminded the next day that he had done it. Her fall had rubbed out all his other thoughts.

More were arriving outside, and he took another peek. He saw Dunbar standing about holding the reins of the horse Leo was meant to ride. A liver-chestnut gelding, an alert horse but steady, and fast when he was under way: an Irish hunter, white-socked, with a star on his forehead. He was still blanketed, but tacked up underneath. Dunbar was walking him round in a tight circle on the lawn, keeping him warm. The temperature had levelled and there had been no further frost, but it was still cool. The man would wait for him in vain. Leo wasn't going to ride. He was astonished that anyone should expect it now. Who had asked for his horse to be saddled? He supposed it must have been Celia.

Leo shut the curtain again and paused. Why had she done that? Why on earth might she wish him to ride? It was a gleam of doubt and he set it aside. There was no room for doubt now. He would not ride alongside her and Charley Sutton. Without her he had nothing.

He went back to his desk and picked up the gun, wiping it down with a soft white cloth. He got up on to his chair, reached up to the top shelf and pulled out a book: behind it were his bullets. Celia insisted he keep them hidden because of the children. He took out a handful and dropped them into the pocket of his green tweed coat.

Standing up that high, he had a sudden memory of his father making him stand on chairs as punishment after he had been beaten. Why had the man done that? Beaten him, then made him stand up on a chair. His parents would carry on as normal. His mother was complicit. So were the servants, in particular the nannies, who caught on with indecent haste to his father's trick. He supposed he was made to stand there so that he shouldn't behave as he felt, which would have been to curl up into a tiny ball and whimper, sobbing. He was made to stand up there like a statue, and that proved something to the old man. That a person could still live without emotion; their heart could stop but they would still go on.

There would not be treats when he came down, but strange allowances: yes, he could take down his great-grandfather's sword that day, and no, he wouldn't be rebuffed this time for asking how many wicked fellows that man had chopped up with it when he was in the Hussars?

Leo stood there. The bullets had grown hot in his hand. He clenched his jaw and tried hard not to remember the one time in particular when he had been beaten and made to stand there that he most longed to forget. But it wasn't possible. Although he had falsified it – thrown everyone off the scent, even Celia, who knew nothing of it – the memory was still there. It was the first time he had been beaten, and he had been seven years old, and it was because of his older brother. Leo gripped the bullets and shut his eyes.

His father had wanted Leo's brother to kill a white hart deer, and the boy had read somewhere that it was unlucky, and had refused, but had been made to do it, the method simple: his father had held up the rifle, pointing it first at his son's horse, then the stag. 'Choose.'

Leo's brother had not, as Leo had claimed to Celia, drowned as a small child in the stream, but had shot himself with one of their father's guns at the age of thirteen. He'd done it just outside the gates, his body falling into the stream – that part was true enough. The nanny had been drunk, too – that also was true. She was supposed to have been in charge of the house that afternoon, but had left the boys alone and gone off with her lover in the town, returning, horrible with gin and threats, just before their father.

It was the day after the episode with the stag. Leo had found him, and was punished. He remembered that beating very well. He had been made to stand up there for hours, until it was dark when, reluctant, his father at last had allowed him to come down. A year later he was sent away to school.

Leo got down. He kept such secrets to himself, for what good could it do in confessing? The hussar's sword was his and in the library now; his father was dead; he had taken over the house.

The horses were restless outside, and he leaned across to see them gathering as though, in the next county, a battle was waiting and they were all off to it without him. He moved the papers about on his desk, threw a few things into the bin and locked the drawers. He wanted everything to be in order. He noticed, on the top, a large brown manila envelope, and he hesitated as he picked it up. He looked inside.

He had repressed the memory of many things but he had not forgotten this. It was only last night that he had thrown these papers on to the fire. He remembered the sparks flying when he kicked the burning timbers. Now here they were, still pristine. He set them down carefully. The place where he had asked Celia to marry him, the beechwood and the bluebells, scentless until April. It meant nothing to Celia, but he had given away his soul there and now he didn't want it back. He would keep that bit of land at any price. The house and everyone in it could be destroyed before he'd give it up. He tore the contract decisively into four and dropped it on to the desk.

Now, from outside, he heard the pack approaching, the high pure bugling of the horn, the hounds far off but in full cry. His blood leaped on instinct at the noise and he picked up his gun. Charley Sutton would be along with the pack.

He had left word with Marjorie that Anna should be ready with the girls. He was going to take them with him in the Land Rover; they would follow the hunt; the dogs would come too, caged in the back.

He looked again out of the window. Dunbar had obviously given up with Leo's horse and returned it to the stables. The line of command had been decisively sundered: Leo had given one order; Celia another. Eastleigh was divided. He gritted his teeth, cursing at the dogs as he held them back so that he could get out. He'd return for them, and for his gun, just before the field moved off. He went through to the hall and stopped for a moment at the front door.

There was a huge turn-out. Leo could see Dunbar up on Celia's grey Arab mare, the soft mane long and fluttering like a pennant where it caught the wind. The horse was no good for hunting. It was too delicate, though it was fast. He watched it prancing now, Dunbar light and expert in the saddle, the horse reined in with one hand and already working up a sweat. He caught sight of Gerald chugging back sloe gin aboard a roan hireling, and Henry, too, on a skittish black mare, working off some of its mood on the drive. Will was blowing kisses at his girlfriend, Isabella. Leo turned away from that sight in particular. He thought them very foolish. He couldn't see Celia mounted yet.

He went through to the dining room to fill his flask from the brandy kept in decanters in the cupboard there. The fire had been damped down after last night and, although it was no longer smouldering, a single plume of fine white smoke rose from the centre. It caught his eye, and he remembered, and went across to it and crouched down, turning over the embers and charred wood with the iron poker.

Some bits of plastic had been thrown on, and he frowned, annoyed. People should know better. He turned the ash, and noticed the edge of some photographs, melded together with the heat. He knocked them out into the hearth and considered them. He could tell what they were, could see the edge of a familiar dress, limbs, a smile or two, unmistakably Celia and the girls. But he could not read them. He did not know what they might mean. Why had they been thrown there, and who had done it?

He stood up slowly as he realised. He heard the pack approaching, and a group of people applauding, it sounded like that, and cheering, too, up on the road. It wasn't theatre. He turned from the fireplace to go back for his children, dogs and gun.

He saw himself throwing the envelope on the fire last night. He had thrown them. He had taken them from her. No wonder she had hoped to conceal them: she had been meaning to give them to Charley Sutton.

30

Pausing only for the two world wars, and even then not absolutely, there had been a meet at Eastleigh almost every season for the last hundred and fifty years. Charley Sutton's great-grandfather, General Gordon Sutton, had also been master of the Royal Fusiliers, as had Leo Domeyne's uncle. Photographs since the late eighteen hundreds were displayed five high in the downstairs loo; in the boot room, numerous cartoons from Punch extended the theme; there was a decent Stubbs in the library, and Edwardian hunting prints adorned the walls of the cloakroom behind the kitchen – a fox's brush also dangled there. Beneath it, a silver hunting horn, bent out of true, sat as paperweight atop a pile of *Country Life* and *Field* magazines. To imagine the house without this paraphernalia would be to imagine a different place.

Over the years, the number in the field at Eastleigh had risen and declined. On this, the first Saturday after the ban against hunting foxes with hounds, the number was greater than at any time since before the First World War. There were around two hundred riders; a similar number had turned out in support for the meet of whom a hundred or so would follow on foot or by car. The driveway in front of the house, which usually contained them all, could not that day. Celia had instructed that people should feel at liberty to spill out across the grass and into the park, saying that she did not mind if it was ruined as a consequence: it could be repaired.

They were a rag-tag bunch, saved from being a rabble by good manners and surprise: it had been supposed that, at the eleventh hour, the meet might be called off or, thinking it would be, that people would stay away. Because in the end this did not happen, they were held together by disbelief as much as conviction. It was as though they could sense their own absence, and what that no-show might have looked like, just beside them. It was this that made them cautious: without each one, there would not have been a crowd.

As it was, because they all turned up – unfit horses rapidly reshod and brought back into service, children on unclipped New Forest ponies, muzzles bristling, farm horses limb to limb with slick thoroughbreds – the idea of what they might be there for, now that the past had been declared void, the line drawn to finish it, seemed to spring instead into the future. After all, they were there, weren't they? The law would bend with time beneath their weight. The mosaic, for that day at least, had been perfected: seen from a distance, the pieces made up a picture that was seamless, the pattern unbroken.

Marjorie, Ellis, Cook and her two women from the village, dazed but elated at the magnification of their duty, were carrying round the silver trays: sloe gin, smoked-salmon sandwiches. Everyone from Eastleigh who would ride that day was mounted: Lady Domeyne, Henry, Gerald, Will, and James Dunbar. This left Isabella, the girls and their nanny, Anna. Leo, it had now emerged, would not be riding but would drive them along by road in the Land Rover. He had not yet come out.

Marjorie had been the one to inform on him: she had overheard him telling Anna to prepare the girls, and she had passed this message to James Dunbar, so he could put away Leo's horse; he was, she thought, the most dashing man in the field, she had seen him walking round with it. 'Good, fine.' Dunbar had been curt as he weighed up this information and appeared to find it satisfying.

Marjorie swept on with the salver of sloe gin, but saw Dunbar pause to tell Gerald, who similarly appeared to find the news appropriate. He nodded and moved off. Marjorie was relieved. Everything was settling down again in that department. They had their way of doing things. Going after the others in the car was obviously to be approved of: it showed willing but revealed remorse. Tearing around the countryside on a great big steaming horse might, she supposed, have looked like he was having too much fun, and after everything he'd done she could see, indeed, that that would not have been quite right.

There was also Amir, who had decided to stay at the house, not minding that he would be alone, as everyone else, even the staff, would be out on foot. Smiling, he had complained to Gerald of a headache and asked to be excused. He would only have been there as an observer anyway, he protested. Gerald had seemed relieved. Amir, having heard of the shortage of horses, didn't think it would be good manners at that point to mention that he was in fact an exceptional rider. His great-grandfather was from the Al'Khamees tribe, famous for their Asil horses; he supposed it had always been in his blood.

Now Amir was in the library, lying down on the *chaise-longue* by the open window that gave on to the back lawn and the herb garden.

He was not reading, although he had taken down a book: Cobbet's *Rural Rides*, a passage in it that reminded him of one of his favourite Persian stories, *Vis va Ramin*, where the boy is thrown from his horse at just one glimpse of his beloved Vis.

He was listening to the goings-on at the front of the house, his slender legs boyishly propped up, his head fallen back on a yellow brocade tester, one hand reached back idly to trace the pattern in the cloth. There were angels painted on the ceiling, swimming through foamy water at an island's shoreline, tumbling among blue and gold. Amir gazed up at them. He liked the trumpets, conch-shells blowing in the corners; but the angels he found perilous, too vulnerable in all their pinkness. They reminded him of Lady Domeyne's two girls.

Earlier, he had gone to take a look, popping out of the front door to find a huge crowd gathering, and had darted back inside. It had been like opening the door on to an opera in mid-performance. He had expected everyone to turn in disapproving unity and go, 'Hush!' One glimpse, anyway, and he felt that he could see them all perfectly well from where he was, lying down on the velvet plush, a cup of peppermint tea within arm's reach, remembering them, as he listened to the sound crescendo. Sunlight fell from the garden on to him, and on to the Persian rug beside him. He gazed down at it, admiring, and, finding the flaw, was reassured.

The field would leave at half past eleven. There would be speeches first, and photographs: press had come from London for the occasion. Saboteurs were expected; either there would be a big turn-out or a poor one but, whichever way it went, it would be news. So far, however, no saboteurs were in evidence, although that might not mean they had stayed away: often they came in disguise, which meant they dressed to fit in; saboteurs usually had excellent country wardrobes. Nor were there any police. Their absence was notable: they had been expected. In their case, staying away was a sign of support: it would be business as usual in the country-side. London could have its laws; it did not follow that they would enforce them.

Lance Ash arrived just after the speeches. He parked outside the gates at Eastleigh and walked down, where he was offered a glass of sloe gin and a sandwich. He took both, one in each hand, and walked on to the house. Reverent, because to him it felt like stealing – this was the enemy, he was in their camp – he ate and drank, reminding himself to smile; a harassed-looking woman in a brown tweed skirt smiled back at him, raising her glass.

This was Cook. Her nerves were murder. She had set the tray on a large stone urn and, supposing she was well hidden behind a cedar, had helped herself.

It made a picture, and someone took the photograph. The camera had looked as if it belonged to a professional, and Lance half choked on his smoked salmon. He cursed under his breath, imagining what would happen if that picture made it into the papers – himself standing outside the large house tucking into the food, a grin on his face as he hobnobbed with the hunting set. He prayed he had just been one of the crowd. Cook prayed that she had been, too. She resumed her duties, sighing.

People were starting slowly to move off. Lance swallowed the remains of his sandwich, which, despite the choking, had been delicious, drained his gin and turned to leave. Even not knowing the form, he could sense the mood rising and the pack of dogs was swarming, disciplined as nature, unified as a shoal of fish or a flight of birds drawn magnetised towards the poles. Dogs and horses would gather outside the gates in the field, and then they would be off.

As they moved away, Lance was caught up in the vanguard. He overheard a young man laughing as he pointed at a cluster of particularly wild-looking ponies, cropping the grass, the equally wild-looking children on their backs flashing their whips and looking untameable, their raucous giggles like the cry of feral pups. 'The whipper-in will have his work cut out with that mob.'

Lance was startled: he had heard an almost identical expression in the House the week before.

He headed up towards where he'd parked his car along the drive. As he did so, he felt himself watched by a tall blond man, good-looking fellow, his expression fierce but oddly puzzled, who, Lance couldn't avoid noticing, and was alarmed as he did, was carrying a rifle.

This was Leo. To him, Lance was familiar. A man from the town? Perhaps it was that. He seemed in a hurry at any rate. Leo watched him dart back up the driveway to his car, which, Leo observed, was covered with birdshit: yes, a townie, definitely – only someone like that would be unobservant enough to park beneath a tree.

Leo went to the back of the house to get the Land Rover. He drove it round; the girls were waiting with Anna by the front door. He asked them to get in, then went to get the dogs; they jumped, silent, into the back.

Isabella had been with Anna and the girls and now that the others had gone, and the rest of the field was already moving, she had been left alone in the doorway of Eastleigh, not quite sure where she should be.

To Leo, she looked expectant but at the same time half afraid, and he supposed it was because she was in love. He cursed under his breath and started the engine. He wished she wouldn't stand there like that. He almost expected a young Charley Sutton to emerge from the house at any moment to stand beside her. What was it he'd asked? Where was the loo? For God's sake. Leo was exasperated to have this memory emerge.

He supposed he could hardly leave the girl hanging about there without asking if she'd like to come. But that wasn't part of the plan. He was about to drive off when Gerald, unexpectedly, decided the matter for him.

Mounted, he approached Isabella. 'You're going along with Leo?'

'Do you think that'd be all right?' She was glad that Gerald had rescued her. She hadn't liked to be left there when Will was riding off.

'Would you mind giving these to Henry?' He handed Isabella a pair of ladies' riding gloves. 'She left them inside and she'll be missing them otherwise. She's up at the top of the drive, likes to get off in front. I'm more of a hanger-back.' He tipped his hat at her as he rode away.

Isabella got into the front seat beside Leo. 'Is it all right if I come along with you?' For answer, he drove off.

31

Promptly at eleven, the hounds arrived in full cry from the kennels a mile distant, led by the master, Charley Sutton, and the whippers-in; the kennelmen, also mounted, followed and behind them, in their Land Rover, the terrier-men, their dogs noisy in the back.

Cutter was of this number. He had the dead fox with him for the scent. It was wrapped up in a brown canvas knapsack. He sat in the passenger seat with it on his knees. In that day's weather, the scent should be good for at least half an hour, less if the wind picked up, more if the day continued mild and dampish. On the command from Charley Sutton, they'd be away on the bike with it. They'd drag it behind most of the way, across the fields, and then, over the rougher ground, he'd be off with it on foot, as though he himself were being chased.

They stopped on the verge in the Land Rover and waited. Cutter had an eye open for the girl, but he hadn't seen her yet.

Charley had dismounted: he'd wanted a quick word first to remind the men of everything they'd discussed the night before. There were tactics in place that, with a degree of cunning, might be employed to dodge the letter of the law. He smelt beer on the men and he was strict with his instructions. Cutter, he felt, required particular attention. It wasn't that he was unruly, and he had never seen him stupid with drink, only silent with it, and more sullen. When he was in that mood, he took matters too much into his own hands. They had almost had a stand-off last season over when to send in the dogs. Charley would tolerate nothing of that nature this time. He would see that the man kept in line.

Cutter, carrying the knapsack, climbed down from the Land Rover at a word from Charley – the crowd pressed in; horses jostled close by – and one, a young black mare, recently lame and just declared fit, so therefore green and skittish, scented the dead fox, was spooked and reared. The rider, expert, came down cursing.

This was Henry; she turned her horse swiftly, moving off up the driveway to calm her down. She did not see the face of the man carrying the knapsack with the dead fox, but she noticed Charley, and called over her shoulder, 'Tell that idiot to look out, would you? Someone will get hurt.'

Cutter, of course, had recognised her perfectly. He had stopped in his tracks, a word of greeting left dead on his lips for the simple reason he had never learned her name. He could hardly shout out, 'Oi, you! Lady!' He stared after her as she moved up the drive, her horse dancing nervy on the grass. It was her: she was exactly as he remembered her, if not a little more so – her thighs a little plumper, and her cheeks more flushed. He watched her go away from him, oblivious, up the drive.

Before, he had not minded that she just said, 'Hush, no need,' when he asked what she was called. She had giggled and it had provoked him, because he had not seriously thought she would go away afterwards without telling him. But she did. It would have made him feel like a girl to call after her, protesting, 'Tell me, what's your name, will I see you again?' Rather than do that, he had kept silence, and let her go.

Now he felt the withholding of that name like a kick in the belly, half winding him, and that she had not even noticed him now seemed to blank him out. He would track her down and make her remember him. He would bide his time, but he would have his sign.

Leo had emerged now in the car; he had driven round from the stables at the back, and was approaching, driving towards Henry. He stopped when he saw her and got out. The two girls were visible from where Cutter stood with Charley. Cutter watched as Henry leaned down to Leo, who reached up to give her something.

'Henrietta.' Leo was curt. She wondered if he was doing the rounds of apologising for last night. But he held up her gloves to her and did not meet her eye. 'Gerald had these. He said they were yours. You left them in the house, and asked me to give them to you.' Henry could see Gerald in conversation with one of the whippers-in, a Devon man; he was raising a hand from a distance, pointing to his own gloves. Good, she had them.

Charley cleared his throat. The man was plainly not paying attention.

Cutter turned back to him: 'Who are they?'

Impatient, annoyed at the interruption, glancing towards Leo's car, Charley said, 'Family, they live here, now you do understand . . . ?' He went over the details again. He hadn't time for any nonsense from the terrier-men. Today had to be well run or it would not come off; it would end in disaster.

Cutter knew it all already. So that was her husband, those her children? There was no reason beyond that brief episode, just glimpsed, to believe it. But nor was there anything to disprove it. He uttered an oath under his breath. He had been duped. She wasn't a guest: this was her house. She belonged here, had been married all along. He knew what he thought of such women.

Leo drove on towards the gates. To do this meant that he passed Celia. Neither gave any sign of recognition. Their faces remained impassive. Observing them, there was no evidence that they were married.

Cutter broke away from the field, striking out alone with the dead fox on his back. His strong legs pushed uphill against the tide of long grass, the hedgerows soon concealing him. His shot-gun was slung on a leather strap across his back. As he went, his deep poacher's pockets rattled with metal on metal. His knife and cartridges. It was the noise of a convict, shaking in anger at his chains.

He had a head start. Half an hour later, everyone would follow. For now, though, he was on his own. He pressed on uphill and felt the damp air cling, his thick trousers wet already about the knees and his hands alert to pull himself past the rough ground now that he had breached the first covert. The earth was hard after yesterday's frost; it was cold to the touch, and gave him solid leverage.

There was a low mist here above the beech leaves fallen last autumn and the ground smelt mushroomy and fresh, with a richness he knew would turn rank when the bluebells were over. He thought of the way they were felled once they had flowered, as though a storm had passed across them. They just keeled over when they were dead. He strode across the new growth now, and smelt the weak sap ascending, too young to interfere with the stronger, brackish smell he'd detected, like a tart's armpits; he sniggered to himself. It was how he thought of it. A smell no perfume of nature could conceal. Nothing else was like it. It was pure fox. They might yet have another kill.

He pressed on through the beechwood, then broke out into the first ploughed field. He would cross this one and the next, and tran-scribe a big loop that touched again at its low point on this covert. As long as he did that, he would be following orders. Beyond that, he was free to do as he saw fit. He chose a route along the loamy far edge of the field, boxed in by a new fence, one of Charley Sutton's by the look of it for he'd gone against the proper hedgerows on his land and instead preferred this modern fencing. Cutter glanced at it in disgust. The countryside round here was getting all prissed up.

He quickened his pace and felt his thigh muscles working and warming. The huntsmen could do as they pleased. Without him, there'd be nothing. Soon enough they'd know about him. He would lay the scent.

32

On Friday night, when Amir led Celia from the dining room, she thanked him at the foot of the stairs, and went upstairs alone.

Her pace had been even and composed. She shut the bedroom door quietly behind her, and crossed the room to remove her jewellery, intending to place it as she always did in the Chinese bowl, which, for that purpose, stood empty in the middle of her dressing table.

She unclipped her earrings, held them in her hand and stared at them before she put them down. Then she reached round to unhook her necklace, releasing the catch, and set it alongside the earrings in the bowl. Her fingertips replaced her husband's: this was his nocturnal task. She closed her eyes and felt the echo of all the times he had performed that tiny task of love grow faint until there was no sound left. She drew in her breath. She listened. They were gone.

She raised a hand to her right ear, which was ringing with another noise, as though the glass had hit her, as he intended it should, and smashed against her, shattering her and not itself against the wall. She pressed her hand to the side of her face, sensing the blow, and — but how could he have known? He did not. She had never told him — she felt the heavy thump of landing on the rocky ground when she'd been thrown down before.

She had picked herself up that time, too, when the man had gone, and walked the mile back across the Hampshire fields towards her aunt's house. Just before she reached the high brick wall, the limits of the garden, wisteria tumbling over, purple effervescence of cultivation into the wilder meadowlands and fields, she had stopped and looked down at herself and her dress, which was torn and dusty, marked.

There was a horse trough nearby, beside the gate, and a soft-bellied Friesian drinking at it, backing off suspicious as she approached, perhaps scenting blood. Celia went to the trough and washed her face, did what she could with her dress. She didn't want to scare her aunt. When she went to her, she saw that she was sleeping among the roses in the shade. The back gate had been left open, and before Celia woke her she had hesitated, gazing at the older woman with a clear, accurate premonition: I will never lie sleeping and trustful in a garden with a gate left open.

Now she looked down at the bowl and then away. She could not feel Leo's fingers gentle against her neck, nor his kisses as he leaned over with a word of love for her. She crossed to the dressing room, unhooked her dress, hung it back alongside the others in the wardrobe. She stood naked for a second, then went to his chest and, opening the bottom drawer, took out a pair of his pyjamas and put them on. It shamed her to do it, but she had to have something.

She buttoned them, and turned up the sleeves, decisive. If she thought about it, she would not do it. And if she reasoned at all, she would not allow herself the indignity of this undertow of love. But there it was, and she sank into it, and she slipped into their bed – he, of course, not in it – and as she lay there, unsleeping, flat on her back, she remembered him having told her, years ago now, she supposed he would have forgotten, of how his father used to beat him and then make him stand on a chair so that he could not crumple. That was how he put it. Could not crumple and be as he felt – finished, beaten, destroyed by the stronger man.

It would be her method now. She was perfectly still and flat and she did not cry. She heard everyone going up to bed; and she heard him, too, the latest of them all, going eventually along the corridor to the far room where she heard him shut the door. No, she had not been waiting for him. It was then that she wrapped her arms round herself in his pyjamas, once, then jumped out of bed. She felt the decision coming to her and she wanted to elude it a moment longer. She darted over to the dressing-table. Embracing herself, she had felt her rings dig hard into her skin. She took them off, leaving just her wedding band, dropped them into the Chinese bowl and returned to bed. But by then the decision was taken.

She could not remain standing on that chair for ever. She could not pull it off. It was too much. It was not life to live without love, so she did not want to live. Her lips parted with a fast in-breath. She felt her heart hammer violently in her chest. It should not take a child to stand as proof of her own innocence. She screwed her eyes tight to stop the tears. They did not fall. She had no further use for herself without him. Tomorrow she would ride.

Waking on Saturday morning – Marjorie had disturbed her bringing in the tea, shutting the door sharply behind her – she had got out of bed, washed, dressed, been before the mirror again, brushing out her hair, when she noticed – it had caught the light, the bright day flooding in – a fine crack running from the lip to the base of the Chinese bowl. She stared down at it. It must have happened when she dropped her jewellery there last night.

She paused, and then she left the bedroom. Descending into the house, she felt as though she was sinking into poisoned water, and she did not drown, she drank it in, and by the time she entered the kitchen to find Marjorie and Ellis, gazing at her dumbstruck, she felt the malign energy of deep grief well inside her until she felt lit up with that perverse vitality. Her life seemed to have run up full tilt behind her, and it urged her on. She had held things off for much too long. This was the price.

She commented on the day ahead, and remarked upon the weather. She slipped into her mended jacket and went out quickly into the hall. She could not stand to see them still believe in her. It was stupid of them to have that kind of trust. Couldn't they see? She had already failed them. She was counterfeit. They had all believed a picture and beneath it there was nothing to be loved. She had been loved on faith alone.

At the front door, she put on her boots and went through to the downstairs cloakroom to tie her stock in front of the mirror. She did not want to go back upstairs, as though returning might be to reverse the decision.

She tightened the stock and buttoned her black jacket. The new button was stiff in the hole. She peered down at it. The thread was not true black and looked weak. She supposed it would last one day.

She held the edge of the sink and leaned closer to the glass. For a split second she felt a pang of memory and missed herself. She hoped she wouldn't be sick. Then there were footsteps outside in the hall and the sound of horse-boxes crunching over gravel and she went out. She missed herself no longer. She was gone. There was nothing left to break that was not already broken. The picture was worthless to her now.

She stood in the doorway, and although the driveway at this point was almost empty, two horse-boxes pulled up, Dunbar's voice carrying from the yard, she could see another scene entirely: a tennis party, herself in whites, Leo coming without hesitation to claim her.

Now Henry came downstairs. Celia turned and saw her sister's face seem almost to grow younger in her concern. Celia touched her arm for reassurance, and felt with the gesture that she had said goodbye. They spoke briefly. Time was getting on. She went outside and round the house towards the stables.

33

When Lance Ash left the garden at Eastleigh, he jumped into his car, and started to head slowly to the gates with every intention of going straight back to London: that business over the smoked-salmon sandwiches and the possible photograph appearing in the papers had put the wind up him, and he was nervous as he set off, fudging first gear, his palms damp even in the cold weather.

He did not, however, get far. It wasn't just that the driveway was crammed with other cars, people and horses. Something else tugged him back – a small hook of doubt. With the exception of the children – of whom he was a little envious, because in their wickedness they were clearly having so much fun – not all these people looked to him like monsters. Not all of them, either, looked like toffs. He had an impulse to say, 'Cheer up,' to a few, because they seemed so glum, but he said nothing. How could he? Their misery was partly his fault.

Of course, his was only one of many votes cast. But trying to get away in his car, he overheard someone say, 'Well, you've got to do your bit,' and was gripped by the aptness of that remark: he had done his bit, too; and if enough people did it, look what happened! They were a crowd, but it was all about those numbers and how they added up: it was as though he'd personally made it illegal. He felt as though he was at a state funeral: unexpectedly, someone much admired was dead, and he was in his way to blame. He remembered his earlier intention to do something, possibly rough things up, and he was relieved not to have had the call that morning from the other man.

Now, the engine labouring, Lance felt torn. He couldn't just go home, but he didn't have anywhere else to be. No one would know if he stuck around for a while longer, would they? To go now felt like leaving a party early: there was a sense that with just one person's arrival it might become even more exciting. Something at once inexplicable to him yet very definite was going on here, and he was fascinated. It was life. He might not like it, but – and then he smiled at himself.

He turned out of the gates and drove a short distance along the road, pulling in beside some others where the verge banked down into a ditch. People were milling around, and he supposed the hunt would soon pass by. The seat beside him was empty and, as he turned the engine off to wait, he thought of Alison, and saw, clearly, that he did not want to lose her. There was no doubt in his mind on that score. The strangeness – sitting in his car in unfamiliar countryside, the windows down – was that in that moment of pausing to think about her, he realised that it was something he rarely did, and he felt chastened. He should do it more often. She had not died, he had not lost her absolutely, so he should be thankful for that much, and give some thought to how he might win her back.

The crowd had gathered and he could hear their voices, hushed now and expectant. Instructions were being issued down at the house. Everyone was listening to find out how things would go.

He wished he could be given a lead about what to do with Alison. What would bring her back to him? What made her happy, gave her pleasure? He could not work it out. There must be something he could do. He sat and pondered for a while, idly watching the families clustered, drinking from flasks, the cold air steaming and the sky above them very blue.

Then he heard the horn, a trumpety bugling, antique and serious, the dogs replying, the strike of hoofs on the driveway clattering upwards, and felt himself physically tipped forwards. At his back he had the top layer of Wiltshire to cushion him with its sloe gin and its smoked-salmon sandwiches, and then he felt the rest gathering beneath, and suddenly he could discern great armies. Saxons, Celts and Romans and beneath them all barbarians and he was also one of those. His blood was rising and the armies were approaching. He clutched the steering-wheel as though someone had given the command he should be off. Even the birds had stirred at the sound of the horn and flown off to the woods. He collected himself and laughed out loud.

He saw the first horses coming by, the men on them severe and glorious, boots gleaming, the horses triumphant in their glossiness as though nothing on earth could snuff them out. They were vividly themselves and all aflame with life. He'd seen pictures. It was nothing like this. They passed so close by the car that it shook. The pack was ahead and concentrated, running up towards the brow of the first field, working. He leaned over the wheel and felt the speed of them rush by as the first horses bolted, disciplined, towards the line of sky, the riders' pink jackets blazing pure against the green. The noise as they crossed the strip of road was of an army fording a river undaunted. The wicked children were on the flanks, their ponies kicking up mud, heads down, crashing through tall grass and thickets, swarming, regrouping at the brow of the hill, and then they, too, were out of sight. He sat back. They were away. He finally took breath.

He felt bruised and bloody, and he wiped his face, as though he might actually have been spattered although, of course, there was nothing. After all, this was England, the year 2005. Suddenly he felt very peaceful.

The cars started to follow the field by road. Lance, much calmer now, was focused. He was able to mock himself because he had realised what he should do for Alison and, thinking of it, he felt very much a man. He had dodged it, blamed her, blamed himself. He would do so no longer. He knew she wanted children. It was the subtext of her going; it would be the draw to win her back. That was what she wanted him to do to make her happy. It was what he wanted too.

The lane ahead was empty. Everyone had cleared off. He got out of the car and stood tall, looking around. The verge fell steeply to the ditch and the ground was soft, the grass lush and marshy beneath the trees. There were meadow flowers and some irises growing wild among the reeds. She loved those. He went down to pick some and, because no one was watching, snapped off a branch of something blossomy, then scooped up an armful of the long grass. It made a nice bouquet. He took it to the car, laid it carefully on her seat. He would go back to London with it and reclaim her. He had forgotten Valentine's Day but he had remembered this: he loved her; he loved her very much; he didn't want a life without her.

He smiled as he started the car. The engine roared into life, but the wheels spun, found no purchase. He turned off the engine, tried again. He gripped the wheel and gunned the engine in his frustration but it only made it worse and he felt the car settle deep into the soft earth of the verge. He turned off the engine and the countryside seemed to hum about him in its massive emptiness, only a faint wind in the trees overhead and the brook running along the gully, the water dripping into silence.

He leaned forward over the wheel and punched it hard, shaking it. Everyone had gone. They were probably miles away already with the hunt. Even his phone was useless here: there was no signal. He looked ahead, down the lane, and tried to remember how far it was to the main road or the next village. Ten miles? Further? He had lost track. He had been absorbed in watching the green banks rushing by, melodious and soothing, and all his thoughts had been on the day that already now was gone. He had been left behind.

He noticed that the way ahead had become, by a faint degree, less clear: a mist was rising; or was it falling? He peered upwards at the sky, which in places was still bright blue, but elsewhere, lower down, was whitening, as though someone was clearing it to paint another picture: the mist was rising from the earth. He frowned as he looked at it, and then, behind him on the road, he heard what sounded like another car.

34

Amir woke to a sky of drowning angels and something, somewhere nearby, screaming.

It was only one of the peacocks. It had jumped up on to the window-ledge of the library where he'd gone to lie down and read while the others went out hunting. He had fallen asleep while they were still gathering outside. They were leaving now, and it had been the sound of the pack that had made the peacock cry out.

But it made him nervous, and when he leaped up from the *chaise-longue*, he knocked over the remains of his peppermint tea and panicked. He could hear the large clock whirring but not striking in the hall and the bird was pressing, curious, against the window, its face and then its feathers brushing across the glass.

He went in search of a cloth to clear up the tea, walking in his socks across the marble, glancing out of the windows at the front of the house to see the last horses, stragglers, trotting away up the drive. He liked the house. He felt at home there. It was a bit like a place where he'd been put up for a month in Eaton Square: another patron, richer, he supposed, than Henrietta, although he preferred her because she was impulsive and undemanding. The others, an elderly American couple intent on philanthropy, had regarded him as half caretaker while they were away, and half poet laureate, for they expected a tidy house and a slim volume, dedicated to them, no doubt, on their return.

They had been disappointed. He had spent the whole month on their *chaise-longue*, running through their supply of Fortnum & Mason canned peaches, and reading. Their library was very good, better than the one at Eastleigh, which, aside from Cobbett and a row of Hilaire Belloc, was mainly farm and shooting records, Greek and Latin. In Eaton Square he had got to grips with *Ivanhoe* and the Waverley novels, puzzled over stories of King Arthur, and alighted finally on *The Seven Pillars of Wisdom*, after which he brooded.

He didn't brood now, for he had met Dunbar, who, he thought, was the real thing, and he was happy. He fetched a cloth, cleared up the tea, and stood, indecisive, at the window of the library. The peacock had gone, and in its place it had left one long feather. He set down the cloth and raised the sash. He went across to the mirror above the fireplace and tied the cloth round his head so that he could stick the feather there. He examined the effect, and found it pleasing. Thus attired, he strolled, impatient, through the house. He wondered when they would be back. As he stood at the front door, the countryside ahead seemed unlikely to produce anyone, perhaps for years, and he had a vision of no one ever returning. He liked this thought a good deal, until he thought of the people, one by one, and in particular Dunbar, and then he saw that that was the reason for his impatience: he lacked human company.

There were boots left out under the coats, most of them huge, but a variety of sizes, and at last he found a pair that fitted him perfectly: Celia's size sixes, riding boots, well worn in. He tucked his trousers into them and went outside. He could see the mist approaching – the line of trees was less dark than before, as though it were a photograph, developing in reverse, the given light gradually being taken away.

He shut the front door, and did a quarter-circuit of the house, feather quivering, and arrived at the stable-block, where he could hear a horse that had been left there. Understandably, he thought, it was in bad spirits to have been left out, and he went to it. It was Leo's horse: Dunbar had returned it to the stable, taken off the saddle and bridle, and thrown a rug over it, thinking that now Leo was following in the Land Rover, the horse would not be needed. There hadn't been much time, and in his haste Dunbar had left the tack-room door open; the tack was visible on the stand.

Amir stood beside the horse, tickling its neck with the wide end of the feather. The horse seemed to like him, and nuzzled his ear. He didn't suppose the others would be back until nightfall. 'A good day's hunting,' he had heard people announce. A good day was surely a complete one.

He went back to the tack room for the saddle and bridle, put them on the horse, who stood still, appreciative, and mounted. It was cold, so he wrapped the heavy red wool blanket round himself like a cape, and set off up the drive. The mist, which he had seen earlier at the line of trees, now crept close and, just, had reached the limits of the lawn. As he rode through it – and higher up it was knee-deep, rising – he thought he finally understood what the word Arthurian meant, and swept his cloak about him as he clopped up to the road.

At the top he paused, wondering which way to go. The horse swung slightly to the right, and as it lived there, Amir let it. They set out along the lane. The mist had come in further and, after only a few yards, he found he could see nothing. Although it was exciting, he suddenly felt that really he shouldn't be there, and where 'there' was he wasn't certain either, beyond a place called Wiltshire. He reined in the horse, and they stood very still in the road. Why am I here? Because Amir did not know the answer to this question, he did what anyone would do: he whistled.

*   *   *

After the field had moved off, Leo began slowly to follow. He didn't want to be caught up in all that hullabaloo. He knew which way they were heading, and meant to meet them on the uplands just beyond the strip of pines. They'd draw a scent in there, then move off if none was found. Either way, from higher up there'd be a longer vista – one of Capability Brown's introductions – and he was hampered in the Land Rover by having to stick for the most part to the roads. He wanted a clear view of them. If necessary, he'd leave the others behind and go off on his own, on foot.

Anna was in the back with the girls: she knew nothing of what had happened the previous night, although she had gleaned some hints. Oblivious, she was in good spirits, and was already chattering to Isabella, who was relieved to have someone to talk to, as Leo, sullen, she found quite frightening. This morning, he appeared to her essentially to be sulking, and after she had got over the shock of having been wrong about him and Celia, she had drawn the conclusion that perhaps they often fought, but still continued, and that that explained why today no one had mentioned what had happened. Celia had been perhaps paler, but otherwise no different. Still, she was glad at the thought that later on she would be free to return to Primrose Hill: she intended to lure Will back there with her.

They were waiting at the end of the line of cars, the last to turn out of the driveway. Leo was silent. Anna was asking Isabella what she did for a living. He wasn't paying much attention. His left hand was on his gun, his right in his pocket on the bullets.

Isabella had just mentioned that she was a painter – 'Landscapes, portraits, that kind of thing.' She found Leo's silence disturbing. She hoped to bring him out. 'Actually, it was why I thought I'd been asked down here, to do a portrait of Lady Domeyne and you two.' She leaned over into the back, addressing the girls. They were subdued, huddled together, sensing something had gone wrong with their father.

'They'd never sit still for long enough.' Anna tried to tickle the girls under their chins. The joke was flat: they were very still. Leo looked at them in the mirror and frowned.

'Often I paint from photographs, of course,' Isabella went on, and Leo glanced across at her. 'Not many people have the time to sit about having their pictures done, or sometimes it's a gift, wanted as a surprise.' She didn't mention that this had been her understanding of the commission this weekend. It seemed incredibly remote now. She turned to look out of the window as the last horses, the children's ponies, trotted out past the gates.

Leo was looking in the other direction, but he had heard the mention of photographs for portraits, and wrestled with it now. Nothing came of it. He thought of the photographs in the grate, smouldering, and he was glad he had thrown them there, more glad still that he had ripped up the agreement for the land. His anger came up hard again inside his blood and stuck there, holding. He restarted the engine, and they edged further up the drive. He had noticed the mist coming in and doubted they'd have a full day's hunting after all. He wished the car ahead would move along. He had to get after them.

'It's quite a day isn't it? Wish I was out there.' Anna was chattering – stupidly, Leo thought, for he had seen the girl on a horse and she was no good. He wished they'd all be quiet.

'Actually, when we arrived yesterday, Lady Domeyne very kindly offered to lend me her horse,' Isabella laughed, 'but I don't ride, so . . .' Finally, she confessed, 'In fact the only time I've been on anything remotely horselike was when I was about your age.' She turned to the girls.

Belinda, haughty, corrected her, 'Equine,' and Hettie giggled.

Isabella had done that deliberately. She wished she could cheer them up. She hated to see them so forlorn. 'And anyway it was a donkey.' They both giggled. 'I was in Greece and he was called Zorba.' Anna smirked now. 'Unless that was for my benefit, which, no doubt, it was.' Isabella turned back. Leo was staring at her, not smiling.

He turned away, speaking half out of the window: 'There's nothing on earth would stop Celia hunting today. I'm sure she was just being polite.' But then he turned back to her, and Isabella thought she saw a lessening of his anger as it was replaced by something a shade less certain.

She thought it was rude of him to correct her on this point, so she insisted, gently, because she had thought it was, by contrast, particularly kind of Celia to have done so – especially now that she had seen the day's significance – and if he was still so intent on her taking sides, even over this, she knew where her loyalties would lie. 'No, I'm quite sure she meant to lend me her horse. She said her mare would take care even of a novice like me, and I thought it was very good of her.'

Leo started the engine, his expression inscrutable. 'Right, about time.' The other cars had all moved off. The lanes were now almost silent and the mist had started to come in across the fields on either side, although the sky overhead was still bright blue. Leo was gruff when Isabella commented on it. 'Often happens. Quite normal. It's nothing.' But she noticed him glance sideways across the stubble, and his face was set. He'd brought his gun with him, it was propped up between them on the seat, and she thought better of commenting on it. She supposed that that was normal too.

Just past the first bend in the road, a car was parked far over on the verge, tilted at an angle, its back wheels deep in the wet mud of the ditch. Suddenly a man leaped out of the driver's seat and into the middle of the road, as though Leo might not have been meaning to stop, although he'd already started to slow down, cursing.

'Goddamn townie,' he muttered to himself. 'Shit.' He had remembered the bird-droppings.

Isabella caught Anna's eye in the rear-view mirror. He really was ill tempered.

He sighed heavily and got out into the road. The dogs started jumping in the back, and he cursed them too.

The man came over to the Land Rover, and from inside, they could hear him explaining that he'd got stuck in the ditch, although by then Leo had already taken out the rope and crossed to the Cavalier, tied it to the front. 'I'll pull you out in reverse. Get back in.' Lance did as he was told. Leo got back into the Land Rover, and the Cavalier slipped easily from the ditch. He climbed back out to unhook the rope.

Lance was ecstatic: he was on his way home; he was going back to claim his wife; he had flowers, and was relieved also that these had gone without comment. He recognised Leo from earlier, and was glad that this time he was not carrying the gun. Leo untied the rope, and Lance spoke up, waving out of the window to thank him. 'You've no idea what a service you've done me. I'm most grateful.' He was eager to be off.

Leo was almost back at the Land Rover but, hearing the man's thanks, turned to see the man framed now in the window of the driver's seat – the frame like a head-and-shoulders shot on television. Leo stood in the road, effectively blocking the man's way, holding the heavy coil of rope, staring.

Lance peered at him. What was he staring at? The countryside really was full of nutters. He'd tell Alison. It'd give her a laugh. But he wasn't laughing yet and he wished the man would budge. He could hardly sound his horn, as though he were a cow or something.

Leo could not move. He had remembered. He felt returned sud-

denly to the previous morning, when he had seen this man on television: the backbencher, Lance Ash, on the news. He had asked
Marjorie to turn it off because he hadn't liked to see him, and he
hadn't wanted Celia to see him either. It would shake her confidence, he had thought. But when he had gone out into the hallway
to find her, she had been already leaving. He had wanted to kiss her,
and he had wanted to tell her he loved her, and say something tender
to her because he knew how much she minded about the ban, and
because he had remembered about the accident before. The timing
of it had spooked him. Five years. He had gone after her to take
hold of her, but by then she had been gone, and somewhere in her
absence the madness had taken hold of him. Now it let him go, and
he staggered back.

He turned round unsteady, reeling. Isabella saw his face and drew
breath. It was murder and the anguish of murder all at once. The
girls, cheered by the chatter earlier, and by their father's heroism in
saving the townie, were laughing and applauding in the back.

Leo was staring at them, and Anna, he could hear, was going,
'Hush,' to keep them quiet. They were all afraid of him, and with
good reason. He felt like the giant in the winter garden, his rage a
bad spell that had held the seasons from their natural fall. He could
hear the car behind him, the Cavalier, the engine revving, impatient,
though that man, too, was afraid of him, no doubt, because he wasn't
calling out to tell him to move along.

But Leo could not get his limbs to work. He had helped a
stranger who before had been his enemy when he might have
driven by. He was, just, still human, but it felt like a slender thread
indeed. The mist was coming up faster now and he felt his mind
grow cold. What had he done? The landscape was dissolving and
with it his conviction, piece by piece, was clouding over, as though
he had pulled himself up to this terrible place of certainty with
images of guilt that added up to nothing. Snapshots burning,

chequebook stubs and pots of honey. He had looked for proof of guilt and been blind to the picture of love with which his whole life shone. The black points melted into white. He shut his eyes, the ground felt unsteady beneath him, and then from somewhere close by he heard the sound of hoofs, and someone coming along the lane behind him whistling a high tune. He did not recognise it, but the music woke him from his stupor and he moved out of the way of the car.

Leo half raised his hand as the man drove off. Lance waved back and then was gone. The horse approached, and riding it was Amir.

Leo broke into a run. 'Get down, quick, come on, off!'

Amir leaped off the horse and stood bewildered in the road. Leo jumped up on to it and kicked it into a gallop, down the lane and, skidding, sharp right, clearing the ditch and off up across the middle of the field. He had to find her. The fog had come and only now could he see clearly. Celia had not meant to ride, that girl Isabella had just told him so, and suddenly he knew why. Nothing but a child would stop her. But it did not take a child to prove her innocence and he felt damned for everything he had done. She could not forgive him. It was impossible, and he rode on into that.

He kicked the horse on faster. If he could outrun his wickedness, if he could just get clear of it. To do it he'd need heaven's help and he had no right to ask for it, although certainly he did, pounding uphill across the ice-bound furrows, the fog thickening so that almost straight away he could not see, but he rode on into it to find her. He had no compass left now but his faith that she would be there, somewhere, at some point, and he rode faster because it wasn't soon enough, and the fog was coming heavier now, and the way ahead was blank. Everything depended on it. He had given her his soul and she had kept it safe and he had not believed her. It had been him stuck there, standing frozen on the chair, not her. It had been him all that time. She had known. They hadn't needed words to do it.

It was why she'd given him that gift of silence, which was love: they had met there.

He rode on fast uphill towards the beechwood. Cresting the top of the ridge, calling out to her, he heard two gunshots and his heart stood still.

35

When the hunt set off, Celia was close to the front of the field, which ran swiftly away from the start at full gallop up the hillside. The ground was soft there: the snow had not settled; that part of the hillside had not suffered in the previous day's frost. In the shadows it was icy; where sun shone the air was heated. Shade and light did not seem to intermingle, as though the lack of breeze meant that they could not stir. The going here was fast and fair.

On the uplands the air was clearer still, the way wide open, though almost at once as they'd breached the hilltop, pausing as a scent was drawn in the covert, they could see that a mist was coming in across Salisbury Plain, and had gathered already along the narrow gullies and was thickest in the far part of the shallow valley, swallowing the view of Eastleigh. Charley Sutton's house, Sanbourne, could still be seen from where they'd stopped on the brow of the incline. The sun appeared to favour it, and the slate rooftops shone back silver.

A scent was picked up and they were off again, the going rougher now on the hillside under trees, the branches low, the earth hard and flinty where stones had been chucked out into the lane from a field that in summer would be golden. Now the earth was grey, turned in solid furrows, greasy-looking in the dampish light where the mist, even here, started to come in. The scent led them back on to the road for a short stretch. A few cars were there, pulled over as the horses came thundering by, some at a canter, most trotting, metal loud on Tarmac, the engines idling or cut dead. Celia waved thanks at a black car, the man inside it craning out and smiling. She caught sight of wild flowers bunched on the seat beside him and rode on.

They turned off sharp into a lane, heading fast downhill again, the mist thickening, sudden as water thrown on to anisette. Her mare was sure-footed, but many were slipping, and Celia cantered past them, urging the animal on. They came to a stream that was once Leo's: for many years, he had fished for trout there, and she had gone with him. It was no longer his. They crossed it, heading uphill again now beneath low-hanging trees and then, at the top, the horses were suddenly off fast along the perimeter of the field, once more flat out at full gallop.

There were fences ahead, dry stone walls and hedges, and some of the horses hung back, slowing, to take the long way, going round back to the road. The field became divided. Many surged on. Some refused. None had fallen yet. Celia took the fences, cleared them, rode on. Her mare was blowing now, her flanks shuddering with effort when they landed, but she had a day left in her, and was fit and strong, not tiring yet. The mist ahead was dense, dead still, no longer moving, the water settled potent in the anisette, the air steady and blank white, and this they entered, galloping.

Celia was still close to the front of the field and the gallop was downhill now towards the beechwood – they'd come right round and back on to the first loop where, hours earlier, Cutter had laid the scent. It wasn't far from Eastleigh, less than a mile, although the house was now invisible. They approached the beechwood, horses skidding, swerving back, and slowed up along the wire fence that circled the edge.

A couple of the terrier-men had come by road in a truck, another had a bike, and he was the one now to take the fox off for the scent. Cutter, on foot still, had been told to set up here where, had there been no fog, he should have been able to get a clear view of how the pack was running. The mist meant he could not. But he had waited. He knew that soon they'd be coming along, and he heard them rumble uphill and wondered if she'd still be with them even in the fog. He heard the horses pull up, riders cursing, panting.

'What do you think?' A man's voice, disembodied, called out in the fog. It was Gerald. 'Won't get much more out of it today.'

Someone, a woman, was cursing. 'Look out!' It was one of the children, who, somehow, had kept up, and his pony was backing, chaotic, into her cob.

'I'm going to go down,' Gerald again, who had thought he was addressing his sister, Henry, as she had for a long time been riding near him. 'Henry?' There was no answer. It didn't perturb him. She was a good rider. Some chap would see her down anyway he shouldn't wonder.

Henry had been separated from Gerald earlier, though her thoughts were now running along the same lines. She was fed up: she wanted a hot bath and a large glass of brandy. She had had quite enough of this weekend. Her horse had gone slightly lame. She had wondered before if the animal was fit enough to go out, but there wasn't another to be had. It was the mare's first outing of the season, and she was nervy, too, stumbling like a two-year-old. She'd picked up a stone some way back along the track, and Henry had urged her on to a gallop to see if the beast was bluffing. They sometimes did. But it was clearly not that, so, reluctantly, and cursing the silly thing, she'd drawn up and jumped off.

Now that she was walking, the others had left her behind. She was terrible at geography, her instincts about such things as direction had always been abominable, but they were matched only by her confidence – a combination that had often got her into terrible scrapes, rushing headlong in the wrong direction, into the arms of the wrong kind of man, she thought, trudging along a narrow path that led into the beechwood. She was sure it was the short-cut down-hill towards the house, although so far, if she was perfectly honest, the ground appeared to be tilting slightly upwards. She pressed on.

Gerald called, at the sound of a retreating horse, 'Hi, are you going down?'

From a different direction, someone from the village, hearing him, called back, 'We are!'

'Well, you'll not get down that way. Follow me.' He had just recognised the line of trees, and knew that, although it was a long way round, it was the safest and would lead them back eventually to the house.

'Oh, thanks!' a young woman's voice called out, grateful; some children followed, and more stragglers after that. Gerald, pleased to be leading the way, set off at a careful walk. He had had a damn good gallop, after all. Now he fancied one of those cigars and a bit of quiet feet-up before everyone came home.

The field was gradually dispersing. Charley Sutton was torn: although the weather had intervened, they'd had a good turn-out, which boded well for next season. He was, after all, an optimist. And he was confident that the fog would soon clear and they'd have some more good hunting even today. What people were left had gathered round him. By now, only thirty or so were out and, reduced, they carried on at a slow pace, along the line of trees.

Will had been riding along the flanks, and had it in mind to turn back to Eastleigh along the first clear way that opened up, but he was in no great hurry: he had had a good ride, and was content, plotting things he'd like to do with Isabella. He hadn't been home in a while, and although he didn't wish to frighten her off, he would like a long weekend with her in Oxfordshire.

A slight wind had picked up, and the branches rustled, the horses passing slowly by, the riders sightless.

Suddenly, in the fog, two rifle shots were fired close by. Crows flew up, black marks against the white, the sound like sheets flapped out upon a bed.

Celia also had been riding in this group, along the outer edge of the beechwood. She had been looking between the branches as they walked solemnly by, but there was no sign of bluebells yet and she had not expected it. She was exhausted and nauseous. She had ridden hard and taken risks, and at every jump had anticipated the disaster that would end it all; she had shut her eyes and in the darkest part of her a voice had agreed with Leo's accusations and said, 'Yes, I am frozen, finished, so bring it on. Nothing matters now.' She had felt so far back in that ice age that she saw no way of melting, no way down.

Celia's mare, however, had been nimble, never once stumbling, relentlessly sure-footed, and when the fog came down it was as though nature had conspired against her, wrapping her in safety, for now they were obliged to walk. It was unlikely they'd have any more hunting that day. She had been thwarted by the weather. Frustrated, she urged her mare along, kicking her hard without need, so that she jumped forwards unprotesting, mild, then Celia reined her in. She felt vicious towards the animal for taking such good care of her, for she could not see the point.

They were almost at the far end of the beechwood where the line of trees gave out and, on a clear day, the view stretched down towards the house, which would look beautiful, all its shabbiness remedied with distance.

Now the fog concealed it, shabbiness and beauty, and Celia missed the sight of it. They came to the end of the trees. It was then that the two shots rang out.

Celia thought first of her daughters. Shot one, shot two. Her breath stopped dead and the curtain seemed to draw back. The mare reared, jostling fierce to be off, leaping heavily forwards, spooked, and a third shot hung suspended, imminent, and Celia thought of the new life barely started in her and on that instinct of love called out her husband's name.

The air was blank and empty, and her horse, steadying, breathed heavily, gasping, as Celia was, to draw in life, and suddenly there he was, and he came out of that emptiness riding alongside her and they embraced. She held him tight against her, and his arms were strong, the circle unbreaking: he would not let her go. He was begging her never to forgive him, but already it was too late. Love was time and memory and, together, that meant forgiveness also: without it there was nothing, and there could be no future. She held all that inside her, and he felt the heat of it, and it warmed him too. He dismounted, he helped her down; they landed together on the earth in safety.

People were calling out to one another; the fog wrapped round.

36

Isabella, gingerly, had avoided Leo's gun, left behind, as she crossed into the driver's seat, and drove with Amir, Anna and the girls back to the house.

They stood together on the steps, uncertain what to do next. Amir, thinking the best course would be at any rate to remain dressed as he was – no one had mentioned his feather, or his cloak, so perhaps they thought it usual – had been talking to them about his morning's reading, and it made him think again of *Vis va Ramin*.

'It's the Persian version of *Romeo and Juliet*,' he had explained, and this made him think of last night's cigars, but he kept quiet about that. Leo's behaviour he had found inexplicable: he had a family, a house and, above all, Celia, yet he was in a rage over the wrong cigars. Amir had been thinking this, indignant, when the shots were fired.

For a moment, no one spoke. Anna was the first to rally. 'It'll be nothing.' She turned the children round. 'Pigeons. They often get shot around here. Or a car backfiring.' The children scoffed at this explanation, and, illogical, claimed, 'We're not children,' as they were shepherded inside.

Anna glanced at Isabella, who didn't quite believe her, although she was prepared to pretend so until proved otherwise: Will was still out there somewhere in the fog.

'Of course, the pigeons.' She said this to reassure Amir, who was thinking now about Dunbar.

They were able to do nothing at the house but wait, so they did, and while they waited they drank tea. The children had orange juice, sucked through straws, such was the mood of chaos, and Anna made everyone jam sandwiches.

The house, like an island, received the shipwrecked hunters back one by one. Ahead of them all came Marjorie, Ellis, Cook and the two women from the village, who instantly took charge, and within half an hour the kitchen was out of bounds: they had reclaimed their territory. They positioned themselves in the vanguard against all rumour of catastrophe. Tea now came in silver pots; the sandwiches, without their crusts, issued forth from the kitchen and were delivered to the drawing room, where, although it wasn't quite the hour, the housekeeper had decreed that tea should most certainly be served. Ellis served it.

Gerald came back, and with him he brought a line of stragglers, who, hearing only the shots and not the cause, lined up with cups in frigid wonder. Gerald marshalled them. Outside, horses were being tethered, or stabled where there was space. Amir gave up his blanket; it was needed. He went out to find Dunbar, which was easy for he was efficient, working in the stables. Amir helped him, and was useful. He had left his feather behind, but he meant to claim it later.

It was they who first saw Celia and Leo, returning together, briskly down the drive at a swift clip, bringing their horses round to the stables, then helping out. 'Let Isabella know I saw Will, and he's fine.' Leo mentioned this to Amir who, because he could not resist it, had been already on the point of darting back to the house with the news that he had seen Celia and Leo. He added this to his stash, and ran with it to the drawing room. Isabella, who had been poor at concealing that she was frantic – she had already smashed a Wedgwood cup, and was fretful about that also – was relieved, and sank back on to the sofa, hoping Will would hurry up and come back to her.

This, however, Will could not do as fast as Isabella would have liked: he had been caught up. One person from the party that weekend had still not returned: Henrietta. Another, though not of that party, would never do so, for by this time he was dead.

Afterwards people put together a picture of what had happened, and all the pieces seemed to fit. They were satisfied. Even those who could not possibly have seen it recognised it, and claimed to remember that, yes, that was just what it looked like; that was exactly how it happened.

The horses had drawn up at the edge of a small beechwood. The two gunshots were fired from somewhere inside there. But no one claimed to have seen the gun being fired. Exactly what went on there remained concealed for ever. Naturally, they embellished their involvement as far as they were able but then could go no further: the fog prevented it. People drew their own conclusions.

This was the disputed beechwood, the agreement to sell it to Charley Sutton – although that man was not aware of this – that morning torn up by its current owner, Leo Domeyne. Had Charley known the significance of the patch of otherwise almost worthless woodland, he would never have offered to take it off his old friend's hands and, moreover, with a price-tag well beyond its market value. It had been merely a favour to help Leo out of a tight spot. He could well afford to bestow it without the reward. But he had not wished to be insulting. He'd simply mentioned he'd had his eye on some of Leo's woodland for some time, been vague; Leo had been vague too, neither of them comfortable in speaking about such things, and Charley's farm manager had drawn up the agreement; Esther had failed to post it; Charley had delivered it himself on Friday morning.

None of those who claimed to have been there, witnesses, mentioned anything of this. It was never spoken of. It ceased to exist as a relevant detail: the land was never sold; no one but Celia and Leo knew of its significance.

Thirty or so were there, halted at the wood when the two shots were fired. If the so-called witnesses were believed, and they often were, at least two hundred must have been in attendance. But this was false. Some riders had dismounted, this was true, and the fog, also true, had descended fast enough to cause alarm. It seemed dangerous to be charging about blind, and many of the horses had grown skittish, sensing their riders' anxiety.

Henry also had grown anxious. By this point her horse was lame, and she was on foot, leading the mare along what she took at first to be a track through the beechwood, expecting that it would lead her out on to the other side, and then on to a sloping field and from there up to the road that led to Eastleigh. She thought she had seen a couple of other riders take that way, and she meant to follow them.

But her compass was off, the track began to peter out – it was just an animal's path – and the low branches scratched at her face where she failed to duck them, one snapping back into her eye, making her call out in annoyance.

She was infuriated at the way the day was turning out. She stumbled on a tree root concealed by crackling beech leaves, turning her ankle, bending over to rub at it through the leather of her boot. It wasn't serious. She stood for a moment, trying to see up through the bare treetops to the sky with some vague notion of being able to judge the best direction by the light, but it was now blanked out. Her anxiety increased. The noise of the hunt was very far off, and she decided to retrace her steps.

It wasn't so straightforward as she had imagined. Things looked different from the ground. The perspective was all off-kilter for her. She pressed on for a short distance and then, hearing the noise of metal rattling ahead, the bundling crack of footsteps that sounded like those of a large animal – she supposed a horse, another rider inside the wood – she called out to them, 'Hey, over here!'

There was no answer at first; the noise became cautious, not a horse's motion at all, but light and deliberate, hard to catch – like a poacher at work to set his traps. She drew breath. Why had they not answered? And then, suddenly, Cutter stepped forwards out of the blank page of the fog. He came quickly towards her on foot, shotgun under his arm, the barrel not cocked for safety but bolted and ready.

What happened next Henry, who survived it, never fully related to anyone. She addressed the man, whom she recognised instantly, as though she had never seen him before, asking him bluntly, because she was afraid, which direction she should go to find the others. When he did not immediately reply, she started to go past him, as though he was of no consequence to her if he could not supply her with the answer.

When she drew level, Cutter spoke: 'You know me. Don't make like you don't.' He darted out his free arm and took hold of her. 'Where's your husband now then?' She stared at him in fear. The wood was silent. He shook her. 'Go on, I've seen him. Give me your husband's name.'

Confused, she stammered, 'I don't have one,' which was true, but he mistook her meaning.

'Yes, you do. Come on, give me your name.'

She was crying now with fear. She didn't know what to tell him.

'Well, then, you'll never know my name either. I'll not give you my name and I'll say we never happened.' He dropped her arm, letting her go. 'We're nothing. We never were anything at all.'

She stumbled forwards, and – this was how she described it – turning to escape, was knocked over flat by the force of the shot entering her right shoulder. He had shot her in the back as she turned to go. He had brought her down, and must have thought she was dead. He staggered away, his voice bellowing once in the wood, and then the second shot rang out, fatal, as he fell on his gun.

Later, and whenever she had cause to tell the story, which was often, Henry related it always, as it were, in silence — she omitted everything that had been said.

She presented the story, but the trick of it was in the vanishing-point: the inscrutable heart of the picture, the meaning of it all about which everyone had a different view.

Epilogue

Now it was summer. Will and Isabella had gone down to spend the weekend at Eastleigh.

They had been down a number of times since February: Isabella was giving Celia painting lessons. Celia had anyway been, as she put it, 'a closet water-colourist', and Isabella was instructing her in oils. Celia had had the brilliant idea – Leo's expression, not her own – of attempting a family portrait. Will kept quiet. Celia would not begin, however, until that winter, by which time she could include them all: her son was due to be born some time in October.

Henry was also there, stopped off before continuing on to meet Gerald down in Devon: the cousins, after all, had been glad to budge, and had been wanting to leave the place on account of the bats, the ha-ha and, in particular, Wilmot, who, in their opinion, was a menace. He had not handed in his notice, but had stuck. Gerald had persuaded him. It had been easy. Wilmot's family had always been loyal to what he called 'the proper Stevensons', by which he did not mean the cousins but the sons. Order was restored in Devon.

The family was in the drawing room, the french windows open on to the garden. The two girls had gone out after lunch to play, disappearing some time ago into the tall grass of the meadow. It was June, a hot summer. The family had been discussing, as they often did, the accident that day in February. Henry brought it up whenever conversation lagged: it was her war-story; her shoulder was still bandaged; her grouse-shooting days were over.

'But did he come from Wales or Shropshire?' Will had addressed this to Leo, who shrugged.

'They didn't find out in the end. No fixed abode. Shropshire, I think. Charley said so. Though the best ones are from Wales.'

Isabella looked up. She had been drawing earlier in the garden, and was glancing over the sketches now. 'The best what?'

Will's arm settled more comfortably round her. He drew her in, kissing the side of her face. 'Is that me?' He pointed at a sketch of a man looking out of one of the top windows of the house.

'No, silly, it's Ellis, surveying. Haven't you seen him do that?' Isabella smiled. Ellis had let her in on his secret: he had bought a bit of land for Marjorie; it was just visible from the top floor, and when he retired, Vodafone permitting, he was going to build a house for her there.

'The best what?' Isabella pushed Will away; he had been kissing her neck and it was distracting. Leo had been trying not to look.

'Terrier-men,' Leo answered. 'Charley has always maintained that the best terrier-men come from Wales, and he was one of those.'

'He was a ferocious, towering, huge dark brute of a man,' Henry, lying back on the sofa, piped up, extemporising, for Cutter had not been tall, but certainly he had been strong. He had been quick, too, though a poor shot: shooting had never been his speciality; he had not meant to miss.

Cutter's identity often metamorphosed in this way. He had had no home, and no family had come forward when he died with photographs of him as a doting husband, happy brother, smiling child. Nothing of that kind had ever therefore appeared in the press. Henry was free to describe him as she wished. People seldom picked her up on the details.

Will, laughing, moved off by Isabella, now decided that he would. 'But you said he was red-haired before. I remember because you'd thought he might be Scottish. It was why you said you couldn't understand his accent or tell what he was trying to say to you.'

Henry wafted this remark away. 'One of those, red, dark. Dark red. It hardly matters now. He thought he'd killed me!' Her voice was indignant. She did not, naturally, like to remember the episode too clearly.

For a moment, face down on the ground, she had thought she might at any second be finished off, and when the second shot came, she had seemed to feel it too, and had passed out. She woke up – thanks to Will, who had been the first to find her, and Charley Sutton, who had known the way, and the other terrier-men, who had had a truck nearby the wood – in the cottage hospital and, gazing straight ahead of her when she came round, had seen the words: Domeyne Ward, and had thought she was still dreaming or, indeed, dead. The cottage hospital received donations from Celia's garden. Her big sister, obliquely, had had the upper hand again. This time, Henry did not mind in the slightest: it was an immense comfort. She sank back in a stupor. When she was convalescing, Celia took her in and was angelic; she knew just what to do.

'Come on, Henry, which was it?' Will, mischievous, had picked up Celia's sketchbook and pretended to take down the details. Isabella took it from him. 'Go on, describe him properly.' He turned back to Isabella. 'Do one of those court-room drawing things, go on. Let's see how he turns out.' He pulled a face and stuck up his hair. 'Maybe he looked like this.'

Henry, exasperated, gave in. She stood up, gesturing with her good arm, groaning ostentatiously, although by now she was in no pain. Briskly Isabella sketched. When it was done, she turned the book round to show Henry, who, genuinely alarmed for the portrait was horribly exact, sat down heavily again, addressing Will: 'There. There he is. I hope that will settle things now.' She badly wanted a stiff gin. She had been attempting to cut down and had given herself a six o'clock rule. It was just after three now. She stared longingly at the drinks tray, and then, unexpectedly, Celia seemed about to come to her rescue. She had already stood up, and was pouring a glass of brandy with an unsteady hand.

Pregnant, she knew she shouldn't, but she had just had an immense fright, and her nerves required it. She knocked it back. For a moment she stood facing away from the others. The last piece of the mosaic had fallen into place. The picture was complete. She shut her eyes. That was the man. She opened them and the picture was gone. Her husband spoke her name. She turned back to the room.

People had become used to Celia's slightly altered behaviour since February. She had become less seamless. It had improved her. People didn't like to comment, but by contrast, it was felt that perhaps before she had been too perfect. Now, with these odd quirks — a stiff brandy suddenly at three, taking up painting, inviting Henry's Iraqi, Amir, to live in the gatehouse so that he could help Dunbar with the horses — it was felt that she had grown warmer, and was more alive.

Leo went to her. He did not understand these things about her. He pondered them, and they made him love her more — these strange mysteries about his wife that he would never fathom. He didn't like to draw conclusions about the reason for such things. He knew too well the perils of doing so. But the other week, Amir had been telling him about something or other in Persian literature, and he himself had made a comment about carpets, and Amir had mentioned the flaw that must exist in the best carpets, so that they do not come too close to a perfection that should be reserved only for the divine, not for mortals.

Leo liked that idea. He thought of Celia now a bit like that. He had tried to say something about it to her only last week. They had been going up to bed. She was standing by the dressing-table, brushing out her hair, and he had gone to stand beside her to unhook her necklace. He hadn't noticed it before, but as she placed it alongside her earrings in the Chinese bowl – it was where she kept them – she pointed out to him that the bowl was cracked and, as it had been in his family for a long time, perhaps they should see if it could be fixed. She would hate it to break.

He leaned over beside her to take a closer look. 'You're right, there is a crack.' He turned back to her to kiss her, leading her to bed. 'But let's not have anyone mess with it. It's still beautiful.'

Celia turned round now in his arms. Her face was a little paler than before, but otherwise she was composed. They went to stand by the open french windows that led out into the garden. The fields beyond were very quiet, nothing stirring in the heat; even the peacocks were in hiding. She heard a door slam clumsily upstairs: the nanny, Anna, who still had not learned to go quietly around the house, as though her clumsiness might almost be deliberate.

They went outside on to the lawn. There was a warm wind here, slightly salty across Salisbury Plain, and England felt very much like an island. It seemed peaceful. They looked out across the meadow and the long grass rising. Celia turned to her husband, shielding her eyes from the sun, for it was so bright that she could not see. 'Darling, where are the children?'

The beech trees ruffled in the wind. Leo glanced up into their tree-house; they weren't there. Celia's hand against his arm was steady, but he felt the heat drain out of her touch and she stood very still, frozen. A blackbird flew down on to the lawn and stabbed at the cut grass, searching for a worm.

They turned at a voice calling from the top-floor window, to see Ellis, framed there, waving. He had been with Marjorie, surveying his land. He thought he had just seen Celia's girls on their way up towards the house from the meadow, and he had laughed at the sight, although he hadn't, quite, seen them properly yet. But he was sure it was them. He'd seen two peacock feathers sticking up, bobbing through the tall grass. The girls were playing at Indians, he supposed, or something of that nature.